Vivian Conroy is a multi-published mystery author with 25+ contracted titles. Away from writing, she enjoys hiking, crafting and spending too much time on X where readers can connect with her under @VivWrites.

 x.com/VivWrites

Also by Vivian Conroy

Miss Ashford Investigates Mysteries
Death on the Rhine
Last Dance in Salzburg
A Fatal Encounter in Tuscany
Last Seen in Santorini
Mystery in Provence

Cornish Castle Mysteries
Rubies in the Roses
Death Plays a Part

Country Gift Shop Mysteries
Written into the Grave
Grand Prize: Murder!
Dead to Begin With

Lady Alkmene Callender Mysteries
Fatal Masquerade
Deadly Treasures
Diamonds of Death
A Proposal to Die For

Merriweather and Royston Mysteries
Death Comes to Dartmoor
The Butterfly Conspiracy

Murder Will Follow Mysteries
An Exhibition of Murder
Under the Guise of Death
Honeymoon With Death
A Testament to Murder

TROUBLE IN THE ALPS

Miss Ashford Investigates

VIVIAN CONROY

One More Chapter
a division of HarperCollins*Publishers* Ltd
1 London Bridge Street
London SE1 9GF
www.harpercollins.co.uk
HarperCollinsPublishers
Macken House, 39/40 Mayor Street Upper,
Dublin 1, Ireland, D01 C9W8

This paperback edition 2025

2

First published in Great Britain in ebook format
by HarperCollinsPublishers 2025
Copyright © Vivian Conroy 2025
Vivian Conroy asserts the moral right to
be identified as the author of this work

A catalogue record of this book is available from the British Library

ISBN: 978-0-00-873709-2

This novel is entirely a work of fiction. The names, characters and incidents portrayed in it are the work of the author's imagination. Any resemblance to actual persons, living or dead, events or localities is entirely coincidental.

Printed and bound in the UK using 100% Renewable Electricity
by CPI Group (UK) Ltd

All rights reserved. No part of this publication may be reproduced, stored in a retrieval system, or transmitted, in any form or by any means, electronic, mechanical, photocopying, recording or otherwise, without the prior permission of the publishers.

Without limiting the exclusive rights of any author, contributor or the publisher of this publication, any unauthorised use of this publication to train generative artificial intelligence (AI) technologies is expressly prohibited. HarperCollins also exercise their rights under Article 4(3) of the Digital Single Market Directive 2019/790 and expressly reserve this publication from the text and data mining exception.

Chapter One

April 1931

Miss Atalanta Ashford leaned slightly forwards in her seat and gazed out of the train window at the impressive mountain view. Even in summer those peaks were covered in snow and now, in early spring, the white was especially copious, reflecting the sunshine with an almost blinding glare. She reached into her purse and extracted her sunglasses, slipping them on without taking her eyes off the view.

Most other people on the train were also staring out of the windows, enchanted by this breathtaking panorama, but if anyone had been looking at her, they would have concluded that she was simply mesmerised. The truth was that she was close to tears and eager to hide her volatile emotions. She would rather have spent these moments alone, hiding away from curious looks and speculative whispers, but it wasn't possible. She had to travel, had to keep going from place to place to find him.

Raoul.

Merely letting his name whisper through her mind elicited a shiver of pain across her spine. Her breathing caught and she clenched her hands in her lap. Ever since the news had reached her, she had been unable to calm down, the anxiety in her chest building to near intolerable heights. She had always known how dangerous his profession was, how, as a race car driver, he gambled with his life, taunted death every time he got into his car. But she had soothed herself with the idea that he knew what he was doing, that he was good at his passion.

The best.

But apparently even the best could be caught off-guard.

Or take too much risk to prove themselves to a new team owner?

Late last year, Raoul had been ruffled when rumours had started to spread that his old team was about to dismiss him in favour of a younger driver – a hot new talent with whom they'd rather work in place of the man who had proved himself and risked his life for them countless times. It was unfair indeed, but logical in a cutthroat sports environment. More and more money was going into racing with wealthy benefactors starting to sponsor the sport; benefactors like the Italian businessman Vincenzo Dulce who had signed Raoul for a new team with a brand-new car imported from across the Atlantic. The offer had been too good to refuse, even if Raoul had not already been under pressure from his old team. But then, with dismissal imminent plus the humiliation associated with such a decision, it had become essential.

She knew all that without him having to explain it to her. She understood because they were friends. Because she knew what the racing meant to him and…

She swallowed hard. He should have stayed away from Dulce though. He wasn't just a rich businessman who had made a fortune in diamonds in Africa. No. That story was merely a cover devised by his close associates to explain his lengthy absence from society and the origins of his wealth. There were no diamonds. His fortune was blood money from theft, extortion and even assassinations. He was a gang leader. A very dangerous man to associate with.

Deadly, when crossed.

And Raoul had signed away his future to that man. Two years, in a racing contract. Two years of smiling at the cameras, talking to journalists, and allowing Dulce and his criminals access to the highest circles for their covert dirty work. Raoul had allowed himself to become the charming cover for their deadly business. And he had known it full well. Had signed on the dotted line anyway to save his career.

Atalanta bit her lip. She would not cry on the train. She would not allow tears to leak from under her sunglasses and streak across her cheeks. She would not have people stare at her and wonder why a young woman with the means to travel was so unhappy that she cried in public.

No.

But she could tell herself whatever she wanted and still her heart wouldn't listen. It was broken for Raoul's sake. He had thrown himself headlong into a new adventure, like he always did, without thinking too much and blindly hoping for the best; trusting in his skill to manoeuvre himself out of danger should it occur. But this time he had overplayed his hand. There had been problems with the car, or one of the mechanics had been a criminal without the proper knowledge of caring for a high-performance engine. Whatever the truth, there had been an accident and Raoul was injured. Gravely.

It was hard to determine just how bad it actually was. The contact of her butler Renard, who had informed him of the events, had said it was so bad that Raoul might not make it. Renard had tapped into every connection he had to find information. One source claimed it was a head injury; another spoke of a broken shoulder. That would be terrible as it could cost Raoul this summer season, but it need not be fatal.

However, Renard had come back from another round of calls with a grave expression and fear had struck ice into her very core. She had asked him what it was and after some evasive answers, he had admitted one contact had spoken of a broken spine.

Would Raoul never walk again?

Worse than that, would he…?

Atalanta would not allow herself to think the word. Death was her enemy, both in the cases she worked to prevent or solve murders, but also in her personal life. She had lost her mother at a young age and had been raised by her father who had died when she was just out of school. She had also lost her grandfather who had left her the detecting business that had taken her to southern France and placed her into the company of Raoul in the first place. It seemed as if everyone she cared for, everyone who could give structure and meaning to her life, disappeared from it, leaving her all alone.

She forced herself to sit up straighter and take a deep breath. Raoul wasn't dead yet. At least, she hoped he wasn't. It was hard to be certain as they had not been able to find out where he was being treated. They had travelled from Germany, where she had been cruising the Rhine with a former colleague's family, into northern Italy where Raoul had been training for a race. There they had learned that he had been moved to a private hotel but no one could tell them exactly where. It seemed to be very hush-hush for some reason.

Perhaps to conceal he was already—?

No. She would not believe it. He was alive, she would find him and she would nurse him back to health. She didn't have the knowledge to heal physical injuries, but she would sit by his bedside and talk to him, put her hand on his and let him know he wasn't alone in this. She would be there for him so he had an anchor as he floated in a sea of uncertainty about his health and his future. That was what friends were for.

More than friends, if he let her. Wasn't this the time to admit what they truly meant to each other? That it was something special between them, not just attraction or having shared danger but…

She cast a quick look at Renard who sat opposite her examining the view. His features were usually unreadable, calm and collected and professional, such as was expected of a man in his position. But now she noticed a little strain around his lips and a twitch at his left eyebrow. He was tense, sitting there like a coiled spring waiting to be released. He was worried. Anxious about Raoul. She knew he had never liked her associating with someone he considered not suitable to be a good friend to her; that he had worried she would get hurt. Renard's concern now could mean but one thing. He wasn't so much afraid for Raoul but for her, and what this blow would do to her. He had worried before, about her workload and her commitment to pursuing justice even at the cost of her own safety. He had not agreed with her decision to get involved with the Rabenhorst family and join them on their river cruise along the Rhine. He had blamed himself for the danger in which she had ended up, a danger from which he had barely been able to save her. He had probably wanted to advise her not to take new cases on for a while, but to travel for her own pleasure and to recuperate and enjoy herself before falling in to a new intrigue. But there was no respite for her now.

Everything she cared for was at stake.

For wasn't it clear that nothing mattered anymore – her wealth, the opportunity to travel and see the world – if she lost Raoul?

It was ironic that his accident had brought her back to Switzerland, where she had taught at an exclusive boarding school for many years, aching to be able to travel, fantasising about the places she'd see and the things she'd do without having any real hope she could ever achieve them. But then her grandfather had left her his fortune and his life's vocation: sleuthing discreetly for the elite of Europe. And suddenly she had been able to go wherever she wanted – explore Athens or Istanbul, go to the seaside or watch the stars in the desert. The whole world had opened up to her. She had known she'd come back to Switzerland someday as it was a beautiful country with awe-inspiring mountain views and much to do, but she had not expected it to be so soon or for such a dramatic reason.

The train started to lose speed and she checked her purse in her lap. Renard would take care of the luggage. She only had to look after her own personal belongings, and with her mind so distracted by Raoul's fate, she had better pay attention to what she was doing.

What was she doing, anyway? Travelling here and there, following insubstantial information, acting like she was entitled to find him, see him, know how he was doing. She wasn't his wife, nor even his fiancée. Her actions might draw attention and that would be embarrassing to him. She could just see the ironic expression on his handsome face as he told her how he had lost the chance to have dinner with a very wealthy would-be sponsor because the man had only sought him out as prospective son-in-law and all her questions had ruined the opportunity. He would tell her off but smile while doing so and she would just be happy that he was able to scold her; that he was still with her. She'd take anything he had to say to her if he were only well enough to speak it.

The train halted and passengers bustled to get out. She waited until the first rush was over, then stood up, clutching her purse. Her entire body hurt from the strain of short nights and the endless worry that she would be too late. Renard gently nudged her to move towards the door.

"The train will leave again in a few minutes and we do not want to be stranded on board."

She got out onto the platform and stood for a moment, breathing the fresh air. The wind that came down from the mountains carried the cold of the snow, but in the sunshine it was nice and warm. The historic station building had the year 1875 laid out in colourful bricks and, right beside it, horse-drawn carriages waited to take passengers to the hotels in style.

Although there were cars around, traffic tended to be slower in these regions, with locals still using a lot of carts and the hotels consciously catering to the sense of history that pervaded everything. Winter sports might have come into vogue recently, but the benefit of thermal springs had been known for centuries. Even the Romans on their way through the Alps to conquer foreign territories had used the hot water to cure their soldiers and provide an attractive resting place for the commanders. She was hoping that Dulce and his cronies had sent Raoul here to recuperate, far from the glare of publicity. This had been Renard's latest information: try Hotel Alpenrot. It was nestled against the side of a mountain, reachable only by funicular, a metal cable car tracking up and down the steep mountainside.

It was a remote location, originally run by a doctor from Basel who had treated lung patients with exposure to clean air and hot spring water. That is, until a rich businessman, who had visited his daughter there, had bought it to turn it into a luxury hotel for those seeking the thrill of winter sports. With spring coming, the season was drawing to an end and the hotel wasn't full, she had been told, although the personal information about which guests were staying there was kept very confidential to protect their privacy. It was just the sort of location that Dulce would choose, she assumed, as he was a man who liked to be in control of his environment. Because the funicular was the only way up to the hotel, he could be certain no one would appear out of the blue or interfere with Raoul.

Once up there, she too would be cut off from the world. There was a telephone line at the reception desk, but all calls would probably be monitored by the hotel clerk.

The idea of this kind of isolation was a bit daunting. Renard had warned her that they were probably going up there in vain, as he had no way of confirming whether Raoul was actually there. She knew he wanted her to stop her search and return to Paris to wait for more reliable information about Raoul's whereabouts and wellbeing, for it was not only unclear how seriously injured he was, but also under what circumstances he had sustained these injuries. She had immediately assumed it had been in a car accident as he had been testing his new vehicle, but Renard had a source who spoke of an avalanche catching him while skiing with friends.

"The funicular is that way," Renard said beside her. He pointed to their left. "We can walk or take a carriage."

"I prefer to walk." Atalanta wanted to work the tension from her muscles and clear her mind. She pulled back her shoulders as she began to walk down the street, past a bakery and a souvenir shop. Normally she would have stopped to admire the offer and select a few items to purchase but now she simply wanted to get to the hotel to inquire whether Raoul was there. If he was not, they'd have to go back down and start all over again.

Her heart sank at the very idea. She didn't know how long she could keep this up, looking for him, hoping, wishing she'd find him and be certain he was not dying. This search pushed her to keep going instead of sinking into a chair and sobbing. But each time she hit a dead end and had to try something else, another piece of her resolve shattered. She was just so tired.

Renard followed his mistress with heavy steps. He had asked a porter at the station to keep their luggage there until he sent word indicating to which hotel it should be taken. He doubted that it would be Hotel Alpenrot and as it was rather difficult to reach, he didn't want to arrange for the luggage to be taken up only to discover half an hour later that Mademoiselle Ashford wanted to leave again.

His heart ached for her anguish. He could tell by the look on her face, the tension in her walk, that she was at breaking point. She had pursued this search with tenacity, never showing a sign of defeat, but always thinking of another place to go to, another logical location where an injured man might recuperate without the press buzzing about. She acted like she was certain she would be successful in the end, but she had to be aware that she was only grasping at straws. Raoul Lemont was in the hands of Vincenzo Dulce, a ruthless criminal, a gangster – someone the Italians would call *Mafia*. He had taken Raoul under his wing for his own selfish purposes, and he would continue to dangle him like a puppet on a string. If he wanted to keep the accident a secret, he would hide Raoul away so cleverly that no one could find him.

Of course there were rumours flying about. The papers were printing column inches but it was all stories without substance, quoting anonymous sources. No journalist had spoken to Dulce nor to one of his team, and no one had seen a trace of Raoul anywhere. The fact that it was also unclear where and when the accident had taken place, added to Renard's worries. He did not dare say it to Mademoiselle Ashford, but he feared that Raoul's accident might not have been an accident at all, but an attempt by a rival gang to assassinate someone they didn't want Dulce to use for his business activities. By allying himself with Vincenzo Dulce, Raoul had set himself up as a target, and despite having no special liking for the rather too handsome and callous driver, Renard did not wish to see him dead.

No, that would certainly be disastrous. Mademoiselle Ashford believed herself to be in love with Raoul Lemont and anything bad happening to him would hit her hard. In fact, as Renard watched her tread resolutely ahead of him, he could already hear her heart breaking bit by bit.

He clenched his teeth. During his term of service as an employee of Clarence Ashford, Mademoiselle's revered grandfather, he had always maintained a strictly professional relationship with the gentleman. He had admired his master and had aided him wherever he could, and he knew that Monsieur Ashford had also valued him and trusted him with tasks beyond what was normal for a valet. They had formed a partnership of sorts and although they had always stayed master and servant, they had still attained a level of confidentiality.

But it was nothing compared to what Renard felt for his mistress. Perhaps it was because she was still so young and vulnerable. She had made great strides in acquiring the skills for successful detecting, but she was also very lonely at times and at risk of falling into the trap of trusting the wrong people. Renard felt a need to protect her, a deep inner urge, stronger than he could expect from mere loyalty to his deceased master and the task he had left behind. She needed someone to look out for her and guide her, even without her noticing. She was proud and independent and he liked her that way. Still, he would be there, on hand, to care for her, if she needed it. And now, being in such emotional turmoil, she needed it more than ever.

But she was steering right into danger. She was determined to find Raoul, and once she had found him, she would be stepping into Vincenzo Dulce's inner circle. She, a detective, an upholder of law and order, would clash directly with a dangerous criminal. Renard wished he could have somehow prevented this, but it was much too late. They were walking to the funicular that would take them up to Hotel Alpenrot. They could already see the brown building on high, with its little turrets peeking out of the snow-covered trees. Alpenrot was allegedly a luxury hotel for those seeking absolute privacy, but if Dulce had found his way there to hide Raoul, it had to be more than that.

Cover for criminal activities perhaps? Was the businessman who had bought it one of Dulce's henchmen? Or had Dulce muscled in later, having gained a hold over the man, through illegal gambling or some kind of blackmail?

Renard could envision many scenarios and none of them were good. He could only hope that once Atalanta had found Raoul and ascertained that he would live, she would listen to reason and leave again, before Dulce was informed of her presence. Renard could only hope that the great man himself would not be staying at the hotel but would leave caring for his injured driver to others. If Atalanta merely paid a short visit and left again, she might be able to go unnoticed. At least, she wouldn't raise such a red flag that Dulce would feel obliged to give her attention.

Because it could be very dangerous once that man started to look your way.

Chapter Two

Atalanta watched the village with its houses and church grow smaller as the cable car moved up the steep track. It maintained a slow but steady speed and the air inside grew colder as they climbed to snowy heights. She dug her chin deeper into her coat's collar. Renard had not brought the luggage. He had argued that it was more convenient to have it brought up later, but she knew what he was really thinking: Raoul was not at the hotel and they were going up there in vain.

She felt a little ashamed that she was dragging him along on this search which had so far been so fruitless. He would never point that out as he was far too polite to openly question her judgement, but he had said last night that she should consider staying in the area for a few days to do some sightseeing, regardless of whether they found Raoul here or not.

"The information currently going around is not very

reliable," he had said in his deep, even voice, "and acting on every new lead is just wasting time and resources. We could find a hotel here and stay until after the weekend, so I may gather some more detailed reports of what happened and what they did afterwards."

Atalanta had not committed either way. She recognised that he was right in his assessment but she was not in the mood to sit still and enjoy her surroundings. Even now, as she regarded the majestic view, her breathing was as rapid as if she had run fast and her hands clutched the strap of her purse. She could not relax for a single moment until she knew what had happened to Raoul. She had to find him first and then she would decide about having some time off. She didn't need it now. She could not allow herself…

"Look." Renard pointed down. "A waterfall."

Atalanta didn't see it. It had probably just been a brief glimpse through the trees. The mountain landscape was wild with rocks, waterfalls, forests and glaciers. It was a world she had never before explored at leisure. While teaching in Switzerland, she had learned how to ski because the teachers at the school were supposed to take the girls on tours and outings and it would not do to be less adept than the very charges she was supposed to look after. At first the speed of it had daunted her and she had feared ending up with a broken leg but after a while she had grown more used to it and had actually started to enjoy it. It was too bad the season was almost over now, or she might have taken a little tour.

The memories of happily frolicking with her charges in

the snow lightened her mood for a few moments and an involuntary smile formed round her lips. She had not thought much about the school in recent months as she had been so busy with her new life, but now that she was back in the mountains, she recalled the good times she had had with the girls, many of whom had trusted her with stories about home and their feelings on being suddenly away from everything they knew. Some of them had promised to write to her when she left, but there had only been one or two letters since then.

She didn't blame the girls. They had probably already found a new favourite teacher to confide in. That was life. Situations changed, people moved on, and it was only natural. Like the water in the waterfall that could never stand still.

A whisper of peace breathed through her heart. She had never been able to hold Raoul. To catch him in her hand, to keep him with her. He had been like sand, slipping through her fingers. He had been like sunlight warming her face without her being able to retain it, lock it in a box to look at later. With him she had to live in the now, without regard for the past or the future.

Perhaps it was as it should be?

She took a deep breath as new anxiety flooded her chest. She was thinking about him in the past tense. *He had been...*

No, he *was*. He was right now. Somewhere in the world he was drawing breath right now and she would find him.

Renard touched her arm lightly. "We are almost there. You must not be—"

"Too disappointed when he is not there? I know. I will be strong."

The cart halted and they got out. The steel platform was attached to the mountainside, a narrow path leading to a plateau on which the hotel was built. It all looked like it was slightly tilting and Atalanta had a strange sensation in her legs as she walked towards the plateau. Having been on a moving vehicle she was suddenly a little unstable – or was it the illusion that the whole hotel was poised to slip down the side of the mountain at any moment?

She reached the double entry doors where a man in blue livery was waiting for them. He looked her over quickly. She had become used to the behaviour of staff at expensive hotels but something about this man was different. His assessing gaze seemed to categorise her. Was she an innocent guest or…?

It made the hairs on her neck stand up. She smiled at him, however, and said with confidence, "I am a close friend of Raoul Lemont. As soon as I heard of his accident, I travelled out here to see him. Could you direct me to him?"

Her heart thumped as she waited for his denial that Raoul was a guest. She should not have handled it this way. She should have gone inside and asked at the desk. This man could lie to her and send her away empty-handed.

But so could the desk clerk. She had no way of knowing whether Raoul was here. In a few minutes she could be leaving again, returning to that funicular, while Raoul was here in the building behind her back. The mere idea caused her to panic. She had to get inside. She had to find him.

"Renard, you explain the situation to this gentleman," she said. "I am going inside." Before the man could react, she pushed through the doors. She assumed Renard would understand her prompt and detain the man so she could get inside to search for Raoul.

Standing in the lobby, with its high, panelled ceiling and mounted animal heads on the walls, she caught her breath a moment. To her left was the reception desk of wood with a clerk who was busy taking notes. He hadn't noticed her arrival, it seemed. To her right were two lifts. The doors were closed and she wasn't about to wait for one of them to come. She walked straight ahead to where a door with a beautifully carved panel led into the next room. Perhaps it was the dining room or a reading room, she had no idea, but she had to remove herself from the entrance. She pushed through the door and stood in a sort of library with bookcases against three walls. The fourth was largely glass and offered a breathtaking view of a frozen lake behind the hotel. There was a terrace with deck chairs and several people lay reading or sunning, draped in warm fur blankets.

At the back, almost at the edge of the lake, was a deck chair on which lay a man. A parasol was positioned to shade him from the sun, but still he wore sunglasses. A woman leaned over the chair, fussing with the blanket that covered him. A second woman stood beside the chair, chatting to the first, making lots of exaggerated hand gestures. A third woman sat on a deck chair, balancing a silver tray in her hand with several cups on it. A fourth was walking over carrying yet another tray with bowls of fruit.

As Atalanta analysed the peculiar little scene, there was a sound behind her and she turned around in a rush. A handsome, dark-haired man of about thirty stared at her with intent brown eyes.

"I have not seen you here before," he said in a pleasant voice, but his gaze was guarded. He spoke German with an Italian accent.

Atalanta forced a winning smile.

"I have just arrived. To see Raoul. Raoul Lemont? I heard about his accident, and I want to make sure he is doing well. We spent quite some time together and…" She let the rest hang.

The man studied her longer than was comfortable, then he burst out laughing. He pointed to the view outside. "If you want a shot at talking to him, you must join the queue."

"I don't follow."

He stepped closer to her. "Every female in this hotel, whether guest or staff, is abuzz about Raoul. It is very hard to keep them away from him, and yet it is essential that he rests. My uncle will never forgive me if I don't bring him back fully recovered."

Atalanta didn't quite know what to say. Relief rushed through her but she was also too tense to fully accept it. "So he is not dying?"

"Dying? No. He did get a nasty blow to the head and he hasn't been quite himself ever since, but…" He studied her closer. "Did you think he was dying? You look very pale."

He reached out and supported her. "Perhaps you should sit down here." He ushered her to a large dark-green sofa and made her sit. "I will pour you a drink." He went over to the mounted wooden globe on a polished oak table and opened it with a click. It contained an assortment of bottles with alcoholic beverages.

"I don't need anything," Atalanta protested, but he poured a liberal amount of something brownish into a glass and handed it to her.

"To cure the shock of finding him better than you thought." He winked at her. "You need not have worried about him. A cat has nine lives, and Raoul is not even a cat. He is more like a lion. Or a jaguar in the jungle. A stealthy creature."

Atalanta sipped the drink. It burned all the way down into her stomach. The hand that was holding the glass shook. She had made it. She had found Raoul. She could see him, talk to him.

The man said, "I don't think I've ever met you before. I mean, at a race or… If you and Raoul are close, we must have met somehow? Or he should have mentioned you to me."

Now she was on thin ice. "We kept our relationship a secret."

"Relationship?" he pounced. "Was it that serious?"

Atalanta wanted to deny it, but that would not serve her purpose. She wanted to stay here and ensure Raoul was well. What was more, she wanted to know what exactly had happened. In how much danger he had been.

This man made it sound like it wasn't all that bad, but still...

However, it seemed like there were too many females vying for his attention already. That would not please the people eager for his speedy recovery. She had to make sure she wasn't just another fawning admirer. She had to make sure her position was somehow special.

"We discussed marriage. So my money could support his career." This was true, even if Raoul had refused her offer, claiming it would only harm their bond if he became dependent on her.

The man's expression changed in a heartbeat. He had previously regarded her with a little amusement and perhaps pity, but now his eyes became warmer.

"I see. Well, perhaps your arrival can cheer him up. He has been a bit down lately. Can't do much. Used to be such an active outdoor man, you know. Hard to sit still." He smiled winningly. "Once you have finished that drink, I can take you to him. We will ask the other ladies to leave. They are just being kind but it is all a little too much exertion for Raoul right now."

Atalanta nodded and sipped anew. This seemed to be going in the right direction.

She didn't want to think about Raoul's reaction when he found out what she had told this man. Suggesting that they were ... practically engaged? Well, she hadn't precisely said as much, but still...

"I don't think you mentioned your name?" she said, looking up at him with a more helpless air than she felt.

"Maurizio Dulce. I am Raoul's team manager. I sometimes call myself his handler. It sounds a little unkind, but … he does need someone to look after him. Ensure he doesn't go to too many parties, doesn't drink too much, you know. All in the interest of the team and getting good racing results this summer."

His last name was Dulce. Family of the great criminal. He had been assigned to look after Raoul. To guard him and keep him in line. He was here to determine everything Raoul did and did not do.

She had to be extremely careful around this man.

He came over and took the glass from her hand. Holding her gaze, he said, "And your name is?"

Atalanta stood up, matching him in height. She smiled easily as she said, "Atty Ford." Her first name was too unique and she had no idea if he knew of the Ashford name in relation to detecting. She was taking a risk by lying to him but she could always clarify later that she travelled under an alias for some personal reason. Safety and privacy? Perhaps Renard could also help there?

He kept looking at her with a pensive intensity. "Ford? Related to the motor car company?"

"Not that I know." Atalanta moved past him to the door leading onto the terrace. "Shall we?"

"Of course. I will take you to him." Maurizio Dulce put the used glass on a table and accompanied her outside. The women were still gathered around the deck chair, clearly attempting to push food and drink on the prostrate Raoul.

If he had indeed suffered a nasty blow to the head, could

he still worsen and die? Hadn't she read somewhere that head injuries could cause internal bleeding? Or break the skull? What side effects could they expect even some time after the initial injury? Was he truly safe?

"Ladies, ladies..." Maurizio waved a hand as he approached the little group. "I must ask you to let Raoul rest. He needs total quiet to recover."

"He needs herbal tea," said the woman with the tray and cups. She was in her thirties with sunglasses perched on her platinum-blonde hair. Her bright red dress was a little short and her silver heels didn't seem appropriate for daytime.

"No, he needs pineapple and peach," insisted the one with the platters. She was about the same age, but with dark hair and a tasteful ensemble of a teal blue silk blouse and brown corduroy skirt.

"He is too cold," said the woman fussing with the blanket, her hand brushing Raoul's cheek as she straightened the edge by his face. She was in her forties, her brown hair combed back into a bun at her neck. Her dress was decorated with a peacock-feather pattern of bright blues and greens and her shoes echoed the green with a blue bow for contrast.

Maurizio put his foot down and said with a stern look, "Away with all of you. Now. If he does not rest, he will get worse and we will have to move him. You do want him to stay, don't you?"

"Of course."

"Oh yes."

Suddenly the ladies were in a hurry to take their leave. Atalanta almost had to laugh as they bustled past her. The woman in the peacock dress wore expensive jewellery studded with emeralds while the platinum blonde had several golden bracelets and rings on her fingers. This hotel catered to an exclusive crowd.

But Atalanta didn't have the time or inclination to analyse them further. There she was beside Raoul and he was alive. Staring down on him, she suddenly felt at a loss for what to say or do. Normally he would have jumped up and taken her hands in his to greet her, but now he lay there listlessly, his eyes hidden behind his sunglasses. It was almost like he hadn't even heard the discussion with the women.

Maurizio leaned down over Raoul and said, "Raoul, *amico*, you have a visitor. A lady who is most anxious to see you. You must make a little time for her. She has travelled a long way."

The head moved and the impassive face was turned towards her. She could not see his eyes nor any sign of recognition.

She forced a smile and said, "Hello there."

Her voice was wobbly. She had to swallow back tears. Here he was. Not healthy obviously, but not dying either. At least, she didn't think he was. She wanted to lean down and hug him, feel him close to her and confirm that her worst fear had not materialised. But he didn't make any move towards her and she stood there clumsily.

"I will leave you two alone," Maurizio said. He nodded

at her and whispered, "Don't exert him. He tires easily and we must promote his recovery, not a relapse." Has he relapsed? Atalanta wanted to ask, but Maurizio was already moving away. One of the women had waited for him and they went inside together, chatting.

The other guests were on deck chairs closer to the hotel and Atalanta felt like she was caught in a bubble alone with Raoul. But he didn't seem like Raoul. It felt like a stranger was staring up at her, with that impassive face.

She lowered herself to sit on the edge of his deck chair. "How are you?"

"Tired. Headache. The same every day." He spoke in a low, monotonous tone. Words without life to them or feeling.

"I had no idea where they had taken you. I've been looking everywhere to find you." Tears clogged her throat. "I was so worried. I had no idea how serious it was and—"

She felt something hot course down her cheek and wiped it away impatiently.

"I am not here to become all emotional. I know how you hate that. I just wanted to make sure that you are…"

"Well?" he asked it with a little surge of fervour. "How could I be? I am lying here, like a wreck, all day long. Nothing to do. Reading is not allowed, nor listening to the radio. Do they want to drive me crazy?"

"I am sure they are doing what is best for you. Following a doctor's advice."

"I am sure I would feel a lot better if I were just allowed to do something. This is maddening."

"You need to regain your strength. You look like you haven't slept much."

He turned his face away and stared into the distance. "How can I sleep when I am lying here all day long? I don't get tired. Still, everyone tells me I look tired. As if they want me to be tired."

"Well, I can read to you a little if you like. Or tell you about the places I have been. Nothing too exerting." *But enough to cheer you up and keep those women away from you.*

Raoul sighed. "They won't let you. They are very strict that I mustn't have any real contact with the others."

"But that is different. They are strangers who are only excited because there is a famous race-car driver at the hotel. I am … your friend." She didn't dare say fiancée, as she wasn't and she should never have suggested it to Maurizio Dulce either. But she had just been so afraid to be sent away. To have come so close, to see Raoul from afar, and then to be denied seeing him. It had seemed unbearable.

"Friend?" Raoul stared at her. "I don't know what you are talking about. Have we met before?"

"Of course we have met before!" Atalanta blurted it out without thinking. "Why would you think…?"

She fell silent and stared at him.

At the paleness under his tan, the strange tightness in all of his features. As if he had become a machine rather than a man. A living, breathing machine but without…

She swallowed hard again. "You don't remember me?"

Raoul pushed himself up into a sitting position. He

pulled off the sunglasses and looked her straight in the eye. His beautiful, deep-brown eyes echoed a deep despair. "I don't remember you, no. But then, I don't remember anything or anyone. They had to tell me my name. They sometimes have to tell me over and over again, and again, and again."

Atalanta's eyes filled with new tears. She put her hand over his and felt the tension in the muscles.

"I am so sorry."

She felt a burning pain – for him, for his situation, because he was lost, drifting on an ocean without a rudder, nothing to anchor him to the past. To experiences, friendships, achievements.

She felt pain for what his future looked like without a past to build on, without hopes and dreams.

But also pain for herself. A blinding pain, in fact, as she realised what this meant.

Everything that had connected them before had been wiped away, like a calculation on a blackboard. The slate was empty now. There was nothing to go back to. Nothing to draw on. No confidentiality. No friendship. No feelings of falling in love.

He didn't know her. It was like they had never met.

Chapter Three

Raoul stared at the beautiful woman sitting beside him on the deck chair. Her eyes filled with tears that leaked down her face without her making a sound. She cried so differently from what he would have expected. There was no fuss, no spectacle. He didn't know why he would have expected it otherwise, but he had. Perhaps because someone in his past had always used tears to get their way? It was possible, but he couldn't remember. He couldn't remember anything.

He formed his hand into a fist to push back the wave of fear that attacked him every time he realised the situation. He had become totally helpless, totally dependent on others – on what they told him about his past.

The man here at the hotel who called himself Maurizio Dulce, he said he was his friend, the one who had found him after the accident, the one who had saved his life. But he didn't know if it was true. Something inside him wondered, doubted. But perhaps it was just his bad feeling about everything. His inability to accept things for what they were, at this moment. It might not always be this way. The doctor had told him his memory could return. Bit by bit. Or even all at once. It had happened before, with other patients.

Patients. He was a patient now. One moment in time had changed him from a healthy man with a bright future into a patient who couldn't remember his own name. Who lay here in a chair like a puppet with cut strings, useless and thrown away. He might be exaggerating, as he had no idea what his life had been like before the accident. He merely assumed he had been healthy and strong and happy and full of zeal to make the most of it, but he wasn't actually certain. Because he simply knew nothing. He also didn't know why this beautiful woman was crying over him. The other women fussed and vied for his attention. He understood that. They found him attractive and they wanted to make the most of the situation. He understood that instinctively as if it had happened before. That was helpful; a sort of gut feeling to rely on.

But she was different. She was crying because she was actually hurting. And something inside him responded to that hurt. He wanted to wrap his arms around her and hold her close to make her stop crying.

Did that mean he knew her? Had they met before and ... been close?

"What is your name?" he asked, hoping it would spark

recognition. What if she could help him remember? He could go back to who he had been before...

"Atalanta," she said in a breathless whisper.

It was not a common name. It was rare and extraordinary, like she was, but he could not say he recalled it from anywhere. It was not associated with anything in his too empty mind.

"You don't remember, do you?" she asked in that same soft tone. There was despair in her eyes, the same despair he felt. The sharp loss of something valuable, something that could never be recovered.

He shook his head.

New tears flowed down her face. He reached out a hand and with a careful fingertip he wiped the tears away. She stared at him, her eyes wide open and begging him for reassurance of some kind. But he had none to offer.

"I don't know..." he said, having to clear his throat before he could go on. "I don't know if I will ever remember. Anything. Anyone. You. The doctor was hopeful when he talked to me. But I got up after he left the room and I listened at the door to what he said to the others waiting in the corridor. He said he didn't know and head injuries are tricky and ... basically, anything could happen. I might never remember who I am. Or how I lived. What I liked. What I dreamed of."

She bit her lip, emotion contorting her face. But her voice was strong when she replied, "I will do anything I can to help you. I remember, you know. We did things together. I can tell them to you. You can try to picture them. And perhaps somehow, while talking, a door will unlock and you can get to a memory. Just one to start with, and then we go from there." A smile tugged at her lips. She gripped his hand harder. "I will stay here with you until it is all solved. Until you remember who you are and what you did."

She waited a moment then added, "Until you remember us."

Atalanta stared hard into Raoul's eyes. She sensed that he was afraid and that he didn't know what to think, feel or do; that he was totally and utterly alone now, cut off from anything he had ever had to hold onto. But she was here and she meant what she'd said. She would help him. Step by step, they'd make their way back to the memories. She would—

"Signorina Ford." Maurizio Dulce said as he approached them. He looked at her sternly. "I see that your reunion is emotional for both of you but I must urge you to be careful. Please, signorina, I ask that you go inside now for a while and return later. The doctor has been very specific that we must avoid strong emotions or anything too shocking, and I do see that this meeting has touched Raoul profoundly."

Atalanta squeezed Raoul's hand. "I will be back soon." She rose from the chair. "Take care. Rest up."

Raoul nodded and sank back into a prone position. He stared up at the blue sky with unseeing eyes.

Maurizio led her back to the hotel. "I am pleased," he said softly, "that you got a response from him. He had become so lethargic that I feared we were going to lose him. You are good company for him. But you must be careful. He is not the man he used to be. His strength seems sapped and…" He frowned. "He sometimes says the strangest things. You must not believe everything that he says. He is confused."

"I understand." Atalanta hoped he didn't notice the chill that went down her spine. Perhaps it was logical that he was warning her, but why immediately plant the idea that Raoul might say strange things and she should not believe him?

What was Maurizio Dulce afraid of? Something she might learn from Raoul? If she took what he said seriously… He was trying to undermine Raoul's credibility and it didn't sit well with her. Obviously Raoul had suffered a great shock and it had affected his mind and body. She had no knowledge of such things and couldn't imagine what it was like. But what Raoul had said to her had made sense. He hadn't sounded dazed or confused at all, so why would Maurizio Dulce warn her not to take everything he said seriously?

She didn't know what kind of accident he had. She didn't know where it had happened, or how; who had been present and what they had done right after. They might have been careful to avoid press reports, but the newspapers were speculating anyway so why not release a statement? Why hide Raoul away in this remote location, where Maurizio could control who came to see him and how much time they spent with him?

What was really happening to Raoul? How dangerous was his physical condition? Or was there something else going on, something she didn't quite understand yet?

Inside, Renard stood waiting. He eyed her with a blank expression. "Ah there you are," Atalanta said. "This is my butler. He will arrange for my luggage to be brought up here. I trust there is a room for me available?"

"Oh yes, I will see to it at once." Maurizio walked to the door. "My uncle owns this hotel so there is nothing you could want that I cannot provide." He shot her a charming smile and disappeared.

Atalanta drew Renard away from the door and whispered in French, as an extra precaution, "I lied about my name. I am now Atty Ford. He is a Dulce and I don't know what they know about my grandfather or me."

Renard nodded. "I understand, mademoiselle. Do not worry, I will play along. Have you seen Monsieur Lemont? Is he well?"

"No, he is not." Her eyes burned anew. "He is suffering from memory loss. Oh, Renard, he looked at me and he didn't recognise me. There was no glimmer in his eyes. He doesn't know who I am! I could be anybody in this hotel, just another woman admiring him because he races cars."

Renard touched her arm. "You are anything but 'just another woman'. You have shown great strength so far and you will continue to do so. Now quiet, for there may be someone coming."

Indeed, Maurizio Dulce was returning with the news that there was a room for her which he could show her to right away. He took her and Renard up in the lift to the fourth floor and showed them into a large room with a beautiful four-poster bed against the far wall, a corner with a writing desk and chair near the window, and a balcony giving a stunning alpine view. There were no large fruit baskets or flower arrangements in the room in the manner to which she was accustomed at luxury hotels, but the furniture looked antique and the fabrics used in the bed drapes and curtains were rich and tastefully patterned with gold thread details. Combined with the impressive snowy world surrounding it, the hotel exuded a unique atmosphere and Atalanta understood why the wealthy would want to stay here and why they would take the isolation for granted. It provided a very different experience compared to what one would find at the more conventional hotels, giving the guests something to brag about once they were back home.

Maurizio Dulce explained that Renard would sleep in the servants' quarters.

"They are quite comfortable," he assured her.

Atalanta thanked him profusely for his good care of her.

Maurizio smiled again. He tapped his finger on her arm and said, "We must look after Raoul. He is very important to us. Anyone who can help us with his recovery is important to us as well and worth any trouble."

Atalanta thanked him again and walked him to the door. After he had left, she made certain he had indeed left the corridor to go back down, before she turned to Renard and said, "Is it my fraught nerves or is there really something sinister about his insistence that they must take care of Raoul?"

Renard sighed. "I am not prone to speculation, but in this case I have to admit I also felt a certain ... suggestion behind his words. Almost as if he was trying to warn you not to interfere with what they have in mind for Raoul."

"And if I do?" Atalanta asked, her heart heavy with foreboding.

Renard shrugged. "Then you might stop being important to them. Instead you will become a nuisance. A burden. A risk even?"

He paused before adding, "A risk that needs to be removed?"

Chapter Four

Renard left to see to the luggage and Atalanta was alone in the room. She had faced difficult situations before, such as posing as a distant cousin to investigate a mysterious *comte* who had lost his first wife in an alleged accident and was about to take a new bride. It had been her very first case and she had been a bundle of nerves. She had feared not playing her part right or not picking up on the right clues to conclude anything worthwhile about the case. She had been totally new to detecting and, looking back on it, it was very special she had actually been able to solve the matter to satisfaction.

That is, if one could speak of satisfaction when there were murders and hurt parties and broken trust. After the revelation of the killer's identity, there were always people who were vindicated and people who suffered the shock of discovering a loved one was not the person they had thought. It made her work hard to do. Apart from the constant tension when being on a case, there was the added pressure of what her revelations might lead to and how nothing would be the same.

Here she had to tread extra carefully. Raoul had signed an agreement to race for Vincenzo Dulce's team for two years. He was their top racer, the front for their entire operation, the cover for their criminal activities. They would not want to lose him or allow anyone to interfere with their hold on him.

However, Atalanta thought as she paced the room, there might be a chance now to wean him away from these dangerous people. He was not well enough to race so they could not use him in the way they had intended. If his recovery took a lot of time, or his memory loss proved to be inconvenient, they might be forced to pick another driver to work for them. After all, the season would start soon and Raoul was supposed to perform at various races in May and throughout the summer. They could hardly expect him to get into a car while he wasn't fit.

Yes, she had to keep reminding herself that the current situation could be good for Raoul; that the longer his recovery took, the more Dulce and his men would be forced to look at other options.

It wasn't pleasant to think Raoul had to stay as he was – unwell, afraid and drifting – but she had previously tried to convince him to break it off with Dulce and he had told her it was already too late, that he was bound. Caught in a trap. This might be his only way to escape.

There was a brief knock on her door and she turned to it

with a jerk. Her heart hammered as if someone had been listening at that door, as if they had heard her thoughts and become aware of her plan to take Raoul away from them.

"*Herein,*" she called, using German as she assumed it was one of the staff.

The door opened and on the threshold stood one of the women she had seen hovering around Raoul outside. It was the platinum blonde in the short red dress who had held the tray with cups. She took in Atalanta's appearance with a quick assessing glance from head to toe. A slight smirk around her lips seemed to betray that she didn't quite see her as competition.

"Hello," she said in German, "I just wanted to come up and meet you. You will be staying here, won't you? I am glad there is someone new moving in. It had started to get a bit dull."

"It could hardly be dull while Raoul Lemont is here," Atalanta said, determined to draw the other woman out at once.

The blonde laughed softly. "Oh, I'm sure it would have been wonderful had he been healthy. But he suffered a blow to the head and they are all fussing over him. He mustn't lie in the sun, can't skate or ski, shouldn't talk too much. I can't believe my bad luck. Finally I get a chance to meet a celebrity and he can't even dance with me." She stepped closer as she said, "Have you ever danced with him? It seemed like you knew each other from before."

"Yes, I do know him." Atalanta reached out her hand. "Atty Ford."

The woman squeezed her hand with surprising strength. "Eva Reuter. My doctor sent me here for my health."

"I thought it was no longer a health resort."

"It used to be until a few years ago when it became more of a regular hotel. But there are still a lot of great facilities – thermal baths and sports. Not to mention the clean mountain air."

"So you have lung trouble?" Atalanta inquired.

"It is more of a general health issue. I am always tired. My doctor says it could also be in my mind. That I am too high-strung. It wears me out." Eva shrugged. "I don't understand all the difficult words he uses. But I do like the mountains and I came here to have a good time."

"This hotel must be quite expensive," Atalanta said. She wondered if Eva had a rich husband who paid for all of this or whether she had money of her own. "I have no idea really as my butler takes care of everything when I travel."

"You travel a lot?" Eva asked with a curious gleam in her eyes. It seemed this new information increased her interest in Atalanta. "You must have a rich husband."

Atalanta laughed softly. It was amusing to realise others wondered about her as she did about them. "One does not always need a husband to be able to travel."

"You have money of your own? That must be wonderful." Eva waited a moment before saying, "Oh." The way in which she moved her hand to her mouth to suggest a sudden shock was too exaggerated to be real. "You must be related to Henry Ford, the motor car manufacturer?" She appeared giddy at the idea of making an acquaintance with someone from that illustrious family.

"Unfortunately not," Atalanta said. "Our family fortune doesn't come from trade." She said it with a hint of disgust.

"Oh, you are old money. You may even have a title?"

"I don't like to use it when travelling. It attracts the wrong kind of people."

"The wrong kind of men, you mean." Eva went to the stool in front of the writing desk and perched herself on it, crossing her legs. Atalanta blinked as she had hardly invited the woman to make herself at home in her hotel room. But Eva seemed to think nothing of it and cheerfully continued, "I know what you mean. When my husband was on his deathbed, he said to me, Eva, you must be careful when I am no longer there to protect you. You must hide what money you have or you will be fighting off fortune hunters. I guess he was a bit sour at the idea that he would pass away and I would go on to enjoy life with all of his money in my pocket. But then, he did marry me when he was seventy-five."

Seventy-five? Eva looked to be in her thirties. How large an age gap had they had?

Atalanta didn't know how to respond but Eva didn't seem to want any kind of reaction from her. She continued, studying her right hand with perfectly manicured nails: "I was his secretary, you know. I typed up all of his letters. He had just divorced his third wife. Or was it his fourth?" Her brows pulled together in a deep frown. "He did marry once when he was very young. A youthful indiscretion, he used to call it. That must have been number one. Oh well, it doesn't really matter. He divorced them all and they had to be happy with the settlement they received, whether modest or generous. I got it all."

With a little squeak of delight she jumped up from the chair and walked to the window. Her silver heels tapped sharply on the wooden boards.

"You have a far better view than me. Maurizio must like you." She leaned on the windowsill and gazed outside. "Maurizio is quite a handsome man, don't you think? The others deny it but they are all looking at him in passing. I suppose they have to be discreet about it if they are married. I, however, don't have such reserve. I fully intend to enjoy my stay here. My doctor will be pleased when I come back in much better spirits."

She turned to Atalanta and smiled.

"When my husband was ill, the doctor was very kind to me. He supported me a lot after the death and advised me on what steps to take to keep the children away from the fortune. Yes, with four ex-wives, my husband also had some children. I never met all of them, but the ones I did meet were quite annoying. They didn't think I should have the money as I had come in last. But they were never kind to their papa, and I treated him very well." She smiled. "Anyway, the doctor was quite helpful but then he proposed to me because he had fallen in love. You must understand how awkward this was. With my station in life, I cannot possibly marry a doctor, no matter how attentive he has been. So I had to tell him no and he took it quite hard. But now we are the best of friends again, as I set him up nicely in a much bigger practice close to the Italian border. He can afford a summer house on Lake Maggiore now."

Atalanta blinked. The constant stream of information was a bit overwhelming. It was beyond her why anyone would want to share this much personal detail with someone they had barely met. She wanted the woman to leave so she could be alone with her thoughts but perhaps it could be useful to learn more about what had happened before she had arrived?

"Has Raoul been here long?" she asked.

Eva blinked a moment. It seemed her thoughts were still with her doctor at the Lake Maggiore summer house. "I don't really know. I only arrived last week. I learned from Margot that he is a famous race car driver. I had personally never heard of him, but he is good-looking, like a film star."

She came closer to Atalanta.

"Margot should not be looking at him. She is married, you know, and trying to convince all of us how happily married she is. Her husband visits her every weekend."

"Every weekend? That sounds like she is here for a long period of time."

"Oh yes. She has weak lungs. She has been coming here for years, on and off, even in the time before it was a hotel. I don't know all the details but she is like the matron. The Queen of Hotel Alpenrot." Eva laughed softly. "I find her interest in Raoul quite amusing. An older woman trying to interest a younger man." She pulled a face. "In her position she should be more discreet about it. Her husband might take offence." She waited a moment and said, "He is quite a handsome man. A fiery Italian type. If I were married to such a man, I wouldn't look at anyone else."

Atalanta made a vague, confirming noise, trying to look for a way to lead the conversation back to Raoul. But as Eva Reuter had only arrived recently, she would probably not know anything worthwhile. Margot was the one she had to talk to.

A sound rang out and Eva turned to the door. "That is the bell for cocktails. See you later." And she dashed away, leaving the door open.

Atalanta went to shut it. In the corridor she saw the other younger woman, the one in the silk blouse and corduroy skirt, waiting for Eva and the two linked arms and walked down the stairs together. Further down the corridor another figure approached. It was the woman who had fussed over Raoul's blanket. She had accessorised her peacock dress with a shawl of glimmering gauze and carried herself with grace. But the look on her face was positively venomous as she stared after the younger women.

Atalanta quickly closed her door behind her and went over to the woman.

"Excuse me? I heard a bell. Is that a signal of some sort?" Eva had just told her but it was a wonderful conversation starter and the other woman took the bait at once.

"It is the bell for cocktails. We have a lovely bar here. There is often dancing at night." She gave Atalanta a sharp, inquisitive look. By contrast with Eva who had looked her up and down to assess her posture and her clothing, this woman only looked closely at her face, as if trying to read behind her eyes. It made Atalanta uncomfortable. She felt ... almost caught out.

The woman said, "I saw you arrive. Maurizio sent us away so you could be alone with Raoul. I confess I watched the two of you out of the window. It was a touching little scene. You were crying and he..." She fell silent and had to swallow before being able to go on. "He seemed quite tender towards you. It made me miss my husband. Dieter does try to visit me as often as he can, but ... he has business to attend to."

"I see." Atalanta reached out her hand. "I am Atty Ford."

"Margot Bergreiter." The woman squeezed her hand. "Do tell me that the two of you are in love. It looked so sweet and ... I think he needs a strong woman by his side. Most men do, even if they will never admit it."

Atalanta felt a flush creep up. "It is complicated. Raoul is fiercely independent and with his racing..." She dropped a silence. "I think it is so dangerous. I am afraid to lose him. Now with the accident..."

"But it didn't happen on the race track. Isn't that funny how life works? You worry too much about one thing and then another happens." Margot shrugged. "It goes to show that you should never let yourself be guided by fear. If you are in love and you think he is the man of your dreams, the one you want to spend the rest of your life with, you must act. Regardless of the consequences." She reached out and put a hand on Atalanta's arm. "You may think I am overstepping a line by saying this to you because we are perfect strangers, but love is a rare thing. There isn't a whole lot of it in this world. When it comes, you must feel lucky and not think of the hardship or what you might need to sacrifice for it. Not even at how it might hurt to lose someone again later. No. You must take it and guard it because you are one of the few people who will ever have it."

"Is love so rare?" Atalanta asked. "I thought it was pretty common for people to fall in love."

"Oh yes, to fall in love, to feel attraction. It happens all the time. But forging a deep personal bond…? Fusing one soul with another? Feeling their pain? That is different. It doesn't happen often and when it does, you must be grateful, not shy away from it or think you cannot handle it. Because you always can." She smiled widely. "You can."

Her insistence was a bit awkward as they barely knew each other. Atalanta did not know what to say and pulled her arm away by stepping closer to the stairs. "Shall we go down to cocktails?"

"Yes. You must forgive me for being a sentimental old woman. Well, I am not that old, but that is sometimes how I feel. Being with younger people who have their lives ahead of them and can still make all the choices – whom to marry, where to live, what to do – it must be wonderful." She smiled again as she walked down beside Atalanta. "I may be exaggerating how wonderful it is as I have never had much of a chance to enjoy my youth. From a young age I had lung trouble and I was sent from one place to another to recuperate. It is not easy as a child to be told you can't run and play or have ice cream because it is too cold and you will start coughing again. But in the end, it was my salvation because I met my husband here."

"Here in this hotel?"

"Not at the actual hotel but in the region. I was allowed to take a boat trip on a lake and Dieter was also on the boat with a friend. We ended up chatting and… That was the start of it." Her eyes shone with a warm light. "It was a beautiful sunny day and the mountains were reflected in the lake. I can still feel the chill of the wind on my face. There is always wind on the water, you know. Dieter told me stories of what he and his friend had done, walking along narrow paths and going all the way up to a viewpoint. I had been to the region often but I had never done these things because I couldn't. Him telling me about them was wonderful."

They were at ground level and Margot turned to go through a short corridor towards an open door, from where the sound of voices emanated.

"I will never forget," Margot whispered as they went through the door to join the other people. Eva was at the bar picking up a cocktail that had an olive bobbing on top. She laughed too loudly at some remark made by a handsome, dark-haired man of about thirty. Behind the bar, a good-looking man in his forties was mixing the drinks. Maurizio Dulce stood beside a table on which sat a record player, chatting to the two women who had also been with Raoul earlier.

Raoul himself was nowhere in sight.

Margot went to the bar and said to the barman, "This is my new friend Atty Ford. She arrived today. I think you should mix her your famous welcome cocktail."

"As long as there isn't too much alcohol in it," Atalanta said quickly. "I can't stand alcohol on an empty stomach."

"I am sure Franco will be careful." Margot said with a wink at the bartender. He winked back.

Looking around the room, Atalanta realised that all the men here were incredibly dashing. Did Maurizio's uncle, the hotel owner, select them based on their good looks? She could imagine that the female guests appreciated this, but how would their husbands feel about there being so many attractive men around?

Then again, it might be natural to wink or flirt a little but ladies of standing would not resort to anything more with a member of the staff. There was an invisible line drawn and one did not cross it.

Then again, not all ladies here were married. And some people might think it quite deliciously adventurous to cross the line.

The bartender handed Atalanta a glass filled with a bright orange liquid. There was sugar on the rim and a piece of pineapple wedged on the side. Atalanta took a careful sip. There was orange in it, pineapple and something else fruity. There was also the burn of alcohol but she had no idea what kind. Margot, who had accepted a green cocktail, lifted her glass to toast Atalanta. "To a wonderful stay, Atty. May your dreams come true."

Atalanta touched her glass to Margot's. "Thank you. The same to you."

"All my dreams have already come true," Margot said. "I am married to the man I love and I can do things I enjoy."

"It sounds positively dreadful..." Eva's voice cut into the conversation. "To have all one's dreams come true. I mean, what is there left to hope for, to wish for? To work for and to fight for?" She looked at Margot with a strange, challenging glow in her bright blue eyes. "Life is for those who dare live it, not for those watching from the sideline."

Margot blushed painfully. She didn't seem to know what to say.

Maurizio Dulce appeared by the group and said in a forced tone, "With the beautiful day we've had, the sunset will be stunning. You must not miss it."

"The sunset is still hours away," Eva said with a hitched brow. "You sound like a stern tutor who wants to send his pupils to bed already."

"I am merely ensuring that everyone is enjoying themselves," Maurizio said. Although he was smiling, his voice seemed to hold a subtle warning tone.

Eva's eyes flashed as if she were gearing up for a sharp retort but then she relented and toasted Atalanta with her glass. "To a wonderful stay. You will like it here. I can show you all there is to do, both at the hotel and around it."

Maurizio said to Atalanta, "Can I speak to you for a moment? In private?"

Atalanta removed herself from the others. They left the bar through a decorated door on the other side of the room and found themselves in a room with several sofas and window seats each offering breathtaking views. There was no reading material in sight, which made Atalanta wonder if the seating was actually only intended as a means to enjoy the panorama outside. How wonderful it would be to sit here and watch the sunset. She knew from her boarding school days how snowy peaks could be bathed in a breathtaking reddish glow. *Alpenglühen* the locals called it.

Maurizio said, "Raoul has retired to his room and claims he has too much of a headache to join us for dinner. I cannot force him to sit at the table with us, but I can try to make him eat. He must not lose his strength. Will you eat with him and try to engage him in some light-hearted conversation?"

Atalanta's heart leapt with joy at the prospect of eating alone with Raoul. She would be able to quiz him about what happened. If he knew…

"Of course," she said. Maurizio gestured for her to leave the room through a narrow panelled door. "I will take you to him. Do bring your cocktail." He added as she walked ahead of him, "I hope you do not find Signora Reuter too annoying?"

"I have only just met her."

"Yes, but you must have realised already that she is determined to create a stir wherever she goes. My uncle insisted we receive her because she is the widow of some German count or duke or earl, I am not sure which. The Germans have too much small nobility – people who have large country estates and peasants who bow their heads respectfully when they pass." It sounded like he was ridiculing Eva Reuter.

"So you are only doing what your uncle requested by being friendly to her?" Atalanta inquired. They had come into a broader corridor with oil paintings on the walls. She let him overtake her so he could lead the way to Raoul's room. Maurizio cast her an amused look. "Who says I am being friendly to her? I must be polite because my position here requires me to be. But I do not like her type. She is a predator."

It takes one to know one, Atalanta thought. As a Dulce he was probably knee-deep in criminal activities.

She could not be certain, of course, and perhaps he was just some distant cousin who had been pulled in by Vincenzo Dulce to play team manager to Raoul, but his last name made him a suspect in her book and she would watch herself around him.

"I always distrust people who talk too much," Maurizio continued, "they talk and talk to hide something they do not want others to notice."

"Perhaps it is only insecurity on her part? I understood her husband was a lot older and his family did not support her marriage to him."

"She already told you as much? That is exactly what I mean. If the woman had only an ounce of decency, she would not flaunt the family difficulties like it is something to be proud of. Italians would never do so. Family is everything. You do not humiliate family members. You do not tell tales about them, or make them look bad. You do not betray them."

Atalanta nodded as if she were following along with interest and approval. But she wondered if he was also making another point here. As a Dulce, his loyalty lay with his family, not with Raoul or with her. Was this story only superficially directed at Eva's talkativeness but in reality a warning to her?

Another one, after his rather sinister words earlier.

Perhaps she had taken too much risk in coming here. It was the lion's den, and with Raoul suffering from memory loss she could not even do much for him.

But she was determined to use what little wiggle room she saw to get him out of the criminals' clutches.

"Here we are," Maurizio said and knocked on a door. There was a reply that sounded much like *"Go away"*. Maurizio knocked again and called something in Italian. No reply this time. He knocked again and tried to open the door but found it was locked on the inside. Maurizio turned red in the face and began shouting abuse in Italian.

Atalanta lightly touched his arm. "May I?" She raised her voice. "Raoul? It is me. We can have dinner together. May I come in?"

There was a brief silence and then the click of a lock. Maurizio pushed the door open at once. Raoul, who stood right behind it, staggered back.

"What do you think you are doing?" Maurizio barked at him. "You cannot lock the door! You might feel unwell but we would be unable to come in and care for you. You do not lock the door again, you understand?"

Atalanta blinked at the violence in his tone. She cast a quick look at Raoul, who looked pale and intimidated.

She said to Maurizio, "You asked me to be gentle in my approach but you yourself are far too forceful. You could have injured Raoul just now and caused him to fall. He could have hurt himself even more. You must be much more careful."

Maurizio took a deep breath as if gearing up for an argument. Then he hung his head and ran his hand through his thick, dark hair. "I am sorry. I just feel so responsible. Vincenzo is not happy about the accident. It happened when he was in my care and … I am sorry, Raoul. But I must look after you now. You must cooperate."

Raoul nodded vaguely. "It is fine." He walked back with slow, careful steps to sit on the edge of his bed.

Maurizio said, "Signorina Ford will dine with you here. I will have my staff arrange for it immediately."

He looked at Atalanta. "*Grazie.*" He retreated with a bow of the head.

She wasn't certain what he was thanking her for. That she was having dinner with Raoul? Or that she had pointed out the error of his approach?

"He seems very highly strung," she observed to Raoul.

Raoul shrugged. He rubbed his face and closed his eyes a moment. "Maurizio is always like that. Intense. I don't know if he was like that before. I don't remember. I just feel like … he is always watching me." He looked up at her. "Do you think I need watching?" His question seemed urgent, and she tilted her head. "How do you mean?"

"Do I need to be watched over? Am I unstable? Dangerous? To myself, to others?"

He lifted a hand to wave in the air. "I can't remember things. Could I do something and not remember it half an hour later? Or is it only that I don't remember things from before the accident? I don't know because I can't make out what is up or down." His face flushed as he continued, impatiently, "I lose track of time sometimes. I don't even know how long I have been here. Everything is a blur. I feel like I should know something to get back on track." He gestured to the bedside table. "I have started to make notes so I can read what happened earlier and sort of remember that way."

Atalanta looked at the black notebook that sat there. "Does it help?"

"Not with actually remembering, but at least that book can tell me when I arrived here and how I felt at the time – things my mind won't recall."

Atalanta nodded slowly. "That is good. I mean, it must give you some reassurance."

Raoul laughed softly. "Does it? Or does it only make me feel worse? In two or three days, I will pick it up and read what I just wrote." He moved around the bed carefully and picked up the notebook. He opened it and read to her, "I just met a woman called Atalanta. You would think I would remember such an unusual name but I don't. I should know her because she cried upon seeing me. She was hurt to see how badly I am doing. I could see it in her eyes. She knows me. She really knows me. But I don't know her. I don't remember a thing. And tomorrow I might not even remember having met her here either. At least, I am afraid of that. I am afraid that every new day is a new torture of trying to find something to hold onto while everything just slips through my fingers. Who am I? What did I do? Who is friendly and who is not?"

He stopped and looked at her.

"I think I have enemies. Does that make me mad? Am I suffering from delusions because of the blow to my head?"

"I don't know." Atalanta stayed where she was, observing Raoul as he stood there with his notebook, quivering with tension.

He kept looking at her. "How do I know I knew you before if I can't remember? How do I know you are not someone Maurizio asked to come and sit with me and chat to me and get me to open up? I feel like I am a clam he is trying to pry a pearl out of."

Interesting.

Raoul continued, "I have no idea who I can trust. I don't want to have dinner with you, thinking you might be some spy for Maurizio. But then again, I don't want you to go away either."

Atalanta's heart broke a little for his anguish.

"I can't tell you anything, for how could you believe me? If I am Maurizio's spy, I will of course deny it. But if I am not, I will also deny it. There is no way for you to know if I am telling the truth. There is no way for me to convince you we do know each other and have shared many adventures and—"

She fell silent, flushing.

Raoul kept looking at her. Then he shut the notebook and put it back in place. "I will have dinner with you, because having dinner together is better than having it alone. I will figure out a way to test you."

His resolve made her smile.

"Good. I look forward to it."

While they sat at the table which the staff had laid with damask, fine linen, crystal and candles, Atalanta just wanted to enjoy the intimacy of the moment without talking about the past. The flickering candlelight threw shadows across Raoul's handsome face and she tried to remember whether they had ever sat quite like this, so dependent on each other. He had always had his racing and his appointments to get to. He had never had much time for her and she had not expected him to cancel his entire life for her, but ... some investment, some proof of his affection would have been nice.

"What do you think happened to me?" Raoul asked suddenly.

She frowned. "Excuse me?"

"What do you think happened to me? I had an accident, they say. What do you think happened?"

"To tell you the truth, I don't know. The newspaper reports vary wildly. Some even claimed you were dying. Or already dead."

"You came here thinking I was dead?"

"I looked for you in several places. It took me more than ten days to actually locate you."

"And you thought I might be dead?"

"I was telling myself it could not be. But I was very afraid." She sat up straighter. "Not that it matters now. You are not dead."

Raoul grimaced. "At least I know that. But Maurizio has been very reticent to furnish me with details of my accident. I hoped you could fill in the blanks for me."

"I can't." But she could have Renard look into it. She would not say as much now, but first see if they could achieve anything Raoul could work from.

"What did Maurizio tell you?" she asked Raoul.

He gestured over his shoulder at the notebook by the bed. "Read it for yourself. Page one."

Atalanta got up and fetched the notebook. She reseated herself and opened it. It felt a little uncomfortable to be reading his innermost thoughts, but at least she had his permission.

She swallowed hard at the sight of his familiar scrawl.

I am in some mountain hotel. There is nothing but snowy

peaks around me. I also see a frozen lake. I have no memory of ever having been here, but then I have no memory of anything. They told me my name is Raoul Lemont and I had an accident while skiing with friends. Apparently I went downhill ahead of them and hit a tree trunk or stone hidden in the snow. I rolled over a couple of times and then lay still. They had a scare thinking I was seriously injured. But I only had a dislocated shoulder and was bleeding from a cut under my hair. They took me back to the hotel where we were staying and looked after me. It turned out I had lost my memory. Therefore they moved me and set me up in this place to recover in private. It seems I am a society figure who is of interest to the press and they don't want pictures of my bandaged head and my vacant eyes in the papers.

Atalanta had to smile as this cynical tone was typical of Raoul. She continued to read.

So here I am, locked up in a hotel that I can't get away from without asking someone to accompany me. There is but one way down in a funicular. It is probably best to keep those journalists at bay, but I feel like they have put me in prison. I can't do anything without being watched.

He had felt watched from the very first day. She frowned as she turned the page to read on. The next page only held three words scrawled in large angry letters.

Who am I?

Her heart hurt for him, but she must not let her feelings overwhelm her now. He needed her to be strong and practical, to help him navigate this unpredictable situation. She lowered the book and looked at Raoul. "Have you been taking any kind of medication? Painkillers? Something to help you sleep?"

Raoul nodded. "For the first few days my headaches were unbearable. I took pills and I was sleeping most of the time. It is a bit better now."

"Do you feel like the pills make you more ... languid? Drowsy? I mean, they are meant to sedate pain, but ... could they also be increasing your sense of confusion? The lack of memories?"

"I wondered about that myself." Raoul scoffed. "Yesterday morning I didn't take the painkiller, but I was so sore by lunch that I had to take it anyway. I am not sure whether they could be tampered with. I mean, why?"

"There could be several reasons." Atalanta went back to the notebook. The next page was a diary entry again.

I quizzed Maurizio about the accident. Apparently he was there and rescued me from lying facedown in the snow. He also got my shoulder back in place. But I don't remember any of it. I feel like there is something he is not telling me. I can see it in his eyes. He is worried. Not just about my health, but also about what I might find out.

She looked at Raoul. "Do you doubt you had a skiing accident?"

Raoul leaned back in his chair. "I can't even judge. You see, normal people know whether they have been skiing before and how well they can ski and how likely it is that they would suffer an unfortunate fall. But I don't know. I can't say, 'Hey, I am such an expert skier that I would never make a grave mistake.' I mean, at that speed…"

"You do remember the speed?"

"I can see people skiing from the windows here. With binoculars. It goes fast." He smiled ruefully. "Easy to overlook an obstacle especially when it is hidden in the snow. And I do have a very sore head."

"Yes, but that could have been caused by other means." Atalanta turned another page and read on.

> *I feel like I am wasting my time here. There is no trace of my past in this hotel. I want to meet people who knew me before. I want to talk to them, to see if I can unlock some memories. But I am stuck here with Maurizio who pretends he is my friend, and a bunch of mindless women who crowd me with blankets and herbal tea. One of them is the absolute worst. Her name is Eva Reuter and she talks all day long about her late husband who left her a fortune. About liking the men here because they are all so handsome. About the other women who are apparently not her best friends.*

Atalanta had to smile again.

> *I can't imagine why she chose this remote hideout for her vacation. I can easily picture her in Biarritz or Cannes or*

some other place where she can show off her wealth and find a ready audience for her stories. She feels like a Hollywood actress on a village stage.

Atalanta stared into the distance. Eva Reuter did feel rather like an actress playing a part. Everything about her was a little too emphatic. Was it because she had once been a normal girl who married a rich and titled man, and she had had to learn how to perform to certain standards to fit in with her new lifestyle? Or was there more to it? Raoul was so clever to raise the question of what a woman like her was doing here. There were plenty of hotels in the region, more easily accessible and offering more opportunities to meet people. Here she was almost cut off from company except those staying here. What was she here for? Atalanta continued to read.

I don't know how I can convince them that no amount of nettle tea is going to bring back my memory. Especially the woman with the weak lungs who has been coming here for years, she has an unshakable faith in all kinds of things for the improvement of health: sleep with a bag of lavender under the pillow; breathe the mountain air at the window while doing exercises; and something with emeralds? There seems to be a gemstone museum nearby where she bought all kinds of stones to line her windowsill to bring her healing. I feel sorry for her. She is always talking about places she has never been. Places her sister writes to her about. The sister went to America and even Australia. I don't know if she makes it up to seem more interesting. It would certainly be hard to stomach having a sibling travelling the world while all you can do is rest in order to be able to do an hour's worth of something. Looking at her, I wonder what my life will be like if my headaches don't go away. If what I am doing now is all I will ever do again.

Atalanta swallowed hard before looking up at him. "You do sound a bit morose in here."

Raoul shrugged. "I can't help it that I feel rather glum. I can't remember what my life was like and even if I could and it had been fun and exciting, like they are making me believe, I have no guarantee I can ever get back to it. Perhaps I am better off not remembering. Just this morning I looked out of the window at the world around me and imagined I would just stay here and paint the mountains. I would create endless paintings of white mountain peaks and sell them for top money because people would be so interested to own a piece by this mysterious painter without a past."

Atalanta closed the notebook with a snap. "I am glad you have figured out a way to make a living because nobody is going to support you forever."

He looked at her with a sudden, sharp jerk of the head. His eyes narrowed a moment in pain. "What do you mean?"

"I mean that you will have to take care of yourself somehow. It is good you are thinking up ways to earn a living if you can't go back to what you used to do." She picked up her fork. "They told you that you were an important society figure?"

"Yes, but not much more. I don't know why. That doctor must have told them not to overload me with information." He laughed softly. "It feels like a conspiracy."

Indeed, Atalanta thought. In Raoul's condition it was obviously pointless to tell him endless details about his life as he could not remember any of it and would easily forget it again. But why not say outright that he was a race car driver? That he made a living racing cars at high speed around a track? What hurt could that do?

In fact, even if Maurizio had not told him, the others could have. The women who adored him. They knew who he was. Why had everyone been so tight-lipped? She had to find out as soon as possible. Something was going on here, something more than just keeping Raoul away from the press.

And she was determined to find out exactly what it was.

Chapter Five

As they were finishing their dessert, there was a knock on the door. It was opened without offering time for a reply and Maurizio barged in. He was dressed in his finest, suggesting he had himself had dinner with the ladies and entertained them. But his expression was wary and his eyes seemed guarded and concerned as he regarded Raoul and Atalanta sitting together.

"I must ask Signorina Ford to leave you now," he said. "This is very good for you but also very tiring. You can see her again tomorrow."

Raoul leaned back in his chair. "I don't feel tired. I want to have coffee with her."

"You can't drink coffee at night. It keeps you awake. You must wind down and go to bed early."

"I don't feel sleepy at all." Raoul got up to ring the bell by the fireplace but Maurizio blocked his path. "You must go to bed early," he said in a firm tone. "You are recovering from a serious head injury. If you are not careful, your complaints will get worse. I just want you to get better."

Raoul seemed ready to shove him aside and Atalanta said, "He does have a point, Raoul. Why don't you go to bed early and we can have breakfast together in the morning? I am staying here now and I am not leaving again. There is no rush. We have all the time in the world to talk."

Raoul sighed, his shoulders slumping. He turned away from them saying in a dull voice, "Fine. See you in the morning."

"Sleep tight," Atalanta said, her throat constricting at the sight of his lonely figure standing there. He probably felt like she was conspiring with the others, but she didn't want to alienate Maurizio. He claimed to have been present at Raoul's accident. She had to learn more about it from him.

She left the room with Maurizio and watched as he closed the door. He extracted a key from his pocket and inserted it in the lock. It turned with a vicious click. The sound sent Atalanta's heartbeat skittering. "Are you locking him in his room?"

"Only for his own safety. One night he got out of bed and wandered the hotel, muttering that he was looking for a drink. I don't know whether he was merely confused because of his memory loss or actually sleepwalking. I am not a doctor and I can't really judge the severity of his condition, so I lock him in to ensure he doesn't start wandering again and hurt himself."

"I see." Atalanta had to admit that she had no idea what

a head injury could do to a person. Perhaps Maurizio was genuinely concerned about Raoul harming himself somehow. She said softly, "This must have been very hard on you – caring for him after the accident, fearing for his life. You were there when it happened. It must have been terrifying, thinking he was dead."

"Yes, yes, we all thought that. It was total panic. Chaos. Fortunately, it turned out not to be that bad. But still … we have no idea if this memory loss will subside. Until then we must live with the uncertainty."

"You were skiing? I am surprised that Raoul had an accident at all, because he is a very good sportsman."

"Yes, but he was distracted. And there was a strong glare from the sun on the snow. It was so blinding white that it was really not possible to see much, especially at speed." Maurizio knotted his fingers with a grim expression.

"Wasn't it a bit risky to take him skiing at all?" Atalanta wondered aloud. "I mean, he is your top race car driver, the person around whom your entire team is built. The new car was imported from America especially for Raoul. The season is about to start and… You must have thought about keeping him safe."

Maurizio grimaced. "Because there was so much pressure ahead of the season's start, we decided we needed some time away."

"But Vincenzo Dulce must be upset that this accident happened. He put so much money into the new team and car."

Maurizio cast her a sharp look. "Have you ever met Vincenzo?"

"No, not at all, but I have heard that he is a successful businessman. It stands to reason that a businessman wants a return on his investment."

Maurizio threw his head back and laughed. "You sound just like him. He will want to meet you." His expression became serious as he continued. "After all, you told me that you want to marry Raoul. Vincenzo will want to meet the woman who wants to become Raoul's wife."

"So he can decide whether he approves of me?" Atalanta asked with a light-hearted smile she didn't feel inside. "I heard from Raoul that Vincenzo welcomed him into the team with open arms and has been almost like a father to him. I would hope that Raoul's father would approve of me."

She was blatantly lying as Raoul had never said any such thing, but he could not deny it in his current condition and she wanted to see how Maurizio responded to her acting like she had a very high opinion of Vincenzo and could not wait to meet him in person.

Maurizio said, "Vincenzo is like that. When he throws himself into something, he does it with all of his zeal. Racing is now his passion and Raoul is his key to success."

It sounded a little bitter. Atalanta wondered if Maurizio tried hard to please Vincenzo but always came up short, and now was in the position of having to watch how his fickle uncle embraced someone else with the appreciation to which Maurizio felt he himself was entitled. Did he really care for Raoul or did he see him as competition for his uncle's favours?

Maurizio said, "Let's not talk about my uncle or Raoul for a while. It is a beautiful evening and I want to show you the stars." He offered her his arm and they went out on the terrace. It was cold outside, now that darkness had set in, but Atalanta didn't feel it as she looked up at the sky. "I remember that they are particularly bright here. I used to love watching them."

"You were in the Alps before?"

"Yes, I ... it was in boarding school in the Alps." As a teacher, but she need not mention that. Let him think she had enjoyed a privileged upbringing with money at her disposal.

Maurizio nodded. "Boarding school is so popular with rich families. It is a concept that is alien to me. I value family over everything. Family cares for one another. It doesn't send children away from home to live with strangers."

Atalanta was surprised by the emotion behind his words. "I assume it is different in some circles. Where I grew up it was perfectly normal. Parents didn't view it as sending their children away or not caring for them. On the contrary, it was the highest form of caring for them, ensuring they would have all the skills and opportunities required to get on in life."

"And you enjoyed it? You were happy? Or were you lonely and homesick?"

"Perhaps a little, at times." Atalanta thought of her

pupils and how some of them had not taken well to boarding school life. Then again, it was important to learn how to adjust to new circumstances. "I guess I discovered that I could not always have things my way. That is a valuable lesson."

"I am glad to hear it," he said with irony in his voice. He stood with his hands folded behind his back, staring into the distance.

Atalanta breathed in the cold mountain air. She was not dressed for the chill around her and started to shiver. Maurizio seemed to rouse himself from some morose thought and turned to her.

"I am sorry, you are getting cold." He slipped out of his dinner jacket and put it around her shoulders. It was strange to suddenly feel warmth around her. His warmth. It was perhaps only the kind gesture of a man used to catering to other's needs but to her it felt awkward – as if she were enjoying the attentions of another man while Raoul was in a room nearby, getting ready for bed.

Maurizio said, "There is a lot to do at and around the hotel. You must make some plans to explore. Raoul might not be able to go with you, but I am sure some of the others would be willing to show you around."

"I am here for Raoul, not sightseeing."

"You cannot be with him all the time. He must rest. Besides, he needs to be cheered up with lively conversation. If you go and explore, you will have things to tell him when you come back."

Atalanta decided that further protest wasn't helpful and

nodded her assent. "I will go and do something nice tomorrow morning and then I can spend the afternoon telling Raoul about it." She waited a moment and asked, out of the blue, "Have you told Raoul he is a race car driver?"

Maurizio blinked. His eyes studied her a moment with sharp intent, then he looked away. His long, dark lashes hid his emotion as he said, "I don't understand the question."

"Raoul had to be told everything about his past, even his name. Have you told him what his profession is?"

Maurizio still didn't look at her. He stared at the ground as if undecided about whether to lie.

She decided to forestall him. "You could of course tell me that you told him and that he forgot again, because he admitted to me that he learns things about himself from others and a few days later it is all gone. But I have a strong feeling you never told him. Is that correct?"

Maurizio stood motionless. She reached out and put a hand on his arm. "I am not trying to make things difficult for you. I just want to understand. He had a skiing accident just before the season started. He needs to recover quickly so he can race again. He loves racing. It has always been his great passion. It could motivate him in his recovery. Why would you not tell him? Why would you not talk to him about what he loves in life."

Maurizio shook his head. "It is not that easy."

"Ah there you are," a female voice said, and Eva Reuter came over to them. Her sharp eyes took in the scene quickly, going from Atalanta's hand on Maurizio's arm to the jacket around her shoulders. Atalanta's cheeks flushed as if she had been caught red-handed.

Eva said lightly, "We are going to play charades. Do you want to join in?"

Atalanta let Maurizio's jacket slip from her shoulders and handed it back to him. "Thank you. I will follow your advice." She said to Eva, "Maurizio encouraged me not to sit here all day long feeling anxious about Raoul's condition but to go out and explore the surroundings. Will you help me do that?"

"Oh, of course. I can take you to see lots of nice things. We don't have world marvels here, but ... it is nice enough." Eva smiled at her and gestured for Atalanta to follow her inside.

As Atalanta did so, one question played on her mind: Eva was obviously a woman who wanted excitement and she was the first to admit that it wasn't to be found here, at the hotel or in the region, so why was she here?

Chapter Six

"I can tell you the names of all the different gems," Margot Bergreiter enthused as she dragged Atalanta along to the small museum on the corner of the street. They had come down in the funicular together, along with Eva Reuter and the other young woman who had introduced herself as Eva's friend, Theresa Hofer. They had met while travelling and had decided to come to Hotel Alpenrot together. Atalanta wasn't certain which one of them had actually made the decision and convinced the other one to come along. Had it been Eva's doing or Theresa's?

Seeing them together, it became obvious that Eva was the driving force, the one who was in charge and Theresa more of the type who followed along. Still, there was something in her quiet, intelligent eyes that warned Atalanta not to underestimate her.

Renard had also come down in the funicular with them, allegedly to shop for her as she needed a few items for her personal use. In reality, he was going to try and contact a few people to find out more about Maurizio Dulce, Raoul's accident and the reasons why he had been brought to this particular hotel. Atalanta knew Renard was in touch with all kinds of useful people and could get to information that was usually locked away to others, but still she doubted whether he could learn a lot in such a short time. He could not ask his sources to contact him at the hotel as the investigation had to be conducted with the utmost discretion. If Maurizio Dulce started to suspect she was somehow here to look into him and his criminal uncle, she would be in major trouble.

Margot stopped and looked up at the museum's wooden front. "That is such a shame," she cried, pointing at the notice on the door. "*Ruhetag*," Atalanta read. "So they are closed for the day."

Immediately Eva threw Atalanta a sharp look. "You must have lived in Switzerland for a while. Or in Germany? Your German is so good. You know all the local habits."

Flushing uncomfortably, Atalanta shrugged. "Boarding schools are good for something, I suppose." She tilted her head and watched Eva as she continued, "Maurizio doesn't agree with the concept though. He told me last night, quite fiercely, that the idea of sending your children to boarding school goes against his ideas of family."

"You discussed sending your children to boarding school with him?" Margot asked, curiosity lighting her face. "But I thought you were in love with Raoul?"

"We are all in love with Raoul," Eva said quickly, "but

he is the unattainable, romantic hero. The man who will never tie himself to a woman. He needs to be free."

With a sharp jab of pain, Atalanta acknowledged how right this assessment was. Eva might act like she was a very shallow person but she had plenty of psychological insight.

Or was her whole talkative, silly widow behaviour an act? To what purpose?

"I genuinely thought," Margot said, "that you were in love with Raoul and he with you. There was something between you when you sat there…"

"You see romance everywhere," Eva said sharply. "But you must not confuse real life with your books." She turned to Atalanta. "Margot writes books, you know. *Liebesromane*. Love stories. They are always very dramatic and take place in the most unusual places. Like volcanic caves on Santorini."

"Oh, have you been to Santorini?" Atalanta asked Margot. "So have I. I really enjoyed seeing the island. It has some very special features."

Margot smiled with a hint of pain in her eyes. "I have never been there myself. It is too exhausting for me to travel, but I have a first-hand source. My sister travels the world and sends me long letters with all the descriptive details that I use in my books. I am very grateful to her that she wants to help me that way."

"The hotel has a few of her books in the reading room," Theresa said. "I've read two of them already. They are very exciting." She looked at Margot. "I love how you let the environment play a big part in their romance. I mean, the danger they get in as their family and enemies oppose their love…"

Eva snorted. "I wonder why it is always seen as some great romantic feat if everybody hates the couple and they must overcome all these obstacles together. In real life, struggles push people apart. They don't unite them."

"Well, that is what people like to hear," Margot said. She nodded with intention. "I give them merely what they want: a dose of danger and excitement in their otherwise rather mundane lives."

"It is odd though," Eva said, "that the person to inject this danger and excitement into their lives herself has the most boring existence ever. I wonder that people don't think you are a bit of a fraud."

Margot blushed painfully. Theresa said, "I think people love the idea of a reclusive writer. They imagine how you sit in a study all day long, thinking up stories and writing them down. They imagine that you are this tortured artistic soul who must create."

"With a full moon overhead and a glass of whiskey at hand?" Eva laughed out loud, a mean little laugh. "I don't think you ever drink anything stronger than coffee." She leaned over and added, "How lucky that you did meet the man of your dreams and had a romance of your own. Now you at least know some details to put in the books. Imagine if you were alone and writing about love! Wouldn't that be sad?"

Margot's eyes lit a moment with a flash of something close to hatred. Atalanta could not blame her. Eva didn't mince her words and she obviously felt superior to the older woman. She might also be the type who had to put others down to feel better about herself. Atalanta feared that this would cause trouble during their supposedly pleasant day out.

"Well," Theresa said, throwing an anxious look at Margot, "I suppose we can't see the gems then. We will have to think of something else to do."

"We should have gone ice skating." Eva's expression was challenging. "The lake is still frozen solid, despite the spring being upon us. It would have been so nice to do a few rounds. Perhaps we could have even enticed Maurizio to join us, or Franco. Or the ski instructor." She said to Atalanta, "He's a really nice man."

Theresa flushed and kneaded her hands together. "We are down here in the village now. We should take a look around. There is a fountain there with stone statues. We can go and see what they are." She began to remove herself from the party.

Eva rolled her eyes. "They are probably mythological creatures of some sort. I don't know their difficult Latin names and I don't care either."

"They are fascinating," Margot said and went after Theresa with firm steps.

Eva threw her hands up in a gesture of exasperation. "They are all so intellectual. Just because they read books and I don't." She looked at Atalanta. "I have never understood why people want to read books about things they can experience in person. Well, perhaps Margot has to because she can't really do anything."

Atalanta watched as Theresa pointed out a female figure on the fountain to Margot. She said softly, "You are not being very kind to someone who can't help it that she is not well."

"She can help it." Eva sounded sharp. "She is using her condition to elicit pity from people and get her own way. Just look at that. Theresa is supposed to be *my* friend and she is now turning against me to support that miserable, manipulative woman."

"I thought you met only a short while ago. You cannot be firm friends." Atalanta decided that, as Eva was very frank, it would serve her well to be blunt too.

Eva stared at her a moment and then laughed. "You are right. I hardly know her, really. We met at a hotel in Basel and she latched onto me. She is nice enough and at least she doesn't pester me for money like most people do once they know I am a wealthy widow."

"A fact you are hardly concealing." Atalanta eyed her. "You enjoy being in that position."

Eva laughed again, more loudly this time. Theresa turned her head to look at them. It was clear she was upset and embarrassed at Eva's derisive comments towards Margot.

Eva said, "You cannot be fooled. I do indeed enjoy it. You see, for the duration of my marriage to my husband, I was cast as a certain type: oh, she was his secretary; she married him for his money; she is really stupid but she pretends to be smart. I was upset about that at first and determined to prove people wrong. But you know what I discovered? People only see what they want to see. Once they have a certain view of you, they only select those bits of information that support that view. It is impossible to sway them in any other direction. So I decided to give them exactly what they want. I am stupid, I am shallow, I am only after money. So much time has passed with me playing that part that I sometimes believe it is who I truly am. Is it possible that they knew it before me? That I am only becoming what I should have been all along?"

"I don't know if I would want to be that cynical," Atalanta said. It was a genuine response to the story, but Eva seemed to feel attacked by it. Her eyes flashed as she retorted, "You don't have to live up to people's expectations. You were born into money and privilege. I never had anything. Everything I have now I got because I *took* it."

She blinked a moment as if her own words took her by surprise. She shuffled her feet uncomfortably, adding, "I mean, I saw a chance to become the fifth wife and I took it. Was that so bad of me? Apparently. But go and read a Margot Bergreiter novel. All her heroines start out as poor girls, working for a living, who meet a rich man who whisks them away to some dreamy location where they have gorgeous dresses and jewels and dinner parties and dances. They all get what they dreamed of. Margot makes a lot of money selling that idea to her audience so why would she need to be so vicious to me about what I have done? I could be the heroine in one of her books."

There was a brief silence while Atalanta contemplated these words. Then Eva said, "Or could I? I may have been young and beautiful when I married my husband but I wasn't naïve. I didn't marry for love, and he wasn't dashing. He was old and rather ugly, he drank too much and he always smelled of dogs – those wretched hunting dogs he kept by his side and who drooled on his knees. Then I came in with the tea and he pulled me to him, grabbing me round the waist and putting me in his lap. My dresses got stained with dog drool." She eyed Atalanta. "I had to pretend I liked it. I couldn't show my disgust. He would never have tolerated a woman who was disgusted by him. Instead of having it all land in my lap I have had to work hard for it. Day by day."

Atalanta nodded. "I see."

Eva continued, with a bitter tone in her voice, "Now, Margot Bergreiter would never write a book about someone like me, a woman who married to better her position in life, accepting the proposal of a man she didn't love, but viewed only as a way up in society. Her heroines all move up in the world as well, but they deserve it because they are beautiful and innocent and badly treated, and the heroes saving them are indeed heroes, not bald, old men who believe money can buy them anything."

Atalanta said softly, "But money can buy them anything. Money bought you. You agreed to it. You paid a price to receive the lifestyle you craved."

Eva held her gaze. "Does that upset you?"

"Not at all. I think you are very pragmatic. Life needs people who use their minds instead of running after feelings."

Eva blinked as if she could not quite believe what she was hearing. "I had not expected you to say so. You came here to find Raoul. You seem to be worried about him, driven by feelings of fear and anxiety."

Atalanta felt her cheeks heat. "It is different when someone is in mortal danger."

Eva laughed softly. "Your reasoning is not quite sound, Fräulein Ford. But I don't mind. I appreciate that you don't judge me as harshly as others do. Or at least, you pretend that you don't." She waited a moment and added, "I wonder what you will say to Margot when you have her alone. That you totally understand *her* too? It is such a good way to win other people's confidence."

Atalanta tried not to flinch. She disliked being dishonest in order to draw people out but it was an inevitable part of her profession. As a detective, she had to get to know people and their motives and it often paid off to play along to gain information.

She held Eva's gaze as she said in a steady tone, "I try to understand other people because I feel it is helpful to see things from their side. If I were in Margot's position, I would probably act in the same way as she does. Considering her situation, she is doing well, writing books and giving her readers an escape from reality."

"The escape she creates because her life is intolerably

dull and boring!" Eva turned away. "I am going to buy a newspaper."

Atalanta looked after Eva as she walked off, head held high. "I wouldn't worry about her," Theresa's voice said behind her. Atalanta spun around. How much of the conversation had the other woman overheard? Had she consciously listened in?

Theresa said, "Eva can be a little rude sometimes, but she doesn't mean any real harm. She is just very outspoken. I sometimes wish I cared as little as she does for what people think of me."

She stared down a moment.

Atalanta asked gently, "Are you enjoying yourself here? Do you find these surroundings stimulating?"

"Oh yes, they are very exciting. I had never been to the mountains before. I usually travel around the Mediterranean." Theresa forced a little laugh. "On boats and all, you know, yachts. I like the sunshine a lot more than the snow. Sometimes it feels like I am freezing." She wrapped her arms around her shoulders.

"Then why are you here?" Atalanta asked curiously.

"I just wanted something different to talk about, to impress my friends." Theresa hugged herself tighter. "If Eva were here now, she'd ask me if I want to impress some man. She finds that amusing. But it is not that. It is not amusing to know he will never notice you and still feel like you have to keep trying."

Atalanta felt a twinge of compassion for the despair in Theresa's voice. She said, "But you must not tie your entire life and happiness to the opinion of a single man. Even if he never notices you, your life is fulfilling and your future full of good things."

"Who says so?"

"Nobody. You will have to tell that to yourself. Start every day by saying to yourself that you are going to enjoy it, regardless of what happens or who is trying to spoil it for you. You must be your own best friend. Your own ally."

Theresa studied her with a frown. "It sounds like something you have learned by experience."

Atalanta shrugged. "I have often wanted to have people around me to support me, or to not feel alone all the time, but it doesn't work to feel sorry for oneself. It just creates unhappiness and even more loneliness. I told myself once that I would always try to see the good side to things. Take Raoul's accident. It brought me here. It is beautiful here. I might otherwise have never found this village and this hotel."

She waited a moment and added innocently, "Eva must have known it as she suggested you two should come here for a stay."

"Yes, she knew it from before, I think. She must have told me but I can't remember because she is constantly telling me things about her past. She is drowning me in details." Theresa smiled apologetically. "But she must have known the owner. Or at least his nephew Maurizio. I saw them together last night and they looked very … close."

Atalanta was taken aback a moment. She was not interested in any romantic advances on Maurizio's part but still the idea that he was close with Eva struck her as unpleasant. As if she suddenly had to watch her back even more.

Which was odd as she had never intended to trust Maurizio to begin with. He was a Dulce and that told her enough.

Still, she had to admit that she had sensed concern in him for Raoul's wellbeing and she could not totally hate him, as she probably should. It was uncomfortable to acknowledge that she might have a soft spot for Maurizio while he was part of the enemy force holding Raoul captive, the very people from whom she had to wrestle him away.

Margot joined them and asked where Eva was. "She went to buy a newspaper," Theresa said. Margot grimaced. "I wager she is going to regale us again with some sensationalist story from that reporter she is so fond of. What is his name?"

"Alexander Hansen," Theresa said in a low voice as if it were a guilty secret. "He does know how to unveil the biggest scandals in society."

Margot pulled her lips down in reproval. "Such reporters create irreparable damage. A few weeks ago, this Hansen character wrote about friends of mine who were allegedly about to divorce because the husband was cheating on his wife with the children's nanny. Well, it wasn't true of course, but now the nanny has been dismissed and the couple are spending their summer apart. She has gone with the children to stay with a friend on

Crete, and he is at home on their estate. I think it is such a shame what such harmful gossip does."

Eva came back to them waving a newspaper in the air. Her expression was exultant. "Wait until you hear what I read here."

"Here we go again," Theresa whispered to Atalanta. "I don't understand how she can enjoy it so much."

Margot said in a dull tone, "We must learn to deal with it. You cannot change who a person is."

Eva reached them and opened the paper to an inner page. "Listen," she said breathlessly. "The famous race car driver Raoul Lemont had a skiing accident while preparing for the new racing season. An innocent outing with friends took a sinister turn when the successful sportsman took a bad fall and sustained injuries to his shoulder and his head. He is now recovering at a secret location, but there are persistent rumours he won't be able to race for some time. This comes as an enormous setback for Vincenzo Dulce who recruited Lemont for his team to drive a newly imported American car."

Theresa waved her hand impatiently. "We know all of that."

"But you don't know this." Eva's eyes sparkled. "The team is said to be negotiating with another driver to take Lemont's place. Several names have been mentioned, but the most persistent one is that of Vincenzo Dulce's nephew, Maurizio."

Atalanta felt her jaw go slack. "Maurizio is a race car driver too? He never mentioned that to me."

"Nor to any of us," Margot said. Her eyes were alert now and her mind seemed to be working at high speed. "Why would he keep it a secret? Wouldn't it have been natural to mention it? Especially as he is here looking after Raoul."

"Well," Eva said with a triumphant smile, "how well will he care for him if Raoul's injuries mean he can take his place? If I were him, I wouldn't be in any hurry to see Raoul's health improve."

"That is a mean thing to say," Theresa protested.

But Margot said, "It is strange that he is not allowing Raoul to do anything. If he is constantly lying in a chair, his muscles will grow weaker. Maurizio is also giving him a lot of medication."

Atalanta noticed that the women were now eyeing each other with a sort of feverish excitement.

Margot said, "If Maurizio is up to something with Raoul…"

Theresa added, "Then we must keep an eye on him and help poor Raoul."

Eva nodded. "Raoul is the driver Vincenzo Dulce really wants, not Maurizio."

Atalanta was reminded that Eva and Maurizio had seemed close just last night and wondered why Eva was now suddenly turning against him.

Theresa clapped her hands together and whispered, "We could play detective a little."

The word "detective" caused a shock to Atalanta. She

was here under a fake name and once Maurizio found out, he might send her away. She had to stay close to Raoul to be able to help him.

Margot said, "Do you think that is wise? Maurizio just about owns the hotel. He is in charge of all the staff and has eyes and ears in all places. We cannot go spying behind his back."

"But we can simply keep our eyes open to see what he is doing to Raoul," Theresa insisted with a nod. "And Margot, you know the doctor who is coming to treat Raoul. You can chat to him innocently and find out what pills he is prescribing and if they are really necessary. You can act like you want to use memory loss in one of your novels and are merely quizzing him. He will probably be delighted to be of interest to a well-known author like you."

Eva seemed to suppress a smirk at the word "well-known", but as this sudden stir was obviously to her liking, she didn't show any disdain. On the contrary, she smiled at Margot and said, "Theresa is right. You can use your position as an author to find out information for us."

"Us?" Atalanta asked, with dread in her stomach.

"Yes." Eva looked past all the faces and then held out her hand palm down. "We are going to find out what is going on with Raoul Lemont. We are going to be the ETAM agency."

"ETAM?" Theresa asked perplexed.

"Eva, Theresa, Atty and Margot. A simple combination of our initials." Eva moved her hand. "Who is with me?

It will be so exciting." She looked at Margot. "Better than waiting until your husband comes around for his next visit."

Margot flushed and seemed to want to step away.

But Theresa put her hand on Eva's and said, "I am in."

Atalanta waited for Margot to deny she wanted to join. Then she could also bow out without attracting too much suspicion.

But to her surprise, and dismay, Margot reached out and put her hand on top of Theresa's.

Atalanta sucked in air. "Are you really intent on doing this? We are not schoolgirls anymore. And I uh ... I don't think Maurizio will appreciate us snooping. His uncle is a businessman with a lot of power. It is not a good idea to cross him."

Eva said, "I thought you cared for Raoul? Doesn't it matter to you that he is being mistreated? That they are perhaps keeping him weak and incapacitated while another is cast to take his place?"

To be honest, Atalanta did want to know why this newspaper story was suddenly being published, where it came from and what it meant – and whether Raoul was really in danger of losing his spot on the team.

She had come here hoping to get Raoul away from Vincenzo Dulce, and now it seemed like there was a chance of the team letting him go, but it gave her no joy. There was fear churning in the pit of her stomach. If Maurizio truly wanted Raoul's place on the team, how far would he be willing to go to get it?

Still she put her hand on top of the others.

Eva cheered. "To ETAM! May we have lots of luck solving our very first case."

Chapter Seven

Night was closing in as Atalanta sat beside Raoul on the sofa in his hotel room. She had just told him what Eva had read in the newspaper. Learning that his profession was a race car driver had excited him for a moment, but the next revelations – that his team might replace him and Maurizio was first in line for this – had immediately dampened his mood. Now Raoul stared ahead, deep in thought.

Atalanta asked softly, "Do you think Maurizio could be after your spot on the team?"

"I have no idea. I don't remember. Was he on the team before? Did he help train? I don't know. I can't even tell you if his concern for me is genuine or not because I simply have nothing to go by."

Atalanta touched his arm. "Don't get all worked up."

"Don't get all worked up?" he echoed with flashing eyes. "It is bad enough to be trapped in a body that doesn't cooperate. Now you also share with me that the man who is supposed to help me heal may be sabotaging my recovery for his own benefit. How is that supposed to make me feel? Should I just accept it? Sink back in the pillows and doze off on another sedative? No. I won't have it. This is *my* life and I have to do something about it."

"But you don't know what to do because you don't know anything. And I don't know either. I am looking into it. Renard put out enquiries, but it will take some time—"

"Time!" Raoul got up and paced the room. "They are all telling me it takes time. The doctor, Maurizio, even that smug bartender. They are all trying to comfort me, to keep me quiet. But what is going on?"

"Listen." Atalanta came over and stood before him. "We do not know if any of this newspaper report is even true. Margot told me that Eva is keen on reading reports by this Alexander Hansen, but sometimes he digs up dirt and prints stories without foundation. The marriage of some friends of hers is in danger because of a callous report about infidelity. This could also just be meant to cause harm."

Raoul looked her over. "Are you defending Maurizio?"

"I am only using my logical mind. If he wanted to take your place, he would not be here. He would be with the team testing the car and getting ready for the first race, don't you think?"

Raoul stared at her. Then he let out a hoarse laugh. "You are right. He probably would be. It doesn't make sense for him to want to do races and not even train for them."

"Exactly. He could have someone else keep you here

sedated while he vied for your spot, but he doesn't seem to be doing that. That reporter is only throwing names around, or writing down petty gossip. And it works because it is selling newspapers. That is the way in which such people keep their jobs."

Raoul huffed. He returned to the sofa and sank down on it. "I overreacted. I am sorry. I don't mean to…"

"Don't worry about it. Just try to think straight. You have to be careful and keep an open mind as to what is happening here. So will I."

"And what about your new friends wanting to look into Maurizio? You are now suddenly part of ETAM." He rolled his eyes as he said it and immediately grimaced as the movement seemed to cause pain.

"I guess it is just a silly idea. It will pass." Atalanta squeezed his shoulder. "You are better off trying to sleep and recover. I keep hoping that fragments of memories will surface."

Raoul rubbed his eyes. "I don't know if I want to go through it."

"Through what?"

"Reliving the accident." He looked up at her. "Last night I had a dream. I was going downhill at a frightening speed. I was unable to stop. Then I hit something and everything went black. I woke up drenched in sweat."

Atalanta's heart clenched for his sake but she said, "It is good that you are starting to remember something. Don't fight it. Trust in your mind to recall what you need to know."

"Do I even want to know?" Raoul sat with his shoulders slumped. "I am worried it will only make things harder."

Atalanta swallowed. On their way back to the hotel, the others had chatted cheerfully but she had been quiet as she watched their slow but certain ascent into the realm of Hotel Alpenrot. It was a secluded world in which they were almost captive, held at the mercy of the man keeping them there. Maurizio Dulce.

If he had some evil plot in mind, could they even do anything to stop it? Was it sensible to try and fight him? The other women did not know that Maurizio was part of a criminal organisation with dark secrets. He might not be averse to violence.

What if the women actually did discover something? Would it put them in danger? But she had agreed to join ETAM and could hardly dissuade the others without a good reason. Disclosing Vincenzo's criminal past was not an option so what could she even say to make them stand down?

Raoul looked up at her. "You mustn't be too worried for my sake, Atalanta." Her name sounded so familiar coming from his lips and yet she was so aware that he didn't really know who she was; that there was nothing left of what they had built.

He forced a smile. "I can see you are a loyal person who will fight for what she believes is right, but you owe me nothing. Not anymore. I can't remember you and I might never recover."

"I want to—"

He rose to his feet with lightning speed. "I don't want pity. Don't you understand? I can't bear you feeling sorry for me. For the man I have become."

"You are no different from how you always were. I never loved you for your fame and fortune, or for the danger you courted. I loved you for you. And *you* are still here."

Raoul stared at her. "You say you love me?"

Atalanta nodded. "I do. I knew it for certain when I thought you had died."

He held her gaze. "Did I ever ... say I love you, too?"

Atalanta held her breath as she looked into his deep brown eyes. She ached to put her hand against his cheek and tell him *"Yes you did, you loved me, and you love me still."* She wanted him to kiss her and let her believe for a few moments that all was well with the world.

But she could not lie to him. She could not betray him in such a monstrous way.

"No." Her voice was hoarse and she had to clear her throat before she was able to continue. "No, you never said you were in love with me. On the contrary, you gave me all the reasons why you could not fall in love with me. And why I should not fall in love with you either."

She fought against the burn behind her eyes. She would not cry now. She would not make him think she was trying to force something with sentimentality.

"But it didn't work. I could not stop growing closer to you."

Raoul nodded slowly. "I see." His smile was wistful.

"I can't remember my reasons for not wanting to fall in love with you. I don't know if they were any good or if they even matter now. But I do know one thing. I am lucky that you care for me. I know you do because you told me the truth. You could have lied to me. You could have said that I did say I was in love with you. That I ... kissed you and..."

Atalanta stared into his eyes. For her the attraction was still there, but if he didn't even remember her, how could she hope for the connection to stay alive?

She heard a sound in the corridor as if someone was coming and stepped back from him. "I had better go downstairs and have a last cup of tea before bed. Choose a book to read that will help me to fall asleep easily. I will see you in the morning. Goodnight." She walked to the door quickly, not allowing herself to look back and be tempted to run up to him to give him a hug. She had to keep her distance and let him work through this in his own way. In his own time.

She had to trust that if their connection was indeed still there, they would find a way back to each other.

Atalanta stood in the reading room feeling lost. Her head was so full of emotions after the exchange with Raoul that she could not think straight. Previously, their relationship had felt complicated because he was a man who didn't want to develop bonds with anyone. He wanted to be independent, and he lived for his sport, for the danger he courted every time he got into his race car. She had often felt like she took second place in his life, or perhaps even third or fourth. He did make time for her, but it was always limited. He wasn't ready to commit, to open up to her and share his innermost feelings.

Now he was more vulnerable than ever. She had even read his diary. She had seen his frustration at his fate and the uncertainties he faced over the future. It put her closer to him than she had ever been. But he had been forced to do this by circumstances. It wasn't a choice. And she should not abuse the situation to coerce anything from him. She should allow him ... to become his old self again? A man she could care for from a distance, never getting to the heart of him.

She felt so helpless to do anything for him, and at the same time she was the one with all the power in their relationship now because she remembered everything, and he didn't even know her name.

She could tell him anything she wanted. She could pretend that there had been something going on between them. It was true that there had been attraction and friendship and the awareness that it could become more if they let it, but there had been so many other things in the mix too: his fear of commitment, his belief that she should have more experience of falling in love without tying herself immediately to the first man who came her way.

And then there were her own doubts about their compatibility and whether Raoul would ever love her the way she wanted to be loved. She had known so little love in her life, so little true connection. She had few memories of her mother, and with her father the bond had been strained by his irresponsible decisions and his need for her to grow up faster than she would have liked. Her grandfather was gone too.

Grandfather... What would he have thought of her situation? Caught up with dangerous people who were engaged in criminal activities while trying to rescue the man she cared for from their clutches... Would he shake his head, thinking she had more sense than this? Sense to see that she could not save him, no matter how she tried?

But Raoul was not able to drive now. He was losing his importance to them as cover for their criminal plans. And if it was true that Maurizio wanted to take his place, wouldn't it be an ideal solution?

If Raoul got out alive.

She didn't want to think about the possibility that the skiing accident had been staged to injure him. That would mean that they had accepted the risk he would be killed. Perhaps they were looking to murder him still? Was Raoul in danger as long as he was here with them?

Atalanta forced her gaze away from the floorboards to the bookcases all around her. She wanted to select a few titles to take up to her room to read. She could use the distraction. There was no point in speculating about Raoul's accident or the position he was in. She could not remove him from here, at least not at this very moment, and she had to hope she could find out more about Maurizio and his plans for Raoul with the help of the impromptu detectives.

She could not really see Theresa uncovering incriminating evidence about someone but Eva had seemed enthusiastic to dig in, and Margot...

Atalanta turned to the nearest bookcase and began to try to figure out how the books were organised. By category or theme and then by author, it seemed. She looked for the section of romance novels and once she had found it, it was easy enough to see Margot's titles. Her name came early in the alphabet and there were a lot of them. Atalanta's gaze browsed the titles. *A Greek Adventure. Holiday in Havana. Danger among the Tombs.*

Was that one set in Egypt? She pulled it out of the row and studied the cover. It looked like pyramids. She felt a genuine excitement to read it and opened the cover to leaf to the first chapter. Her eye fell on the dedication.

To my sister Johanna who made all of this possible for me.

Her sister was the one travelling and sharing all the details with her. Perhaps it had started as a way to let Margot live some experiences vicariously because she could not travel herself. But with the books becoming successful it had actually provided her with a very nice career and a loyal readership.

Atalanta sat down in one of the leather chairs by the fireplace and began to read. Soon she was caught up in the life of the hapless heroine who was living with a stern aunt and uncle and having no excitement in her life until a bad investment by the uncle put him in debt and he offered her hand in marriage to the highest bidder. Atalanta felt this part of the story was a tad improbable, but it did bring the heroine together with the hero, a dashing adventurer out to explore Egyptian tombs and find the treasures of the pharaoh. Once they were on the trip to Egypt, dangers abounded: a scorpion in their cabin, mysterious men lurking about and watching them, and luggage mysteriously disappearing.

Atalanta lost all track of time as she kept turning the pages, eager to find out how the heroine would get through all of this and whether she would secure the respect and even the affection of the man who had married her for personal gain.

"Excuse me, signorina…"

Atalanta looked up with a jerk to see the bartender Franco standing at the door. "Are you aware of the time?" he asked.

Atalanta shook her head and at the same time glanced at her watch. It was past midnight.

"This room is never locked," Franco said in an apologetic tone, "but the manager does appreciate guests retiring to their rooms for the night and not wandering the hotel."

Atalanta agreed that this made total sense and at the same time she wondered if there was a reason why they wanted everyone safely tucked away in their beds at night. She rose but kept hold of the book. "I was so engrossed in this story that I didn't notice the time."

Franco came closer and looked at the book. "Ah, a

Margot Bergreiter title. They are very popular with our female guests." He held her gaze a moment. "I would have thought you a little too sensible for this kind of story."

Atalanta felt taken aback. "Why would you think so?"

He shrugged. "You look like a serious young lady. You travel a lot yourself. Why would you need to read about adventures you can have for yourself?"

He waited a moment before adding, "Or is it that you never meet attractive men?"

Atalanta held the book tighter. The tone of his voice and the look in his eyes didn't seem entirely appropriate for a member of staff. "Whether I ever meet one is entirely my business."

Franco smiled. "Of course. I did not mean to pry. It just seems like you are so serious and ... life is meant to be enjoyed."

"I assure you I know very well how to enjoy life."

"By reading books about it?" Franco stepped closer. His dark eyes sparkled. "Is it not better to see the stars for yourself? To hold the glass of wine and toast with someone the beauty of the night?"

"It is a whole lot better if done with the right person."

His smile deepened. "Why don't you tell me something about this book? Where it takes place, why the hero is such an attractive man to females. Is it because of money? Success? Looks?"

"Money and success matter but little," Atalanta said. "It is the nature of a man that counts. Whether he is truly a gentleman." She wanted to test Franco to see how he would respond to her answers. Was he simply going through a repertoire of stock remarks meant to dazzle the female guests? Or could he actually make interesting conversation? How much of it was innocent and how much intentional?

"A gentleman...?" Franco walked over to the bookcase and pulled out a title. He opened it and read to her, "As she looked out of the window, onto the moonlit lawn, she saw him riding past on a beast of a horse, dark and tall and hard to control. But his strong hands held the reins confidently and his exultant expression betrayed how much he enjoyed this. She had never seen such freedom, such lack of concern for what others might think. This was his terrain, this was his time. He was the knight of the night." He looked up at her. "Is that the kind of gentleman you dream of? A world away from the stuffy types you meet at your aunt's soirees?"

Atalanta wanted to laugh but suppressed the urge. She tried to look stern as she replied, "That is but a book. Real life is very different."

Franco closed the book and put it back on the shelf. "I suppose so. But one can dream. There is no censure on hopes and dreams. At least, not last time I looked." He stood staring at the ground a moment.

She asked, "What does a bartender dream of?"

He winced as she named his profession. It was unfeeling, but she wanted to see how he would respond to it. Whether he was really flirting with her or whether she was just not used to reading men right.

"I haven't always been a bartender. I was born on a

manor such as Margot Bergreiter describes. Only, in her books the houses are full of silverware and crystal chandeliers and beautiful paintings by old masters. In our house the silverware had partly been sold to pay off Father's debts. The ballroom hadn't been used in ages and the piano was seriously out of tune. We all had to do our best to keep up the pretence of having money, but it was just that. A pretence. And with me not even being the eldest son..."

He turned his back on her and paced the room slowly.

"I don't know what is worse: being the eldest son and inheriting the large house that is in decay and having to worry for all of your life whether you can afford its upkeep or whether you will have to sell more land or forests from the estate just to keep your head above water; or being the second son like me and not even having a place there, being expected to marry well or go into the army to make a career, or become a clergyman to have a steady living." He shuddered a moment. "I didn't like any of those options much. From a young age I wanted to get away and travel, to see the world. So one day I packed my bags and kissed my mother goodbye, and I haven't looked back since. I have been everywhere. I've worked at a French chateau, I've been a fisherman on the Aegean Isles. I was even in North Africa briefly. I guess I am almost like a Bergreiter hero – well-travelled, just not rich." He looked up at her. "Does that matter?"

"Money always matters," Atalanta replied. "If you have a lot of it then you must be careful because anyone with whom you associate may be after your money and not care for you at all. If you have almost nothing then you must spend your days struggling to get some and then worrying about how to keep it. There is always in some form or other an element of money at play." She thought back on the murder cases she had solved. Gooseflesh formed on her arms and she sucked in a sharp breath.

"You speak as if you have experience of it," Franco said slowly. "Does your money attract the wrong kind of men?"

Atalanta smiled softly. "What is the wrong kind of men? It depends on what one is looking for, doesn't it?"

Franco tilted his head. "Do you not want to marry?"

"Why would I? It would only tie me down. I would have to dance to my husband's tune. I am an independent woman now and I intend to stay that way."

"I see." His eyes sparkled again. "But there is nothing against having a little adventure on the side?"

Atalanta stepped back towards the door with her book in hand. "It is time for me to retire. I wish you goodnight."

Franco wanted to say something more, it seemed, but she turned her back on him and left the room. Her heart was hammering. She found his advances most peculiar. Did Maurizio know that his bartender was trying to woo the guests?

In her turmoil she took a wrong turn and realised she wasn't going in the direction of her room. She stopped to look about her. This was another corridor. It would probably lead to a staircase she could take to get to the floor on which her room was located. She continued down the corridor but stopped when she heard something ahead of her – a door opening softly. She didn't know why but she quickly stepped behind a large potted palm to avoid being seen. She did not want to be questioned as to why she was wandering the halls at this time of night.

Through the leaves she could see a female figure stepping from a room. The woman closed the door and looked about her in a furtive manner. The low light from one of the electric lamps along the wall shone on her excited expression. Eva Reuter. Why was she leaving her bedroom at this hour? Or was that not her room at all?

What if she came this way and spotted Atalanta?

Sweat formed in her palms, but luckily Eva turned away from her, walking quickly but on tiptoe as if to keep very quiet. Atalanta waited until she was out of sight and then quietly made her way down the corridor to the door of the room from which Eva had come.

She hesitated. Was this a good idea? Then she put her hand on the door handle and pressed down. The door opened with a soft click. She pushed it open a fraction and peeked inside. It was too dark to see anything. Did she dare turn on the light to see what kind of room it was?

No, it was too risky. But she did push the door open wider so the light from the corridor could get in. By the outline of the furniture – a writing desk and chairs, a large cupboard with doors and a key in the lock – she determined that it was some kind of office. Did Maurizio work here? Had Eva been inside to find out more about the story that Maurizio wanted Raoul's place on the team? If Eva had been rifling through paperwork then she was willing to take chances to unearth information. Because she was curious? Or was there more to Eva than met the eye?

Atalanta closed the door again and decided to go back the way she had come. She didn't want to run into Eva and have to explain why she was up and about. She would not feel comfortable until she had reached her own room and locked herself inside. And even then…

What was going on at Hotel Alpenrot?

Chapter Eight

In the bright light of day, her worries seemed farfetched and exaggerated. Franco had only been teasing her about her taste in literature. He had not meant to make her uncomfortable or drive her to flee. She had overreacted. And Eva had perhaps just entered that room to look for something she needed. A stamp on a letter home? If she had indeed been sleuthing, she would probably share her findings with the other women soon enough. Atalanta could not imagine someone as direct as Eva being reticent about her discoveries. Perhaps she had already told Theresa something? The two of them had been whispering together right before they started ice skating on the frozen lake at the back of the hotel.

Atalanta had offered to keep Raoul company at the edge of the lake. She was not a great ice skater and she didn't want to take numerous falls and have the bruises to show for it.

It surprised her that Margot had joined in and that she was quite a good ice skater too. But then, the lake was small and it didn't cost her much exertion to do a few rounds. Theresa was struggling and constantly asking people to skate with her so she could latch onto them. Eva stayed out of her reach, calling out that she was holding her back and she had to find someone else to help her. An older woman whom Atalanta hadn't really met before lent Theresa a helping hand. Atalanta thought she had seen her before, on that first day when she had arrived to find the women crowding Raoul. But she had not been introduced to her, yet.

As if he read her mind, Raoul said with a nod in that direction, "That is the writer's secretary. Her name is Karin, I think. I cannot remember her last name." He frowned a moment and then glanced at her. "Sometimes I hear her typing. I think Frau Bergreiter dictates her books and then the secretary has to get it all on paper for the publishers. She told me a day or two ago that there is a deadline for a new novel coming up."

"Oh, I see." It was good that he remembered all this information. It seemed like it was becoming easier for him to recall normal events that happened on a day-to-day basis, but he was still struggling to piece together his past. "Did she mention where this one is set? Last night I read part of a book set in Egypt. It was fascinating with a lot of mythology and bits about grave robbers. I don't know how accurate all of it is but I had a good time reading it."

"And you didn't dream afterwards that you were stuck

in a tomb?" Raoul asked cynically. He looked at the skaters as he continued, "I had another nightmare where I was trapped. Something was pressing against my chest and I couldn't get away."

"Perhaps it's memories of the accident. If it surfaces, little by little, you may also start to remember other things." Atalanta rubbed her hands together as she formulated the next question. "Did Maurizio decide where you were going to ski?"

"I suppose so. He knows this area much better than I do. But I can't remember much of the preparations, let alone whether he discussed anything with me about the route."

Atalanta nodded slowly. If Maurizio knew the area well, he might have picked a dangerous slope for their skiing trip knowing full well that the adventurous Raoul with his love of speed would go down without holding back. In such a case an accident would be easy to bring about.

Still, she wasn't convinced that was what had happened. If Maurizio wanted Raoul's spot on the team, there were other more reliable methods to incapacitate him.

There was something else on her mind too. With the newspapers speculating about the accident and this reporter Alexander Hansen openly voicing discussion about a replacement, Raoul could learn of it and get suspicious of Maurizio. Would Maurizio have taken those chances?

She asked, "Are there any newspapers delivered to the hotel?"

"I suppose so, but I never see them. Maurizio claims he has to protect me from shock. The doctor has warned him that anything that upsets me might make my condition worse. I cannot imagine that an earthquake or shipwreck on the other side of the world would very much upset me but..."

"He just wants to take good care of you," Atalanta said with a smile. "You are very valuable to the team."

"Is that so?" Raoul glanced at her. "I am not physically fit. At all. Each day that passes takes us closer to the season's start. They should be pushing me to get fit. I could do some things you know. Lift some weights or do a little run." He gestured down a path. "That leads to some grotto. It was used in the past for storage, I think. I could run up and down just to see how well I hold up."

"And get a splitting headache so you have to retire to bed? No. The season may start soon, but you have to think about the entire year. If you force something now..."

"You sound just like Maurizio. Did you agree on this?" He cast her a reproachful look and then suddenly asked, "Do you like him?"

"Maurizio?" Atalanta was surprised. "How can I like him? I barely know him."

"Well, you must have some opinion about him. Doesn't one always judge people pretty quickly? I mean, in general one does have a feeling about them after a few exchanges. What does your feeling say?"

"I can't quite gauge him yet. He seems to be friendly but distant. I am, of course, a perfect stranger to him." She waited a moment and added, "Perhaps he feels I am some sort of threat because I know you better than he does?

I can't tell." She wished she could ask him if Maurizio had ever acted like he was jealous of Raoul's position in the team but she already knew what his answer would be. He wouldn't know. There was no reliable information to be had from him.

"Dieter!" Margot called the name with excitement and waved fervently. Atalanta looked behind them to the hotel. A tall, handsome, middle-aged man was approaching from across the terrace, carrying a bunch of flowers in his hand. He smiled with real warmth as he watched Margot skate to the edge of the lake. She leaned over to take her skates off.

"Don't exert yourself," he called out to her. "I am here to stay all weekend. There is no rush."

Margot huffed in frustration as she lowered herself into a sitting position to remove her skates. The man stopped where Raoul and Atalanta were seated and said, "Ah, Herr Lemont, still here recuperating? Are you feeling any better?"

"Unfortunately no," Raoul said with a grim expression. "My head is still very sore and I am not allowed to do anything. I am bored to death."

"I am sure you will find something to amuse yourself with. Margot can spend weeks here and she never gets bored." The man looked at his wife with a fond expression. She was getting up again to come and meet them. Her breathing came in pants as she reached them. The man pushed his flowers into her hands. It was a mixed bouquet of pink roses and white alstroemeria. She beamed down on them.

"My favourites. I don't know why you keep bringing them. I mean, every weekend…"

"Because you never cease to enjoy getting them." He leaned in to kiss her on the cheek. "I just don't want to rob myself of the pleasure of seeing your happiness." There was a hint of concern in his eyes as he studied her closer. "Have you been resting enough? I know the deadline is approaching and you also want to do things with your friends but…"

"I am fine. I can handle it." Margot sounded a little defensive. Her breathing still rasped and she coughed, holding up the flowers to hide her face.

Her husband sighed. "Well, there is no stopping you anyway, not once you put your mind to it." He looked across the lake. Eva was twirling her arms up in the air. She seemed to be good at everything she did; a very sporty woman.

Margot followed his gaze and immediately her expression changed to anxious. She put a hand on his arm. "Shall we go inside? I want hot chocolate and we can talk." She slipped her arm through his, pulling him along.

Atalanta rose from her chair and said, "Oh, Margot, could you introduce me to your husband? You have talked about him so much and with such affection that I just have to meet him."

Margot flushed. "I am so sorry. How rude of me not to introduce him right away. This is my husband, Dieter Bergreiter."

"The husband of the famous author," Bergreiter said

with a wink at Atalanta. "I am used to people viewing me like that. Of course I have a profession of my own, but it is a boring one."

Atalanta looked at Margot, who said with a shrug, "He is a banker. But don't tell anyone because they always want to borrow money from him." She looked at her husband again and said sharply, "You are not going to indulge anyone who wants to talk about money troubles, are you? I want to have you all to myself this weekend."

"I am here to please you," Bergreiter said and led her away.

Raoul said with a grimace, "A most devoted couple. They are so in love with each other it almost makes me queasy."

"It's good to know true love does exist." Atalanta sat down again. She saw that Eva stood very still on the ice, watching Margot and her husband go inside. There was a look of interest in her eyes and something Atalanta could not put a name to. Glee perhaps? A sort of malign amusement? But why would Eva feel that way?

Raoul wrapped his shawl tighter round his neck. "Are you not cold?"

"Not at all." She was wearing the red coat she had worn when they were together in Salzburg but he didn't seem to remember. She fidgeted with the white fur muffler.

Raoul leaned closer and said, "Red becomes you."

A flush of pleasure rose to her cheeks. "Really?"

"My memory might have suffered, but there is nothing wrong with my eyesight. You are a very attractive woman."

"That is a nice compliment, but so are the other ladies." Atalanta nodded in the direction of Eva and Theresa.

Raoul shook his head. "Eva Reuter is not an attractive woman. Oh, she is good-looking, I agree, but there is something about her I don't like. Something cold and calculating, perhaps?"

Atalanta tilted her head. "Do you feel that way because she married a much older man, apparently for his fortune?"

"No. I had no idea that she had. Someone must have told me but I of course forgot. I am not talking about the past but about the present."

"The present?" Atalanta queried.

"Yes. She is very friendly with Maurizio, but I have also seen her flirt with the bartender, the ski instructor and every man in the place. Even Margot Bergreiter's husband. The poor man didn't know what to do."

Atalanta recalled that Eva had described Dieter Bergreiter as a fiery Italian type. She had even stated that if she were married to such a man, she wouldn't look at anyone else. Had it been one of many such comments or was Eva really interested in Bergreiter and were her advances painful to him?

"Still, he must be used to female attention," she mused. "He is quite handsome and his wife spends a lot of time here recuperating. When he goes to dinner parties and soirees alone…" Atalanta fell silent, wondering with a niggle of suspicion if Bergreiter's kindness to his wife, his attentiveness with her favourite flowers and all, was born from guilt. Did he flirt with other women when his wife wasn't around? Did he have affairs? It was quite common for wealthy men and he was alone a lot. He had also mentioned that he was often seen only as the husband of the famous author. Perhaps that also grated on him? Did he look for ways to assert himself? His importance, his self-worth?

She almost had to laugh. Here she was supposing things about a man she had only met five minutes ago. She knew nothing about him, or about Margot and their marriage. She had to stop analysing and focus on Raoul.

But when she went inside a few minutes later to ask someone to bring hot chocolate out to her and Raoul, she found Dieter Bergreiter at the reception desk. The clerk was nowhere in sight, but he was not alone. Eva Reuter was right next to him. She put her hand on his arm and talked to him in a low, urgent voice.

Atalanta sidestepped so she could stay out of their line of vision but could still see Bergreiter's expression. Was he interested in Eva? Were they even closer than they pretended to be to the outer world? But why then was Eva addressing him here, in full view of anyone who came in?

Eva stepped back and said something. Her posture exuded self-confidence. Bergreiter's features were tight, as if he had heard unpleasant news. Eva turned and walked away with quick steps. He seemed to want to go after her, then changed his mind.

Atalanta decided to approach and take him by surprise. "Herr Bergreiter."

He spun around, his eyes still wide with something

close to shock. "Ah, Fräulein uh... Did my wife mention your name?"

"No, she was so eager to introduce you that she forgot to mention my name to you." Atalanta reached out her hand. "I am Atty Ford. You must forgive me as this is quite forward of me and your wife just said you must not speak to anyone about money matters, but ... I am looking to invest. Not in the stock market, obviously, but in something more reliable. Bonds perhaps? I wondered if you could give me a few recommendations."

Bergreiter blinked. He seemed to still be reeling. But he forced himself to smile at her and said, "I could of course see what I can do for you, but I must inform you that I usually only handle large estates and businesses. I am not the right man to speak to you about small, personal investments, to save a little money for a rainy day."

"Oh, we're not talking about a small investment. I was thinking of something in the region of one hundred thousand pounds? You must forgive me that I think in British pounds but you can of course estimate the number in any currency you like."

Bergreiter stared at her, then he said haltingly, "But of course. Maurizio wouldn't let just anyone stay here." He straightened up and smiled more warmly. "We can sit down together later today and speak about it, Fräulein Ford. I will be happy to help. Now, if you will excuse me, I must not keep my wife waiting."

"Of course not," Atalanta said sweetly. "Margot is such a dear."

Bergreiter nodded and took his leave.

Atalanta's heart was pounding at her bold move. But, like she had said to Franco last night, money always mattered, and she wanted to learn more from Bergreiter about Maurizio Dulce and this hotel. She could only hope he would have some useful information.

Chapter Nine

Margot had never looked so lively as over dinner that night. She wore a vibrant orange dress and was talking a lot, gesturing wildly and drinking more wine than her husband thought advisable. At least, Atalanta noticed his concerned looks whenever Margot took another sip from her glass. But he didn't try to stop her from either drinking or chatting and the atmosphere was relaxed.

After dinner, the gentlemen wanted to play billiards, but Dieter Bergreiter turned to Atalanta and said this was a moment as good as any to sit down to chat about her concern.

Margot drew up an eyebrow. "What concern?"

"Fräulein Ford has a financial matter to discuss with me. Yes, dear, I know you told me not to give advice to strangers, but Fräulein Ford is not really a stranger, is she? She is one of your friends and you know I am always there for your friends."

As he said this, Eva made a ridiculing sound, almost like she was snorting with laughter but suppressing it with an effort.

Margot glanced at her, turning red in the face. Theresa quickly drew Eva aside, suggesting they play cards.

Bergreiter took Atalanta to another room where they could speak in private. Once he had closed the door, Atalanta's stomach swirled with nerves. She really didn't have that much money to invest and she had to prevent him from asking too many questions that would give her away. "This is such a beautiful old hotel," she began quickly. "I understand it was previously used as a health resort?"

"Oh yes, Margot has been coming here for treatments for over twenty years. Her doctor referred her to it when it was still run by one of his colleagues. It was sold to that Italian businessman a few years ago. Margot actually pestered me to buy it so she could stay here year-round and invite friends over. She does love this place."

"But you weren't interested? You do not deal in real estate?" Atalanta asked.

"I do finance real estate purchases but I couldn't see myself buying this and then having to think about exploiting it. I leave those headaches to others." He smiled at her. "Now we must come to—"

Atalanta approached him quickly and looked up at him with a pleading expression. "Herr Bergreiter, I have not been totally honest with you. I do have money to invest but that is not what I want to talk about now. It is my friend Raoul Lemont. I am most concerned for his wellbeing. This blow to his head, his headaches and confusion ... can you tell me whether he will be better again? I mean, you are no doctor, but you have been here before and you saw him then. Is he improving or getting worse?"

Bergreiter seemed to flinch under her insistence. "I am not the right person to ask. I have only met him very briefly. Margot spends so much time here and must have seen more of him. Why don't you ask her?"

"Oh, I did ask her, but she is always so kind in her judgment of others. She thinks the best of everyone. She would never want to hurt my feelings and tell me something unpleasant. And I want an honest opinion." Atalanta wrung her hands. "I have always thought Raoul's profession was so dangerous, and now he really has had an accident."

"I thought his accident happened while skiing."

"Yes, the irony of it. He plays with his life every time he gets into that sportscar and then he takes a tumble while skiing..." Atalanta raised a hand to her temple as if she were still in shock. "I cannot understand how it happened. I wonder if Herr Dulce looked after him at all."

"Oh, I am certain Maurizio takes his task seriously. This racing team is very important to his uncle." Bergreiter fell silent a moment and then added, "You must have heard of Vincenzo Dulce. Everything he touches turns to gold."

"To diamonds, rather?" Atalanta joked.

Bergreiter laughed softly. "Indeed." He shifted his weight. "I don't see how I can help you, Fräulein Ford, other than by saying that I have the fullest confidence in the Dulces to take good care of your friend."

"Thank you, that puts my heart at ease a little. You see, I was approached by a reporter. A very nasty and insistent man. He asked me questions about Raoul's condition and suggested that the Dulces were somehow to blame for it all. I didn't believe him for one moment because I know what the press are like. Always digging for some hidden scandal to sell newspapers…"

Bergreiter seemed to get uncomfortable again. "Yes, well, I would not know. Fortunately, the press have always been kind to Margot. Her books are well liked and … her life is scandal free."

"But have you not heard of this reporter who wants to incriminate Raoul and Vincenzo Dulce? Alexander Hansen?"

Bergreiter's eyes went wide. "Is he now interested in your friend? That is not good, Fräulein Ford, not good at all. He is a predator. He sniffs out secrets and he goes on the attack until he draws blood. A friend of mine…" He fell silent, his cheeks pale.

Atalanta leaned closer. "Yes?" She had already heard the story of the couple who dismissed their nanny after infidelity claims which might be unfounded, but she had to get him to tell her more.

Bergreiter sighed. "He was wrongly accused of some financial wrongdoing and had to flee the country."

Atalanta hid her surprise. This was a different story. It seemed various people surrounding the Bergreiters had been targeted by Hansen. Did that explain Bergreiter's nerves as soon as his name was mentioned?

Bergreiter said, "It was very unpleasant. You say this man approached you?"

"Yes. Yesterday while I was in the village."

"He is here in the village?" Bergreiter seemed shocked. "To look into your friend's accident?"

"I had that impression, yes. How can we guard ourselves against him?"

"Have you told this to Maurizio?"

"No, I have not had a chance to speak to him yet. Besides, the reporter suggested that—"

"Yes, yes, I understand, but that reporter cannot be trusted at all. You must never talk to him again. He will only cruelly misquote you." Bergreiter stepped away from her. "*I* will tell Maurizio."

"No, please don't." Atalanta's palms were sweaty now that her strategy to get information was backfiring in a major way. "I don't want him to know the reporter contacted me. I don't believe his lies at all, but it could look like—"

"I will tell him *I* saw Hansen while I was on my way up here. I will tell him that I know he is in the village." Bergreiter walked to the door. "I will keep you out of it. I won't mention your name at all. This will be handled, trust me."

He left.

So you know what Hansen looks like, Atalanta mused. *That is interesting.*

She had no idea if she was creating trouble by her actions, but it did seem like there was something going on and it involved Raoul. As he was in no condition to stand up for himself, she had to look after his interests.

She returned to the ladies and Margot asked if her financial affairs had been straightened out to her satisfaction. Atalanta said that Herr Bergreiter had promised to look into the matter for her and they might have to sit down again later to discuss it anew. She wanted to leave some room for another conversation with the banker who was clearly concerned about the Dulces and his wife.

The four women played bridge while Franco served them drinks. Atalanta noticed how he kept making teasing remarks to Theresa but his smouldering looks were meant for Eva. What was the mysterious influence she seemed to have on men?

Around ten-thirty, Margot said she was tired and wanted to go to bed. Atalanta rushed to offer to walk her to her bedroom. She wanted to test a little theory and see if there was a response.

As they walked to the lifts, Atalanta said, "You have a very charming husband. And so devoted to you. He told me that he is even contemplating buying this entire hotel for you."

Margot seemed surprised. "Is he? I did discuss it with him, frequently, over the years but he has always decided against it. I was trying to resign myself to the fact that his decision was final."

"Oh it probably was, but since this reporter Hansen is writing about Raoul and the Dulces, it seems he fears there is some dirt to be unearthed and he wants to protect you."

"Protect me?" Margot echoed perplexed.

"Yes, if the hotel were his, the Dulces would take Raoul elsewhere and peace and quiet would descend again. He seems to think you are getting overexcited."

Margot shook her head. "Dear Dieter. He is always so concerned for me. I am of course not well, but…" They got into the lift. Margot turned to Atalanta and said in a sudden earnest tone, "I am not well at all. My condition is getting worse and I have not been able to work on my new book as much as I would have liked. But Dieter must not know. Promise me that you will not tell him anything should he try to quiz you. He is always asking other people how I am because he doesn't fully trust my answers." She smiled ruefully. "There is a reason for that of course. I lied to him before. We were for once travelling together and I just wanted us to see many places and enjoy ourselves. I told him that I was feeling better than I actually was so we would not be forced to go home prematurely but then I got pneumonia and he was really upset with me. Since that time, he doesn't trust me to tell the truth about my health. He asks others about me and, well, it is rather painful. He even asked Eva last time he was here. I saw them from my window talking together. It looked quite, uh … secretive so I quizzed her about it later and she confessed he had asked her to report on the true state of my health."

Atalanta didn't believe it for a moment. Eva was up to

something with the banker. She was playing him somehow. Was it flirting? Was it a power play of another kind?

Raoul had called her cold and calculating.

Margot said, "I am grateful to Eva that she played along and reassured Dieter. But her idea to do a little detecting is really going too far. She showed me some pills she had and claimed she had taken them from Maurizio Dulce's office. She said that they are used to sedate Raoul Lemont, to keep him weak after his accident. She wants me to have them tested by my doctor so she can prove that there is foul play going on. She really believes this story about Maurizio Dulce wanting to take Lemont's place on the racing team. I was so shocked by her brazen actions and told her that I will not be a part of something like that. She took those pills without permission, so it is basically theft. I cannot involve myself in anything like that. If word got out…" She shuddered. "She says I am a coward and that I did promise to be part of ETAM but … she never told us that she would go this far. She will have to find someone else to help her."

The lift arrived and they got out.

Margot seemed to shake her annoyance at Eva's behaviour and said with a smile, "I am probably a silly woman because I find it quite endearing that Dieter is so concerned for me. I should perhaps be annoyed that he is checking with people behind my back but … I know it comes from a good heart. I don't want him to worry so, should he ask your opinion, please tell him I am fine. Will you?"

"Of course." Atalanta forced a warm smile. "You have a

good night's sleep so you are fit enough to go and do something with your husband tomorrow. Goodnight."

Margot walked towards her room. Atalanta could not help feeling sorry for her because she thought she was the one being dishonest with her husband about her health while he was also being dishonest with her about his contact with Eva. What was Eva up to with Dieter Bergreiter?

And why had she been in the office at night? Was it only to search for those pills that were administered to Raoul? Or also to gather other evidence of Maurizio's actions?

Margot was right to conclude that she didn't want to get drawn into this. It was risky. A lot riskier than she knew. She was merely concerned for her reputation, but if Maurizio discovered that someone was prying into his business, what would he do? How far would he be willing to go to ensure that his secrets did not get out?

Chapter Ten

The next morning, Atalanta was on her way downstairs when Maurizio intercepted her and asked her to have breakfast with Raoul in his room.

"He slept badly and now he is as agitated as a bear roused from hibernation. You must talk some sense into him. You do seem to have a positive influence on him."

Atalanta flushed. "I don't know how you can have deduced that."

"It is the way he looks at you. I can see he cares about your opinion. He doesn't care one bit about mine, or about the risk I run of getting into trouble with my uncle because I am not taking good care of Raoul."

"You can hardly blame Raoul for not thinking too much of your uncle. He doesn't even recall ever having met him."

"I know." Maurizio nodded with a grave expression. "My uncle would not believe it possible that anyone could have met him and forgotten all about it. He is so charismatic and influential."

Not to mention coercive, Atalanta added to herself, but she smiled at Maurizio and said, "I am certain Raoul will start remembering again soon. He is having dreams about the accident. That must mean his memory is coming back."

"What kind of dreams?" Maurizio asked. It seemed he was immediately interested – or perhaps concerned? – judging by the tightness around his lips.

"Dreams of being trapped. It must be because of the fall he took in the snow. A hard fall knocks all the wind out of a person's chest."

"Oh that, yes." Maurizio seemed relieved. "I suppose so. We did try to help him straight away and make him comfortable, but it must have been a nasty fall. It looked like that from afar. He was way ahead of us, you know. We could barely even see him."

It seemed he was eager to emphasise that he had not been with Raoul at the moment of the fall, as if he wanted to convince her that he had nothing to do with it. But he could still have chosen a dangerous route or, knowing Raoul would forge ahead of them, hidden an obstacle in the snow.

"Do you know someone called Alexander Hansen?" she asked out of the blue, to see if she could shock him.

Maurizio froze a moment before saying, "I might have heard the name before. Why do you ask?"

"I think Eva mentioned him?" Atalanta frowned as if she were trying to recall. "Didn't he want to interview Raoul? He seems to be some kind of a reporter?"

Maurizio was silent a moment as if he was considering possible answers. Then he said, "Yes, he is a reporter and he has been following the team. I heard last night from Dieter Bergreiter that he is sniffing around in the village. Herr Bergreiter wasn't pleased because Hansen wrote a nasty article about a friend of his that caused significant personal harm, but I am certain he will not write anything bad about Raoul. My uncle would immediately sue him and that would become very costly for him."

"I see. Well, that is a good thing. I want to protect Raoul's reputation. He doesn't deserve unjust criticism or wrongful accusations, especially when he cannot defend himself."

"What kind of wrongful accusations do you have in mind?"

Atalanta shrugged. "It would be all too easy for a reporter to assume that Raoul was somehow the cause of his own accident. That he might have taken too much risk or been drinking... Something wild like that."

Maurizio laughed softly. "I do not think that Raoul taking too much risk is a wild story. He is always taking risks. But it would not be very good for my uncle to have newspapers writing about the team in a negative light."

They reached Raoul's room and went inside. The staff were setting up the breakfast table. Raoul stood at the window looking at the view. He didn't turn to look at them or wish them good morning. Atalanta went over to stand by his side. "How are you? Did you sleep well?"

"No, I did not and you already know that. Maurizio ran

to fetch you like he would ring for a nanny to cheer up a difficult charge."

"I am not your nanny." Atalanta studied his tight expression. "I understand you are tired but you have to stop being such a grouch to everyone. We only have your best interests at heart."

"Then let me go and do something! Anything other than sitting here all day long. Let me go down to the village with you. Please?" He gave her a pleading look.

Atalanta looked at Maurizio who was telling the staff to bring more toast and coffee. "And some scrambled eggs." He turned to her. It seemed he had overheard the exchange because he said with a shrug, "If Raoul insists on going, I cannot stop him but you must accompany him and make certain he doesn't overdo it. I don't want him to relapse."

Atalanta was surprised that Maurizio had agreed to this plan. If he believed Alexander Hansen was in the village, why would he let Raoul go down the mountain and potentially cross paths with Hansen?

Or was that what he actually wanted? So Hansen could see for himself that Raoul was on the mend and then he would have to stop printing lies about Maurizio wanting his spot on the team. Did Maurizio know exactly what Hansen had suggested? Was he far better informed about the reporter's stories than she had thought?

Raoul had turned away from the window upon hearing he could actually go and was now at the table loading his plate with breakfast items.

"Let us not waste any time," he said, around a bite of

toast with jam. "I can't wait to actually see some of the surroundings."

Atalanta shook her head at him but she was also glad to see him a bit cheerier than he had been for the past few days.

Maurizio left the room saying something in passing to one of the staff who came in carrying a crystal jug of orange juice.

Raoul buttered another slice of toast. He pointed at Atalanta. "I don't know how you do it, but you have softened Maurizio's hard heart. He behaves more like a jailor to me."

"All with the best intentions no doubt." Atalanta watched a staff member fill her cup with hot, strong coffee. Another piled eggs on her plate. The service was excellent here and she looked forward to spending the day sightseeing with Raoul. "The gem museum must be open today. We tried to visit there before but it was closed. I think it will be nice to have a look around. It is not big but it must be interesting to learn more about how gems develop in rocks. I heard from Eva that there are locals who go into the mountains around here to look for crystals. I cannot believe it is without significant risk, given the terrain."

Raoul shrugged. "Nothing worth having ever is." He picked up an apple and began to peel it. Outside the room in the corridor she could hear raised voices. Atalanta turned her head to the door to overhear what was being said, but she couldn't make out much. Just that a woman was talking in a high-pitched, excited voice. Perhaps it was Eva complaining about something?

Raoul cut up the apple. "If the gem museum also sells souvenirs, you must let me buy you something. You can keep it with the Christmas ornament I bought for you in Salzburg."

Atalanta looked up at him. "You remember being in Salzburg with me? At the Christmas market? You remember what you bought me there?"

Raoul nodded. "I don't know how I remembered, but I suddenly knew. It is not yet a real memory with lots of details, but I have flashes of it. Images. Crystal clear. Like it had happened the other day. You wore that red coat. I think seeing you in it while the others were ice skating must have triggered something. I think there were stalls? Lots of food and drink?"

Atalanta nodded enthusiastically. "That is good, so good, that you remember." She held his gaze. "What did you get me? I picked it out myself. For my Christmas tree."

Raoul seemed to want to answer, but he didn't get a chance as the door that had previously stood ajar was thrown open and Theresa entered. She looked pale and halted only two steps into the room. She held her hand up to her face.

"Oh Atty..." She stared at Atalanta with wide, frightened eyes. "It is horrible! She is dead!"

"Dead?" Atalanta echoed. A cold sense of dread settled in her stomach.

"Who is dead?" Raoul asked.

For a moment Atalanta was certain it was Margot Bergreiter. She had overexerted herself. She had lied to her husband again about being better than she was, just like she had before when she had pneumonia.

But Theresa said, her voice contorting, "Eva."

"Eva?" Atalanta echoed. Her mind replayed the image of Eva twirling on the frozen lake, waving at them, looking at Dieter Bergreiter with daring in her eyes. She had looked so alive, so full of energy and strength. How could she be dead?

"She was in the reading room all night. Somehow she fell and died there. She might have called for help but no one heard her. It is so terrible…" Theresa stared at Atalanta. "I only wanted to get a book to read. I opened the door and I saw her lying there. I—" Her face collapsed and she sobbed in her hands. Atalanta went over and touched her arm. "You have had a shock. You must sit down and drink something."

"Coffee?" Raoul asked standing at the table with the pot in hand.

Atalanta nodded. She guided Theresa to the chair she had vacated. "Sit here and take a few deep breaths. I am so sorry for you that you were the one to find her."

Theresa lowered herself onto the chair. "She was lying there, so still. At the bottom of the steps one uses to reach the higher shelves. She must have climbed up to get a book and then suffered a dizzy spell or lost her balance and fallen. I just can't stop thinking that she probably called for help and no one heard her. No one came to her aid."

Theresa sobbed again. Raoul had filled a coffee cup and handed it to Atalanta. He looked pale. Did this remind him of his own accident? Did it make him relive the frustration and anguish of being helpless? Of being abandoned, alone?

She had so hoped for this to be a good day, and had been so looking forward to getting him away from the hotel, but with this sudden death she doubted they would be going anywhere.

Atalanta was sitting with Theresa when Margot came in. She was dressed in bright yellow and white, carrying her purse in her hand as if she had been about to go out. Perhaps with her husband? She regarded Theresa and said, "I am so sorry you were the one to find her, Theresa. That must have been quite shocking."

Theresa sniffled. "I will never forget it. The way she lay there... It looked really peculiar. I was aware at once that something was wrong. I went over to see if I could help her and I knew immediately that she was dead. It was the look upon her face. A sort of fear? I can't explain it. But her eyes were bulging and—"

"I don't want to hear it," Margot said quickly. She shuddered. "I am just glad it wasn't me finding her. Poor Eva. She must have drunk too much alcohol and then climbed up that rickety ladder..." She turned to Atalanta. "The doctor is looking at the body right now. They have carried it to her room. Dieter and I were supposed to go on an outing today but I am not certain it is entirely appropriate with this sudden death..."

Raoul said, "We had also made plans." He glanced at Atalanta. "There is really nothing we can do for poor Eva now, and it is not like we knew her that well. She was just another guest here."

Theresa looked up at them. "She was not just another guest. She was a friend. We spent a lot of time together. We had even decided that we would—" She fell silent and glanced at Raoul. Then she said to Margot, "Remember ETAM?"

Margot flushed. "That was just a silly little idea. Nothing serious."

Atalanta assumed that Margot was now even more convinced she had done the right thing not accepting the pills Eva had tried to push on her for analysis. She had seemed eager not to get involved in anything dubious going on at the hotel.

"ETAM?" Raoul queried.

Atalanta was not sure if he was pretending to be in the dark about the meaning of the acronym, or if he had already forgotten what she had told him about it earlier. To avoid discussion, she waved a hand at him and said vaguely, "A project Eva discussed with us. Something she had read about in the newspaper. She was very interested in it. Enthusiastic about it. It is difficult to believe she can actually be dead."

Margot clutched her purse. "I had better go back to Dieter and tell him we are staying here for the day. He can do some paperwork and I will get back to my novel. I do hope I can get a few words down with all this excitement."

She turned and left the room. Theresa looked after her with an angry expression. "I don't think Margot is that sad," she observed snidely. "After all, Eva was flirting with her husband."

Atalanta looked at Theresa. "Is that so?"

"You must have noticed yourself. She changed when he was around. She sort of … acted a little silly. I guess she was just always attracted to older men."

Atalanta recalled Margot telling her about the conversation between her husband and Eva that she had observed from her window. A secretive conversation. Eva had assured her it had been her husband inquiring after her health because he cared so much about her. But what about the exchange yesterday at the reception desk? The one Atalanta had seen with her own eyes? It had left her with the impression that the interaction was not a concerned man asking for a report on his wife's health.

What had actually happened in the reading room? How had Eva fallen off the ladder? Theresa had suggested a dizzy spell, brought on by too much alcohol. Eva had drunk wine at dinner and at least two cocktails over bridge while Atalanta had been in the room, but she had retired to bed around ten-thirty and Eva might have continued drinking after that.

Had she even fallen off the ladder? Theresa had only assumed Eva had fallen because her body had been found at the foot of the ladder, but what if it hadn't been an accident?

Had she been in an argument with someone? Perhaps there had been an altercation that had taken a violent and tragic turn? Eva seemed like the kind of person who provoked strong feelings in others.

Atalanta couldn't help thinking of Franco trying to get a little too personal with her in that very reading room. Had he also tried his charms on Eva? He had been flirting heavily with her while serving drinks during the bridge game and could have followed her to the reading room later to see if she was open to more.

Atalanta tried to imagine the scene: Eva rejecting him, laughing at him because she felt above a flirtation with a bartender. Had he become angry and hurt her?

Theresa dabbed her eyes with a damp handkerchief. "Margot could not stand Eva. She only pretended to be friendly to her. It wasn't just the way Eva behaved with her husband but also that she was so young and full of life. Margot can't accept that other people can travel and do things while she is always chained to this old boring hotel and writing her books. She acts like she enjoys writing them because she lives vicariously through them as it were, but I don't believe her."

Atalanta nodded, more to keep Theresa talking than to actually affirm her words. It was odd how Theresa had seemed to support Margot against Eva's unkind attacks when they had been in the village together but now she seemed to have turned against her, painting her in an ungenerous light. But perhaps the shock of finding her friend dead on the floor and assuming she had cried for help without getting any had done something to her. Perhaps it had created a new loyalty that was making Theresa lash out at others who had not been on good footing with Eva?

Maurizio came to the door. He looked in and saw Theresa sitting there with them. He cleared his throat as if he were uncomfortable. "I would like to speak to Signorina Ford a moment. Alone?"

Atalanta glanced at Raoul and then left the room to follow Maurizio down the corridor. He stopped and looked about him to ascertain they weren't being overheard. Then he said in a low voice, "The doctor looked at the body. She wasn't killed by an injury sustained in a fall from the ladder. He thinks she was poisoned."

"Poisoned?" Atalanta echoed. She had not expected that at all. It did not fit with her assumptions that the death, if not accidental, had been the result of an impulse during an altercation. Poison suggested premeditation, and that opened up a whole different field of suspects.

"Yes, he can tell by looking at her features – her eyes or something." Maurizio waved a hand in the air. "There was a cup of tea with her in the room – some horrible herbal concoction like the ones she was always trying to push on other people. The doctor called the police from the reception desk and they will come to take the tea away for investigation." He clenched his hands. "This is very unfortunate. Raoul is supposed to be recovering in peace, not with a police inquiry going on next door."

"I am sorry to hear that, but why are you telling me?" Atalanta's heart beat fast. She expected him to face her and tell her any minute that he had known all along who she really was and that he wanted her to investigate the case discreetly so there would be no scandal involving his uncle's name.

But Maurizio said, "You must break the news to Raoul gently. He cannot suffer another shock. I will talk to the police as soon as they get here and explain that they must avoid questioning him if they can. His health is all that matters."

"I am afraid the police will not agree. For them, all that matters is the fact that a guest in this hotel was murdered. They will want to know who did it and why, and they will do everything in their power to arrive at a resolution of the case."

"You sound almost as if you have experienced this before," Maurizio said with a keen look.

"I uh ... was a guest at the wedding of the Comte de Surmonne in the South of France. That is where Raoul and I met. The mother of the comte's first wife died on his wedding day, from a fall in the family tomb. She wanted to look at her daughter's resting place and ... it was at first assumed to have been an accident, but then they suspected murder. As you can imagine, the wedding was called off and all the guests were thrown into turmoil. So I know first-hand how disruptive such a police investigation can be."

"I see. And Raoul was there too?" Maurizio looked even more agitated now. "The experience of being part of a new murder investigation could jog his memory."

It didn't seem like he was too pleased at the idea. Again, Atalanta wondered what Maurizio was hiding. Had Eva been right and he had somehow orchestrated the accident to take Raoul's place on the team? Did the pills Eva found prove that Maurizio was drugging him?

But Margot had refused to take the pills to her doctor to analyse. What had Eva done next to get help elsewhere?

Atalanta held her breath when she imagined a scenario in which word had got back to Maurizio about what Eva suspected. Or had she confronted Maurizio face-to-face and accused him of what she suspected? Had he taken steps to silence Eva before things went any further?

Had he known she had been poisoned well before the doctor had said it, because he had been the one who slipped the poison into her tea? Atalanta could hardly believe that he would be standing here talking to her about the death without betraying any guilt, but then, she had faced killers before and they had looked like nice, normal people. No one would have suspected them of having an evil bone in their bodies.

And Maurizio came from a family associated with crime. If he was hiding something about Raoul's accident, then he had every reason to want to keep it quiet, to hide it, even from his uncle.

Or *especially* from his uncle? Had his own life been on the line because Eva had been digging around, and had he decided that killing her was the only viable solution? It was a risk but perhaps he was confident the police would not be able to work out who had done it. There were plenty of suspects around…

Maurizio said, "Do keep an eye on Raoul as this whole thing starts to unfold. We don't want him getting worse."

But what if Maurizio *did* want him to get worse? The murder could be meant to kill two birds with one stone: remove the threat Eva posed with her enquiries and cause Raoul to relapse.

A staff member came to tell Maurizio that an inspector of police was on his way up, and he took his leave. Atalanta went back to Raoul and stood at the window watching as the cart ascended to the metal platform where Maurizio was waiting to meet the new arrival. He paced nervously back and forth but when the cart came into sight, he stood tall and motionless, as if this were any normal visitor. The man exiting the cart was short and stocky. His hair was invisible under a green felt hat decorated with a bird feather. He wore an ill-fitting green jacket and carried a rifle over his shoulder. He looked more like a hunter than a policeman.

Maurizio shook his hand and guided him to the hotel, talking busily and with many expressive hand gestures.

Atalanta saw the cable car begin to lower back down. She kept staring at the track, deep in thought, when she suddenly spied Franco, carrying a satchel and hurrying towards the departing funicular. He went to the platform and used steps on the side to clamber down. It looked quite perilous, and she held her breath. What was he doing?

Then she understood. On their way up she had seen it. Beside the track there was a set of very basic metal steps that could be used by workers to do repairs on the track, but with the snow still covering these higher regions it had to be very slippery and dangerous. Why would Franco risk so much to get away from the hotel without using the cart?

She excused herself to Raoul and ran down the hall then out of the hotel. She reached the platform to find Franco had only progressed a few steps down. He looked terrified and doubtful. The satchel had slipped off his shoulder and dangled against his leg.

"Franco!" she called out to him. "Don't do this! There is no need to run away!"

He looked up at her. "How do you know?"

"I know you were flirting with Eva. Perhaps you even had an affair?" She waited a moment and added, "Perhaps you met in the reading room when everyone had gone to bed?"

Franco swallowed hard. "I swear I didn't do anything to her. She just fainted away in my arms. I put her down on the sofa so she would be comfortable until she came to, but ... she was dead."

Atalanta tried to picture the scene. "You were together when she fainted?"

"Yes. She was in my arms. I was kissing her and ... suddenly her body went limp. I put her on the sofa and went to fetch something to revive her. When I returned to the sofa, there was a strange, glassy look in her eyes. I felt for a pulse but there was none." He blinked fast. "I didn't know what to do. She was dead. Dead!"

As he spoke, the patch of snow beneath his feet shifted and he almost slipped down. He cried out in anguish. His satchel dropped further to rest against his ankle.

Atalanta said, "You have to come back up here. The climb down will be the end of you. It is not worth the risk. You must tell your story to the inspector."

"Inspector? He is just a glorified gamekeeper. A man without a brain. He will simply assume I had an affair with her and that I killed her in a lover's quarrel."

"Why would you do that?"

"He will only be interested to close the case quickly and save the hotel's reputation. Herr Dulce will put pressure on him to do so. The Dulces always get what they want." He slipped again and the satchel fell away into the depths below.

Atalanta cried out, "Come back up here! You need not risk your life. I will help you."

"What can you do for me?"

"I have influence with Maurizio Dulce. Believe me, I will help you."

Franco looked doubtful but he was obviously too scared to continue down to the bottom. With great difficulty, he managed to work his way back up to where he could reach the step of the ladder to the platform. He pulled himself up and when he at last stood beside her, Atalanta heaved a sigh of relief.

"That was very foolish," she scolded. "You could have been killed. Just another pointless death."

Franco's eyes were dark. "I work in this hotel as a bartender. I am not a rich guest. I am a nobody. Before you came, there was a theft and a maid, Sylvia, was accused. She ran away to escape the false accusation. She was dismissed without them ever having asked her what happened or ascertaining whether she did it or not. And this is about much more than mere theft. If I am arrested, I will never be free again. They will lock me up for murder." He stared at her with wide eyes like a panicked animal.

"But you won't be arrested. Let the police do their investigation." Atalanta put a hand on his arm. "Eva fainted in your arms because she was poisoned. It was probably put in her tea."

"Her tea? She drank it before I came into the room. The cup was already empty on the table. I came in and I started kissing her right away. Then she—" Franco stared at her. "Poison, you say?"

"Yes. It will have taken some time to take effect, depending on what it was. But the police will find out about that. You must not lose heart. You must stay here and do your work as you always have."

"They will question me. What do I say? Do I lie and claim I was never near the reading room? But what if they somehow find out I was? I poured her a drink. My fingerprints must be on the glass." Franco's eyes darted in all directions. He looked like a skittish horse about to bolt. "I also arranged her body at the foot of the ladder to suggest she had fallen off it. I had to do something to make it look like an accident." He dabbed his forehead. "It was probably a stupid thing to do. Now I am certainly the main suspect."

"I will talk to the police before you do to find out what kind of man this inspector is. I will find out whether he is reasonable and has some insight. Then we can decide what to do." Atalanta looked Franco over. "Tell me one thing. Did you care for Eva?"

Franco sighed. "What do you mean 'care for'? At least you do not ask if I loved her. Love is the last thing on the mind of a bartender at a hotel. He can flirt with women. He can even steal a kiss. He can have an affair, if he is lucky. That is all. They are rich and well-positioned. They don't look at a man like me, not for a real relationship."

"You see many women here." Atalanta was reminded of Theresa's pleading looks at Franco – her obvious interest in him while he had been flirting with Eva. "Why embark on an affair with Eva? She didn't strike me as particularly ... *kind* in her assessment of people. To her you would certainly never have been more than a temporary distraction."

"Perhaps." He shrugged. "But she was lively and energetic. She had wild ideas. She expected big things of life. She wanted to move on in the world. I liked that. She made me believe in my potential. She didn't promise me anything, never said it would last between us. She was realistic like that. But she did tell me I could aspire to more than just being a bartender here. That was nice." A smile played around his lips before he became serious again. "Who would have wanted to poison her? What for?"

"We have to find out." Atalanta began to usher him back to the hotel.

Franco said, "Why would you help me? Why do you care about the risk I took in fleeing?"

"Raoul told me you have been nice to him ever since he came here." The lie came easily. "He needs support. He has been very glum since his accident. I hate seeing him like that."

Franco nodded. "I tried to cheer him up but I couldn't do much. I wasn't allowed to give him any alcohol or involve him in the card games."

"What card games?"

"Oh, the gentlemen play high-stakes poker at night. Herr Dulce picked that up from his time in Monaco. Just last night they played a few rounds. Herr Bergreiter lost quite a bit of money. He thinks he is good at the game, but he is usually outsmarted."

"I see."

Franco sighed. "The game went on and on which is why I couldn't get away to meet Eva at the time we had agreed upon. I only came to her after midnight. She was cross because she had waited so long. That's why I started kissing her right away. I wanted to make her forget her anger and…" He swallowed hard. "I just wanted to have a good time with her. I had no idea that it would end like this."

"Do not think too much about it. I will see what I can

do." Atalanta touched his arm again before they went inside. "I will help you."

Chapter Eleven

After telling Raoul what had happened with Franco, Atalanta went to look for the police inspector. It turned out he had taken over Maurizio's office in order to question people and was currently busy speaking to Theresa about the circumstances under which she had discovered the body.

Atalanta ensured she stayed close by so she could intercept Theresa the moment she came out from the questioning. As she waited, Renard came down the corridor to meet her. He looked around to ensure they were not being overheard and then said softly in French, "I heard about the death. The staff are all gathered in the kitchen gossiping about how a rich guest can suddenly take a tumble off a ladder and die. Some claim the ladder was rickety, others that she was meeting a lover there and they must have quarrelled."

"But it was not a fall that killed her. It was poison."

"How do you know that?"

"Maurizio shared it with me. He wants me to protect Raoul from the strain of this sudden investigation."

Renard held her gaze. "So you will do just that. You will protect Monsieur Lemont from exertion and not investigate the death. After all, you are here incognito, on private business, not to work."

"I know but … Eva might have been onto some conspiracy surrounding Raoul." She quickly told him about Eva's search of Maurizio's office and Margot's revelation that Eva had tried to push her to analyse the pills she had found. "If there is really something wrong with those pills and Maurizio found out Eva had taken them…"

Renard nodded slowly. Concern creased his forehead. "Monsieur Lemont is at their mercy. So are you while you are staying here. If you believe the death of Madame Reuter is somehow connected to Monsieur Lemont's condition and machinations by the Dulces, you must stay out of it. It can only put you, and Monsieur Lemont, in great danger."

Atalanta saw his point, but at the same time she knew she could not simply ignore the situation. "Raoul is already in danger, whether I investigate or not. Go back to the kitchen and take note of anything you see and hear. Even if the staff do not know the exact cause of death, they may know interesting titbits about Eva's behaviour before she died. We will discuss it more later."

Renard seemed to want to protest, but at that moment the door opened and Theresa came out. Renard retreated and Atalanta went to meet Theresa. As she saw her face clearly, she noticed that there was something of excitement in Theresa's looks, as though she felt important now that she was part of a murder investigation.

Atalanta asked her how she was doing and immediately the young woman's expression changed to sad again. She wrung her hands together. "It was terrible. Having to relive it over and over and tell him all the details of how she lay there…" She shook her head. "I can't believe that someone like Eva could even die. She always seemed so strong and in command. She thought she was in control of everything." Atalanta noted the undertone of spite in her voice. "You called her a friend, but did you really know her well? You only met while travelling, didn't you?"

"Yes, well, but what is a friend?" Theresa gestured with her hand. "We had the same interests, we liked to do the same things. We mostly got along well. If that is friendship…? We never discussed our lives in much detail." She looked at Atalanta. "The inspector asked me about her past, but I know very little about it. She was always sharing stories, but I must confess I never listened closely. She just talked incessantly. It was all a bit much."

"I understand. I am glad this ordeal is over for you now. You have made your statement and the police will take it from here."

Theresa laughed softly. "That man looks like he just came back from a hunting party. He didn't even have a notepad on him and had to ask Maurizio for a pen and paper. He jotted down a few notes but he seemed decidedly out of his depth. I don't imagine there are many murders here."

"I suppose not. Do you know anyone who would want to kill Eva?"

Theresa stopped and stared at Atalanta. "Of course not. People don't want to kill each other. I mean, not nice, normal people like the hotel guests here." She let the silence hang. "Although … Margot wasn't happy that her husband took a shine to Eva. I mean, she was such a vibrant personality that it was hard to overlook her. I guess Dieter Bergreiter does love his wife, but he has eyes in his head and, well, Eva liked to flirt. She didn't mean any harm, I suppose. It's not like she tried to start anything with Herr Bergreiter – at least, I don't think so. I can't be certain of course. She did used to leave her room at night to wander the hotel. Allegedly to read or something."

"How do you know? Did you see her?"

"I went to her door one evening around, oh … midnight? To borrow some sleeping pills. But she wasn't there. I supposed she had gone to get a book. I asked her the next morning and she said she found reading at night comforting because it was so quiet and there wasn't a soul around. But she said it like … like there was more to it. You know how Eva could be." Both women were silent before Theresa added, "She started ETAM. It was another of her little jokes. Like we could uncover a giant conspiracy surrounding Raoul Lemont's accident or something. But … she is dead now."

Atalanta nodded slowly. "Indeed she is. Do you think

she knew more than she let on?" She was wondering whether Theresa knew about the pills Eva took from Maurizio's office but didn't want to ask straight away.

"Eva was always trying to seem more interesting than she was. I don't know how much she actually knew for certain. It could have all been make-believe." Theresa shrugged. "I do know she was interested in the grotto. She went there several times. But I don't see what there was to do there. Or to see. It is just a grotto."

Atalanta nodded again. "I have to get back to Raoul. I hope you feel better now that you have unburdened yourself to the police."

Theresa seemed uncomfortable with the word choice. "I am going to lie down. I need to gather my thoughts. It was all so very terrible."

Atalanta waited until Theresa had taken the lift up to her room and then returned to the office the police inspector had commandeered and knocked on the door. *"Herein!"*

She stepped inside and closed the door. The man sat at the desk writing. He looked up at her with a frown. "Did I ask for you next?"

"No, I just wanted to make a polite request that you be very careful when you question my friend Raoul Lemont. He is recovering from a serious accident during which he sustained a head injury. He is not well."

"So I have heard." The man grimaced. "Everyone has been telling me that, even the lady who was here just now – the one who found the body. She seemed very pleased that she knows a race car driver. A bit superficial, I say."

He studied her. "Are you also impressed with Herr Lemont's résumé?"

"Herr Lemont and I are very close friends." Atalanta kept smiling. "We were even about to be engaged."

"I see. I am sorry for you then that the accident happened. I was told he suffers from memory loss and doesn't remember anyone. Not even you, I assume? That must be hard."

Atalanta nodded.

"And this murdered woman, Eva Reuter, she was also a friend of his?" He put an ironic stress on friend.

"No, I don't think they had ever met before." Atalanta refused to show her irritation at his intonation. "Raoul was brought here to recuperate. Eva arrived later. Last week, she said to me, but she didn't mention the exact date."

"One wonders why she came here." The man looked her over with his watery blue eyes. "There isn't a lot to do."

"The mountains are very beautiful."

He nodded. "Oh yes, our famous mountains." He looked at his notes and then said, "As you are here, I might as well question you. Please, do sit down." He gestured to the chair in front of the desk. "What is your name?"

Atalanta walked over and sat down. This was the moment of truth. "I am Atalanta Ashford. But I am here under the name Atty Ford. It is an alias I use while travelling in order to protect my identity. I am a wealthy heiress and it attracts the wrong kind of people."

"The wrong kind of people?" The man stared down at his notes.

"Yes, men who want to marry a rich wife. Criminals."

There was a hint of a smile around his lips. "You fear criminals and yet you take up residence in this hotel?"

Atalanta hitched a brow. "The connection escapes me." Her heart beat fast. Would he really make such a blatant reference to Vincenzo Dulce's past? Was it common knowledge in these parts?

"There was a report of theft a few weeks ago. A rich lady traveller found some of her jewellery had gone missing. She was certain a member of staff was responsible. A chambermaid. But the girl has disappeared."

"Disappeared?" Atalanta echoed. The wording intrigued her. Franco had mentioned to her that a maid, Sylvia, had been accused of theft and had run away. He had made it sound like it had been a voluntary departure. "Disappeared" sounded somehow different. More ominous.

The inspector explained, "Well, she was not found on the premises. Her things were still in her quarters. She left in a hurry – with the stolen goods, I assume. That was the end of my case. But word gets around and it surprises me that you have come here nevertheless."

"I came here to see Raoul. I didn't choose the hotel." Atalanta decided that the theft and the disappearance of the chambermaid might be worth looking into. She could ask Renard to drop questions to the other staff to see if he could learn more about this girl Sylvia.

The inspector said, "What can you tell me about Eva Reuter?"

"Not much. I met her here a few days ago for the first

time. She told me that she had been married to a wealthy man. She was his secretary before they married. She came into all of his fortune when he died which enabled her to travel, I suppose. She struck me as quite a determined woman when it came to getting what she wanted."

The man nodded. "I have reason to believe she was not alone in the reading room when she died. There was someone with her. Do you have any idea if she was having an affair with someone?"

"I'm sure I couldn't say. I have been here only a few days and I have spent most of that time with Raoul Lemont."

"But you went to the village with Fräulein Reuter and some other women."

"Yes, we wanted to visit the gem museum but it was closed. There was not much else to do." Atalanta tried to sound uninterested and a bit bored. "We came back up here again fairly quickly." Her cheeks went warm at the recollection of Eva's suggestion that they start ETAM. That little trip to the village hadn't been quite as innocent as she was portraying it here. But she was not about to tell him anything about that. First of all, it would probably strike him as quite ridiculous, something only bored wealthy women could think of, and secondly, she wanted to know if any of the other women had told him anything about Alexander Hansen's newspaper reports containing the accusations against Maurizio Dulce. Theresa had seemed to find that so sensational that she had probably shared it with the inspector. He said, "Did you see Fräulein Reuter last night?"

"After dinner we all sat together for a while over bridge and cocktails and then retired to bed. I accompanied Margot Bergreiter upstairs. It was about ten-thirty, I think. I haven't seen Eva Reuter since then. I learned of her death this morning when Theresa came in to tell Raoul and me about it."

"So you cannot tell me anything about the manner in which she died? You did not go into the reading room last night? You were not there with her when she died?"

"Certainly not."

"Did you know she drank herbal tea?"

"Yes, I have seen her do it on occasion. She claimed that nettle tea helped her to keep a clear complexion."

"Do you know where she keeps it? Have you had access to it? Do you carry medication of any kind on your person for personal use?"

"No, to all three questions." Atalanta sat up straighter. Was he thinking of her as a potential suspect? She could understand the logic since he came to this without knowledge of the pre-existing relationships between guests, but it struck her as unpleasant. Her position here was difficult enough, trying to wean Raoul away from the Dulces.

"Your room and your luggage will be searched by my men. You cannot prevent me from doing that as it is part of an ongoing investigation. I will also look into your personal situation to see if anything connects you with the victim."

"I am glad to see you are handling this so thoroughly." Atalanta waited a moment before adding, "It seems some people at this hotel are quite prejudiced. Someone even called you a glorified gamekeeper." She wanted to see how he responded to this insult while making certain he didn't take her as a supporter of this statement.

The man looked up at her. Amusement danced in his eyes. "I like to hunt in these beautiful mountains. I also stuff the animals I hunt. My cousin has a shop in the village where they are sold. There might even be a mounted animal head or two of mine on the walls of the hotel lobby. I only carry out police business when the need arises, and as you can imagine there is not a lot of crime in a small village like ours. People take matters into their own hands. If young men get drunk, and go through the streets laughing and shouting, their neighbours go out and tell them to go home. If something goes missing, everyone helps to find it again. If there is damage, people agree on compensation. It is all very friendly."

"What an ideal world to live in," Atalanta said with a pleasant smile. She knew that crime rates in small villages were low and people could resolve most things by simply talking and agreeing a practical solution. But somehow she didn't fully embrace the idyllic picture he painted. After all, the Dulces had a hotel here. They were criminals – and not small fish, but big, important masters of their trade. This man could not be ignorant of that.

He said, "Yes, Fräulein Ashford. I mean, Ford. I will have to speak to you again later perhaps if new questions arise. For now you may go. I will not need to speak to your friend Raoul Lemont. I may be able to find the killer without even bothering him."

Atalanta nodded as she rose. "That is very good of you. I appreciate it." She turned to the door. "Oh, you have not yet told me your name."

"Tanner. Tobias Tanner. My family has lived in this region for many generations. We have always been hunters and tradesmen. I am the first to have joined the police." He looked down at his notes with a thoughtful expression. "It was necessary, after my predecessor died."

Atalanta imagined a grizzled old man staying in the position until his last day, but Tanner surprised her as he continued, "It was sad because he was quite a young man still – only in his thirties. But he was run off the road by another car. It was quite tragic and we never found out who did it. A tourist probably, speeding where he shouldn't. Likely having had too much to drink." He sighed and shook his head. "The tourists, Fräulein Ford, some call them a blessing for this region as they bring in much needed income, but they can also be a curse. They do not understand our ways. Our traditions. They are not like us. You understand?"

Atalanta felt like he was trying to say more than he actually was with those cryptic words. She held his gaze a moment, doing her best to read behind his eyes, but his expression gave nothing away. On the surface he looked like a scruffy older man, in over his head, suddenly saddled with an inconvenient murder case. But she sensed that he was much more than a local hunter forced into a job he didn't want or like or was capable of handling. She would have to ask Renard to do some subtle digging. Subtle because if word of it should get back to him...? She didn't want to make an enemy here.

Tanner said, "I think I should get on with my business and you with yours, Fräulein Ford." When she reached the door, he asked, "I assume that your host, Herr Dulce, is aware that you are travelling under an alias?"

Atalanta gripped the door handle. This was painful. "No, he is not."

"You are afraid he has designs on wealthy travelling heiresses?"

She flushed deeply. "Raoul has some ... unsuitable friends. I didn't know Maurizio Dulce at all, and I thought it was sensible to find out who he was before I..."

"It is always sensible to look beyond the first impression. And your alias is safe enough with me. I don't know, though, how Herr Dulce would take it if he found out he was being lied to. He doesn't seem like a patient man to me."

Was that a warning? Or just well-meaning advice? She didn't know. She merely said, "I appreciate your understanding. Good day."

In the corridor she stood a moment, pressing her hand to her heavily beating heart.

What had she done by lying about her identity? It had been an attempt to avoid scrutiny by the Dulces but now she was part of a murder investigation and her past would certainly come to light. It would become harder and harder to provide innocent explanations for her behaviour. Still, she wasn't about to reveal herself to Maurizio Dulce now. There had been a sudden death and she knew Eva had been interested in the rumours about his involvement in Raoul's accident. Eva's theft of the pills from the office proved she had believed herself to be onto something substantial. By revealing her real name, Atalanta could lead Maurizio straight to her profession. Once he knew she was a detective, he would realise the danger he was in. Even if he were innocent, the unfortunate fact that a detective was staying at his uncle's hotel would pose a problem to him. She could not know how he might seek to solve it.

With a little poison in her tea?

Chapter Twelve

Renard stood at the window of his room in the servants' quarters and stared at the mountain panorama. Staff members were not supposed to be here during the day, but he was not a member of the hotel staff and he did not need to follow their rules. He had taken a few minutes to himself to think about the situation and the position his mistress was in now that there had been a murder at the hotel. He had thought her decision to lie about her identity was sensible, and at the time he had still had hope that they could somehow extract Raoul Lemont from Vincenzo Dulce's clutches. It had been a small hope because Mademoiselle Ashford had informed him of the two-year contract Lemont had signed, but he had always tried to look for the possibilities instead of the obstacles. If Lemont was injured and unable to race, he might become less valuable to Dulce. There was always money – perhaps a decent sum could free him from his obligations. Renard knew his mistress would certainly pay to help a friend.

But now that they were staying here, he was seeing the difficulties. Maurizio Dulce was taking a very personal interest in Lemont and his speedy recovery, and then there was this sudden development with the murder...

Renard knew that his mistress had a knack for stumbling upon crime on her travels, but this was extraordinary. What were the chances that a simple visit to an injured friend would get her involved in a murder? He was surprised that Maurizio Dulce would take the risk of murdering a guest in his uncle's hotel. But then again, he didn't know for certain that it had been Maurizio Dulce who put the poison in the tea. It could have been any one of a number of people. The gossip among staff members was that Madame Reuter had been with a lover before she died, but no one was bold enough to mention any names in particular to indicate who they had in mind.

As he stood there, trying to settle the uneasiness churning in his stomach, his gaze wandered from the mountain view to the garden below. There, on a deck chair close to the frozen lake, sat Dieter Bergreiter. He was sitting with his head down and his shoulders slumped as if the sudden death at the hotel had utterly shaken him. Of course it had been unexpected and Madame Reuter had been a young woman which made it all the more unbelievable, but still his dejection seemed to be extreme. For a man of the world, a banker responsible for the management of huge fortunes, used to handling situations with self-control...?

Renard sprang to attention when he saw someone approaching Bergreiter. It was Theresa Hofer. She looked around her as if to make certain they were alone. Then she stepped closer and said something. Bergreiter looked up. Theresa kept talking.

Renard could not clearly see Bergreiter's face but he could tell that the man seemed to shrink back in his chair. Theresa, on the other hand, spoke with insistence. She reached out a hand and opened it, to show something to the banker. The sunlight caught the object a moment, reflecting off it in a blinding flash. It was made of metal but it wasn't large. She was easily able to conceal it in the palm of her hand.

Theresa put the item back in her pocket and kept speaking to Bergreiter. Then she suddenly turned and walked away. Bergreiter rose from the chair and caught up with her in a few hurried paces. He arrested her arm and seemed to squeeze tightly. Theresa tried to pull free. Suddenly both of them looked at the hotel and Bergreiter let go of her. Theresa immediately departed. She passed someone on their way out to Bergreiter. It was the bartender Franco. He seemed to ask Bergreiter to come inside. Perhaps there was a telephone call for him or another message he had to attend to?

Renard frowned. What had Theresa shown to Bergreiter? It had obviously upset him enough to go after her and force some word of warning on her – not to reveal to others what she had said to him?

But what *had* she said to him?

Renard thought his mistress should know this, and she must speak to Theresa Hofer about it. She could pretend she had herself witnessed the exchange. He nodded to himself and left the room to go and find her.

Atalanta glanced at Theresa as the cart moved downhill. Immediately after Renard had informed her of what he had witnessed between Dieter Bergreiter and Theresa, Atalanta had made a plan to draw the other woman out. Not only did she want to know what Theresa was up to, but also how much Eva had shared about her investigation into Raoul's accident. Did Theresa know about Eva's nightly foray into Maurizio's office and the pills she had taken? If she did, did it put her in danger?

Initially, Atalanta had not taken the idea of ETAM very seriously, but now that one of their members was murdered, she did feel an obligation to keep the others safe. Margot had refused to be part of anything, so she seemed to be in the clear, so Atalanta had to focus on Theresa.

Not wasting any time, she had asked Theresa to visit the gem museum with her as a distraction from the murder. Inspector Tanner hadn't forbidden them to leave the hotel, but he had emphasised that they were not to leave the area and that he was having them watched to ensure they heeded his orders. She assumed that he had instructed the hotel clerks to call down to the village the moment the cable car left the hotel so that there could be someone waiting to watch them as soon as they got out and started into the village. It gave her an eerie feeling that she was under such close scrutiny.

But Tanner was a policeman. She could trust him, couldn't she?

She ducked her chin deeper into the collar of her coat. The truth was, she wasn't certain she could trust him. There had been something strange about the way in which he had questioned her and revealed certain information to her as if he had specifically wanted her to know it. Who was he really? Why had he been chosen to step up after his predecessor had died in the car accident?

Had it even been an accident? He had been run off the road by another car. Who had been driving that car?

Was it possible that Tanner had murdered his predecessor to get into the position of inspector? If so, to what purpose?

Her stomach tightened. She had come here to help Raoul but the more she thought about the situation, the more she felt that she was in over her head. Could she truly save him from the quicksand he was caught up in? He was angry with her for deciding she was going down to the village without him, but she had to do this to be able to quiz Theresa about her exchange with Bergreiter. She didn't want to do it at the hotel where they could be overheard.

Besides, a relaxed atmosphere was necessary to ensure Theresa was caught off-guard and would admit to something. Raoul, however, had not been very understanding. He seemed to think, just like Renard, that she should leave the case alone. And perhaps they were right. Could this be one case too many causing irreparable harm?

The cart halted and Theresa got out ahead of Atalanta. She took a deep breath of clean, crisp air and said, "I am so glad to be away from there. It is a terrible place. Stuffy and unfriendly."

"I didn't know you didn't like it there." Atalanta leaned closer. "Is it because of Franco? He can come on a bit strong, I suppose."

Theresa cast her a curious look. "Did he also approach you? Did he quote those lines about a woman watching a man ride across a moonlit lawn? It is a bit of a joke among us. I mean, it was." She grimaced. "He uses the moonlit lawn with every female who comes to the hotel. And it is not even a passage from one of Margot's novels. She insists it isn't."

Atalanta was surprised. "Franco made it up?"

"Yes. It is his way of impressing women, I suppose. But he uses the same trick with everyone. It is rather embarrassing."

"He must assume that the objects of his affection won't discuss it with one another as they all believe they are the only one?"

"I suppose so. But Eva wasn't like that. She told us straight away and then I had to admit that he had already tried it with me and even Margot said he had tried it with her. I think she was lying though."

"Why would she lie?"

"Well, it doesn't make sense that Franco would quote her own novels to her, knowing full well that what he is quoting isn't something she ever wrote."

"But she wrote more than thirty books. How can she recall every single line?"

Theresa shrugged. "Apart from that, she is hardly his type. She is too old. And married. I have a feeling he chases younger women who are unmarried and looking for a bit of … an adventure during their stay here."

"I see."

"Franco is quite good-looking and I felt flattered that he was pursuing me until I realised he did it with everyone." Her eyes flashed with a vengeful glow. "He should know better. If one of us complains, he could lose his job."

"But he supposes no one will complain as it is quite an embarrassing thing to admit to. Maurizio Dulce is also a handsome man and … I can imagine that the female guests would rather keep smiling at him than have to admit that they were fooled by a lecherous bartender."

Theresa flushed scarlet. "I wish Maurizio would dismiss him though. Franco deserves it. He is so arrogant. Eva even caught him in her room. She said he was putting a red rose on her bed." Theresa shook her head. "Eva thought it was romantic. She didn't mind him trying it on with all the women he set eyes on. She said she was the same, just wanting to have a good time while she was away from home."

Atalanta wondered if Franco had really been in Eva's bedroom to put a red rose on her bed. It sounded like an excuse for something else. Had he been going through her things? What had he been looking for? Precious jewellery perhaps? There could be a connection with the earlier theft.

The maid, Sylvia, had gone missing. It seemed logical to assume she had stolen the jewels and had run off with them, but what if she had caught Franco stealing and he had silenced her in order to be able to continue with his criminal activities?

Atalanta shielded her eyes from the bright sunlight as they walked towards the museum. It was but a short walk though it seemed longer as her head was so full of thoughts. She had taken Theresa along to question her about Dieter Bergreiter but these revelations about Franco had distracted her. When he had tried to flee the hotel via the track, shortly after the discovery of Eva's dead body, he had acted as if he was afraid of a wrongful accusation of murder. But perhaps he had been trying to flee because he was truly guilty of something – the past murder of the maid Sylvia?

Theresa said, "I have to admit, I was often a little jealous of Eva. She was so outgoing and radiant. People immediately liked her. Men fell in love with her. I felt like I could never be that way."

Atalanta nodded in sympathy. "Eva was indeed very vibrant. Yesterday when she was ice skating ... I watched her twirl and it was almost like a performance."

"Oh, I wager she was showing off for Dieter Bergreiter. She didn't really like him but her flirting with him angered Margot and Eva loved to get people upset about her behaviour. It amused her to no end."

"It sounds like she could be a little cruel."

"A little?" Theresa scoffed. She seemed to want to say something and then thought better of it.

Atalanta studied her. "If she had this darker side, why did you keep travelling with her?"

"Nobody is perfect. I mean, all people have less pleasant sides to their personality. Eva could also be kind."

"And generous?" Atalanta queried softly. "She had a lot of money, I heard. It must be convenient to have a wealthy friend."

Theresa stopped and threw her an angry look. "What are you trying to say? That I took money from her? Made her pay for expenses?"

"Well, didn't you?" Atalanta pushed.

Theresa's cheeks were deep red. "I may have let her pay a bill or two when I was a little short of cash, but … it wasn't like I was using her. Why do I even have to explain myself to you? You don't know how it was. You have money and independence. Wealthy friends who look after you. Once you are in the right place, everything moves your way."

"And you wanted to get in the right place." It was more conclusion than question and Theresa didn't deny it.

"What if I did? Eva married a rich man to move up in the world. It served her well. I was just thinking I might follow her example."

"There is nothing wrong with that," Atalanta assured her readily. She wanted to get more from Theresa and she would clam up if Atalanta alienated her. "But some ways to get on in the world are more dangerous than others. The safer the route the better."

"Is there a safe route? Eva would say one has to endure a little danger to get what one wants."

"Yes, but does one always know how fast a little danger can become so much danger that...?" Atalanta let the rest hang.

Theresa stared at her. "Do you think Eva was murdered because she overplayed her hand?" A little smile tugged at her lips. "Possibly."

"It sounds almost as if you know more than you are saying. Did you tell the police?"

"There was little I could tell them. I found the body."

"And that's it?" Atalanta looked at her again. "You only found the body?"

She meant to denote that Theresa's role had been bigger than just discovering the body by chance, but Theresa flushed deeper and said in a squeaky voice, "Yes, only the body, nothing else."

As she said it, something clicked in Atalanta's mind: the scene Renard had witnessed from the window. Theresa's little conversation with Dieter Bergreiter, and the object she had shown him. She had found something beside the body and it belonged to Margot's husband.

Or had she only thought it did and shown it to him to elicit a response? Judging by what Renard had told her, that response had been almost violent. Did it prove that Dieter Bergreiter was involved in Eva's death?

"It is never wise to challenge a murderer," she said softly.

Theresa pursed her lips and pointed ahead. "There is the museum. Let us not speak about the murder anymore. It is a nasty affair but I am certain the police will solve it."

"How can they solve it when people remove clues?" Atalanta said sharply. She had decided that attack was the best approach and so she continued, "You took something from the crime scene and you are now using it to pressure people. But that is a bad idea. You could get into serious trouble with Inspector Tanner."

"First he would have to find out about it." Theresa looked at Atalanta, standing with her feet planted apart. "Are you going to tell him? Or are you willing to keep your mouth shut if I share with you what I know? Tanner is just an ignorant peasant who got a job he can't handle. They have never had a murder here before." Theresa sounded smug. "I am not trying to derail the murder case or anything. I can still tell the inspector what I know. I just wanted to find out first … whether I am jumping to conclusions."

"And what did Dieter Bergreiter's response tell you?" Atalanta said, deciding to squeeze a little. Theresa was greedy and that could be dangerous. "If you can't decide, I can tell you my opinion. Because I know exactly what happened between you."

Theresa seemed overtaken. "You can't. We made certain that—"

"No one was watching? You are wrong."

Theresa arrested her arm and applied pressure. "You have to leave this thing to me. It is a golden opportunity to get money. He is a banker. He has plenty. He can give me some so I can get away from here and make something of my life. It is not my fault that he got into this mess. He should never have had an affair with Eva while claiming to love his wife so much."

"They had an affair?"

"Of course. Why else would his golden tie clip be lying beside her dead body? They were meeting in the reading room at night."

Atalanta frowned. Franco had been with Eva when she died. He had put her body at the bottom of the ladder to feign an accident. Where had the tie clip come from? Who had placed it there? Or had Dieter Bergreiter come in later and gone over to look closer and leaned down and then the clip had fallen?

"I don't want to hurt anyone," Theresa said. "I don't really care whether he killed Eva or not. I mean, if he did, she probably deserved it. I'm not after his neck. I only want some money. He can give it to me and then I will leave him in peace."

"I don't know if he believes that. Blackmail is a dangerous thing. It can make the victim desperate for a solution. If Bergreiter did kill Eva, he might think he should kill you too."

"He wouldn't be so stupid as to try right after Eva's death. Now he is not a direct suspect. Nobody knows about the affair. Nobody but me."

But you just told me, Atalanta thought.

Theresa didn't seem to notice the incongruity and continued, "He has to pay me to keep my mouth shut and then he can lie back and wait until Tanner arrests someone else for it."

"Like who?" Atalanta asked without fully expecting an answer.

"Maurizio Dulce of course. Eva was looking into the accident that hurt Raoul Lemont. She was convinced it was a scam of some sort. The newspaper article this Hansen wrote only confirmed what she already suspected. She wanted to find evidence for it and deliver it to Hansen."

"She was in touch with him?" Atalanta asked perplexed.

"I think so. When we used to visit the village, she often thought up some errand to separate herself from me and one time I followed her to see what she was going to do and all she did was make a phone call. I don't know to whom or about what, but … it is revealing, isn't it?"

Atalanta agreed but didn't say so. "Did Eva tell you what evidence she had?"

"Of course not. She kept her cards close to her chest."

"She didn't ask you to do anything for her, to help her?"

Theresa shot her a sharp glance. "Why would she have?"

"Oh, you know, because of ETAM, us sleuthing together…"

Theresa shrugged but didn't answer the question of whether Eva had asked her for help with anything in particular.

Atalanta kept pushing. "You say she wanted to deliver proof to Hansen. I assume it was meant to support his allegations that Maurizio is trying to take Raoul's place on the team?"

"I guess so. She never actually told me she was in touch with Hansen. I deduced that myself."

"But if Maurizio is hiding something about Raoul's accident, the murder is only making it harder for him," Atalanta mused. "Tanner will look closely at everyone at the hotel."

"Perhaps." Theresa shrugged again. "Perhaps he will also accept a bribe and choose a convenient suspect on whom to pin the murder in order to close the case quickly. It will not be one of the wealthy guests, I wager, but someone whom Maurizio thinks expendable. Franco would be an excellent option. If I were him, I'd be worried about some evidence being conveniently planted in my room. Proof that Franco was having an affair with Eva or that he was slipping her information about the hotel and its guests."

Franco had been worried about being accused. Had he reasoned along the same lines as Theresa? "And why would he have killed Eva?" Atalanta asked, to gauge Theresa's ideas about motive.

"Perhaps he thought she was getting careless and putting them both in danger? Or perhaps she insulted him with some remark. Eva could be quite vicious. She thought she could get away with anything." Theresa's lips twitched again in that little smile of satisfaction. "Not this time."

Without waiting for a response, Theresa entered the

museum and Atalanta followed. If Eva had indeed been Alexander Hansen's source for his story about Raoul's accident, this opened up a whole new angle in the murder case. If it was true, she had not been snooping merely because she was curious, no, she had been feeding sensitive information to a newspaper reporter who did not shrink from printing sensational stories that hurt people. That made her a very real danger.

They purchased tickets and went into the first room, which had glass cabinets displaying crystals that had been found in the surrounding mountains. There was information about the dangerous profession of looking for these stones, with black and white photographs of the first men and women who had tried. Atalanta tried to focus because she found the gems genuinely fascinating, but Theresa's revelations had left her puzzled. She had sensed Bergreiter's discomfort in Eva's presence last night at the exchange at the reception desk. Had he decided to rid himself of her? Perhaps also to avoid his wife noticing something? He seemed genuinely protective of Margot.

Had he killed Eva by putting poison in her tea earlier in the evening and then returned later to check if she had died – leaving behind his tie clip then?

"Are you even certain that the object you found belongs to Dieter Bergreiter?" she asked Theresa.

Theresa stood at a glass cabinet gazing in. She looked up, snorting. "What is it to you?" She took a deep breath. "You know my secret now. Do you want money to keep it? Or do you feel sorry for Margot that her husband was lying to her? You shouldn't be. She is also lying to him. She claims her sister provides all the details for her books. She claims she gets these long letters that tell her everything she needs to know. Just a few months ago she finished a book set on Crete. Her sister had been there recently and wrote to her, including some photographs. She showed the photos to us. Well, I don't know where she got those, but her sister didn't send them recently."

"Why not?" Atalanta asked intrigued.

"Because they show a building that is no longer there. I was on Crete last summer and I have been to the sites her sister allegedly visited. They are the main tourist destinations. That building was torn down after it sustained damage in a storm. The photos she showed us were old ones, from years ago. So she is lying."

"I see." Atalanta frowned. "Perhaps she is herself confused? Perhaps her sister sent her so many photographs that they got mixed up?"

"No. There was a date on the back. Scribbled in black ink. But I am telling you it was an older photo. She wrote the date on the back herself." Theresa laughed softly. "Perhaps she doesn't even have a sister who travels the world. She could have invented her because it is a beautiful story to support her career. People love her and her books. So sad and tragic that she is unable to do much herself, but her sister writes to her, and they create the books almost together…"

Atalanta made a note to herself to look into this matter when she had a chance. "Did you mention this to Eva?

Did you tell her that there was something not quite right with Margot's story?"

"Yes, as a matter of fact I did. I think Eva also told Margot. She didn't tell her that this was *my* theory, of course, but pretended it was her own idea. She even lied about having been to Crete. Typical of Eva. Always making herself seem more important."

And signing her own death warrant that way? Had Margot Bergreiter lied about having a sister who provided the material for her books? Was it all a beautiful fabrication to entice readers? And what would happen if it all fell apart because of some malicious rumours? Margot had not really liked Eva. Perhaps Margot had felt threatened and concluded that the world was better off without the manipulative young woman.

Or had Eva mentioned to Dieter that she doubted Margot's story about her sister? Had she thereby forced him into action to protect his wife and give Eva the poison?

There were possibilities opening up on all sides and Atalanta had no idea which one was the most likely. Should she not just let Tanner figure it out? She had not been asked to involve herself with this case. Eva had not been her client. No one she knew or cared about was accused of the murder. She had come here for Raoul, to help him recover from his injuries. Was it not better to devote herself to that and leave the murder case alone?

But Atalanta knew that even if that were the better choice, her mind would not let it go. It was working on all the elements, rearranging them like puzzle pieces to arrive at a meaningful whole. She liked the exercise and she was always happy when she got a good result. But she was on thin ice here. The Dulces were dangerous. They were themselves criminals and they had an interest in protecting the reputation of their hotel and their influential guests. They would not want her working to prove that someone of good name and good character had committed a murder at Hotel Alpenrot. They would have to move things in another direction.

Franco? Had Theresa been right to assume he would become a convenient scapegoat?

Atalanta didn't particularly like him but she had no wish to see him arrested for a murder he didn't commit.

Or had he committed it? It seemed he had been more than just a flirtatious bartender. What if Eva had found out something incriminating about him? Could he not have decided to remove her? Could he not have put the tie clip beside the body to point in another direction?

She had to be very careful. There was so much at stake. For people, for the hotel, for Raoul's new sponsor and by association for Raoul himself. This was one case in which she could not afford to make mistakes.

But perhaps she had already made one by revealing to Theresa that she was aware of her attempts to blackmail Dieter Bergreiter.

How dangerous was this inconspicuous woman really, and how far would she be willing to go to get the money she wanted to have an easy life?

Chapter Thirteen

When they got back to the hotel, there was a little commotion in the lobby. Tanner was standing at the reception desk using the telephone. A man who had apparently come with him was speaking to Maurizio, who was shaking his head violently and making dismissive hand gestures. Another man was approaching a few hotel guests with a notebook in his hand. Was there a new development in the murder case? It seemed like the guests were going to be questioned again.

Or had these people not been questioned the first time around? Tanner might have been short on staff, only interviewing the most relevant people at first.

As she and Theresa passed the desk, Atalanta overheard Tanner say, "Yes, I need someone up here right away to remove the remains. Carefully. The doctor can go along."

"Remains?" Theresa said. "I thought Eva's body had been removed already." She looked confused.

Atalanta's heart began to thump in her chest. Had there been another murder in their absence? Who was dead this time?

Raoul? It made no sense to think that, but perhaps it was Maurizio's emphatic denials steering her in that direction. Was he denying all responsibility for his charge's demise?

But just as she was fearing the worst, Raoul came in from the reading room and stopped when he saw the commotion. He looked from one person to another, until his gaze fell on Atalanta. He immediately smiled at her, and she felt the familiar warmth glow in her chest. She was so happy he had survived the accident and was here with her. Even if he could not remember her.

She went over to him. "What's going on? Was there another murder?"

"Not that I know of. The inspector and his men came up earlier to have a look inside the grotto – the one in the back of the hotel grounds. I assumed they were interested in why Eva went there several times." He looked around as if to ensure no one was overhearing what he said, then he whispered, "There seems to have been a jewel theft here at the hotel a few weeks ago. Some very expensive jewellery went missing. Do you think it was hidden in that cave? Do you think Eva discovered it and figured out who stole it? Perhaps the thief killed her to keep the secret?"

"Still, surely the thief would have assumed the police would do a thorough investigation and locate the missing gems in the grotto. Then they'd make a connection between the theft and Eva's death. That would only make it worse for the thief," she said.

"I don't think people reason like that. They only see a present danger and act to remove it."

"I suppose you could be right, but whose remains have they found?"

"Remains? I know nothing about remains." Raoul paled. "If this is a second murder, I want you to leave the hotel. It is too dangerous here." He eyed her with emphatic insistence. "You must not stay where there is a murderer on the loose."

"But Raoul, I have solved murders before." Atalanta said it softly so as not to be overheard by anyone. "You were there. You might not remember but—"

"I don't care what you did before. Now you are here with me, for me, because of me." He began to get agitated, gesticulating wildly with both hands. "My presence lured you here and now there are people dying. I want you to leave."

Maurizio appeared by their sides, eyeing Raoul with concern. "What's wrong with him? Why is he getting so worked up? That is not good in his condition. It will worsen his symptoms. He should go and lie down."

"Forget it," Raoul hissed. "I am not going to bed while someone I care about is in danger."

"In danger? Why would Signorina Ford be in danger?" Maurizio asked with evident confusion. Or was it just good acting? He might know full well what was going on at the hotel if he himself was the murderer.

Raoul glared at him. "People keep dying here." He pointed to the inspector and his men. "They're already looking into a second death. I don't want her to get swept up in this. She must leave."

"She can leave if she wants to." Maurizio glanced at Atalanta. "But I don't think she wants to. She wants to help you recover. As do I."

"I can't recover in a place where people keep being murdered." Raoul wanted to say more but Maurizio touched his arm. "Stop it. You're overreacting. Eva Reuter's death is still being investigated. We have no idea how she died exactly or who is to blame. But I am convinced it has nothing to do with you or anyone you like." He took a deep breath and added, "The remains in the grotto could be from a chambermaid who vanished after a jewel theft. It happened before you got here. If she was murdered, she was probably killed by an accomplice who wanted the loot to themselves. It could have happened at any hotel. It was about the stones and the money they represent. Nothing more."

"You cannot know that," Raoul protested.

But Atalanta said, "Maurizio could be on the right track. We shouldn't rush to conclusions. We'll have to wait to hear what Inspector Tanner has to say. He's calling more people onto the scene to establish some basic facts, such as how long the body has been there and whether anything relevant has been found on or near it. Then we'll know more."

Raoul seemed to calm down a little. He let his arms dangle as if he was embarrassed to have overreacted.

Maurizio said, "I do understand it is a nuisance to have all this activity at the hotel. But you mustn't let it get in the way of your recovery. Go back into the reading room and I will have someone bring coffee and cake for you and Signorina Ford."

Raoul turned and walked away with his head down. It seemed like the energy he had spent had wearied him. Was he losing hope that he could recover?

Atalanta felt for him, but there was also something else on her mind: the almost callous way in which Maurizio spoke about the events at the hotel. She looked at him. "We must not let what's happened here get in the way of Raoul's recovery, you say. After all, what is a murder … or two?"

Maurizio smiled softly. "I can understand you feel a little shocked by my take on things, but consider it from my perspective. I am here to ensure Raoul gets better so he can race for my uncle. I have nothing to do with the deaths of either Eva Reuter or the person found in the grotto. I let the appropriate people handle the cases and I focus on what is my task here, which is protecting Raoul."

"I see." Atalanta took a deep breath. "So your uncle still believes Raoul can get well soon enough to race this season? He is not looking for a replacement?" She studied his features closely.

Maurizio seemed a little surprised by her question. And on guard. He pulled back his shoulders as he said, "Not that I know."

"Are you a race car driver too?"

"I have done some racing in the past but I'm just an

amateur." Maurizio tilted his head. "Where are you going with these questions, Signorina Ford? Do you think I am after Raoul's spot on the team?" He laughed softly. "That would be very presumptuous of me. I am nowhere near as good as Raoul is. Besides, my uncle would never entrust his expensive car to me."

"That's not what Alexander Hansen thinks. He wrote a whole article about Raoul's replacement, featuring *you* as the new driver for the team."

Maurizio's eyes flickered and his smile seemed forced as he said, "Hansen is a nasty man. He has written several scathing articles causing havoc for people. Everyone is afraid of him." He looked past her at the police activity before returning his gaze to her. "It would not be a terrible thing if he were dead."

"But he isn't. Others are and this hotel is now under close scrutiny." Atalanta leaned closer. "Are you worried that some unpleasantness may come to light?" She waited a moment and continued, "Will it affect Raoul's career?" She put a desperate note in her voice. "I am only concerned for him. How he can survive all of this. Physically, mentally. He is not himself. It hurts me to see him so dejected and—"

"There is no big secret here." Maurizio sounded self-assured. "I don't know who committed the jewel theft. It was probably the chambermaid who disappeared. If she is found now, in the grotto, then someone else killed her, to get the stones. That is regrettable but it has nothing to do with your friend Raoul." He eyed her earnestly. "Believe me, we have the same goal. We both want him to recover. To become his old self again."

Atalanta wondered if that were true. Did Maurizio really want Raoul to get better, to regain his memory and remember exactly how the accident had happened? Perhaps he would remember that the *piste* had not been suitable for skiing or that he had hit a suspicious obstacle, one placed in his path on purpose.

Tanner came up to them. He looked at Maurizio. "Herr Dulce, I will need more information on the girl that went missing. Physical description, personal details. Who she spent time with. Perhaps she had a lover?"

Maurizio laughed a little too loudly. "I don't keep track of the personal affairs of my staff. You could ask my bartender Franco. He's quite the ladies' man. He's sure to have flirted with her. In fact, I think I saw them together on the terrace one night. He was smoking and she was talking to him. Intently. There was something going on between them even if it wasn't a love affair."

Tanner nodded thoughtfully. "I see. I will ask him about it. Where is he now?"

"In the bar washing glasses or trying to mix some new cocktail."

Tanner nodded again and took his leave. Atalanta wondered if he had drawn the same conclusion she had. Maurizio had said he didn't pay close attention to what his staff was doing and then in the same breath he described a very particular scene he had seen one night of Franco and the missing girl Sylvia on the terrace. He was clearly leading Tanner to suspect Franco as the murderer of this chambermaid.

Maurizio cleared his throat. "Yes, well, it is all unpleasant, but we must try and survive it as best we can. You had better go to Raoul and try to cheer him up a little. He seems to really enjoy your company."

Atalanta went in the direction she had seen Raoul take, but before she could enter the reading room, she saw Renard gesturing for her. They stepped aside and spoke softly together.

Renard said, "Margot Bergreiter is very upset about the murders at the hotel. She was close to convincing her husband to buy the place for her, but right now he is in no mood to spend money on it. He wants to get away from here as soon as possible it seems. I heard him arguing with Tanner about letting him leave."

"Which Tanner will not agree to, naturally."

"Naturally," Renard confirmed. He regarded her with his deep-set eyes. "Are you well? You look a little disturbed."

"I am just concerned for Raoul. He is not himself and the deaths have shocked him. He even asked me to leave. He seems to think I am in some danger."

"You might be." Renard said it matter-of-factly but she could see the tightness around his lips. "Maurizio Dulce is no man to underestimate. He is very intelligent and must see how the whole situation shines unwanted light on his uncle's affairs."

"Yes, that is what I have been thinking too. Even if Eva

were a danger to him, he would not have killed her here at the hotel. It is much too risky."

"But someone did kill her and now there has been a second death."

"If it is the missing maid and it is connected to the jewel theft, it happened before any of us came here. It could be totally unrelated." Atalanta looked over her shoulder at Tanner's men questioning the guests. "What are they asking them about? If the theft and disappearance happened weeks ago, none of these people were staying here."

"There may be a few permanent residents. They may also be asking who has visited the grotto in recent days. I understand the search was initiated by the revelation Eva Reuter had shown a profound interest in the grotto. Her death could still be related to the disappearance and the theft, if she was onto something."

Atalanta nodded slowly. "I see. I must talk to Franco. If he knew the chambermaid well, he might have something enlightening to say about the whole affair."

When she got her chance to speak to him alone, he was outside smoking just like Maurizio had said. He inhaled hard, staring at the snowy mountains as if he were deep in thought. Atalanta approached without a sound and said suddenly, "Another death at the hotel."

Franco jumped and turned to her with a jerk. He exhaled roughly, blowing out blue smoke. "You startled me." He scrutinised her intensely. She surmised that if she had been a man, or a staff member, he might have asked her directly what she wanted of him, but now there was hesitancy in his expression. Part of him obviously ached to be blunt, but apparently the deceptive charm which seemed to be second nature with him won out because he said, "Do not tell my boss you caught me smoking. He doesn't like it. It could cost me part of my salary. He imposes these cuts when we don't behave."

"That must be against the law, surely?"

"This is his hotel, his grounds. He can do whatever he likes." Franco blew out smoke and watched it rise on the chill air.

Atalanta nodded. She came to stand closer to him. "You must have a hard time here. A man as accomplished and skilful as yourself, trapped in a job he isn't suited to. I mean, you could do so much better."

Franco raised an eyebrow at her. "Are you trying to flatter me, Signorina Ford?"

She shrugged. "I am just making an observation. A man like you must want more out of life than mixing cocktails for rich ladies."

"I am saving money so I can get away from here." Franco shifted his weight. "I assume that the sum found in my bedroom is one of the reasons why Tanner has come after me."

"There was money found in your bedroom?"

"Yes, Tanner had it searched. It is just my savings. I may not earn a fortune here, but then again, I also do not have a lot of expenses. I manage to lay something by every month. It adds up nicely." He took a draft from the cigarette. "But he thinks I am involved in some kind of dark business. Stealing or…"

Blackmail? Atalanta wondered. She glanced at him. "There have been thefts."

"One theft. And I know full well who did that. Sylvia. She told me several times that she envied those ladies for the beautiful gems they owned. And her boyfriend also pushed her to steal."

"Boyfriend? Anyone who worked here at the hotel?"

"No. He operated the cable car for a while. He stopped doing so right after she vanished. I assumed they ran away together – with the stolen stones."

"But now a body has been found in the grotto. Can it be Sylvia?"

"I suppose. Her boyfriend must have killed her and hidden the body and then run off with the stones. Quite clever actually. I mean, to choose the grotto. The body could have stayed hidden there for years to come."

"But it has been found now."

"Only because of Eva Reuter's murder."

"Were you having an affair with Sylvia?"

"I just told you she had a boyfriend." Franco looked at her. "Why all the questions?"

"Theresa told me you tried to flirt with her. And that you do so with all the ladies. Quoting from Margot's romance novels."

"I was just making something up. For fun. I wasn't

serious." Franco held her gaze. "I was not interested in a girl like Sylvia. And I told you before, I knew it was not serious with Eva either. I am in no position to start a real relationship with a guest. Why all the questions? Are you now suspecting me of something? Earlier you induced me to stay here because you promised you would help me prove my innocence."

"I did and I am still eager to acquit you."

Franco blinked. He was obviously doubtful of her intentions, so she pushed on quickly. "Tanner is dead set on accusing you. He thinks you were involved with the missing maid and the jewel theft. Maurizio Dulce pointed the finger at you, claiming he saw the two of you on the terrace one night, involved in a serious conversation. He obviously wants the cases to be solved quickly – once an arrest has been made, peace will return to the hotel. That is good for both the guests and his reputation."

Franco swallowed hard. "Sylvia and I may have been outside together, smoking. And we had conversations sometimes, of course. But we were not involved in anything shady. I honestly never knew Sylvia was stealing from the guests. It must have been her boyfriend who killed her and took the stones. I am certain."

Atalanta said, "I can investigate the matter for you and clear your name, but you must help me with information."

"Why would you help me at all?" Franco asked with suspicion in his eyes.

Atalanta hesitated a moment. She was reluctant to share too much information with him, but she could share something that was common knowledge and use it to explain her involvement.

"Because I can't stand Maurizio Dulce. He caused Raoul's accident. I mean, he allowed him to go skiing where it wasn't safe so he can take his place on the team. It is in all the newspapers. Eva showed the article to me when we were in the village the other day." She had already spoken to Maurizio about the rumours in the newspaper so she ran no risk by sharing this information with Franco. And it did give her a very good reason to want to go against Maurizio and side with Franco to prevent him from being made an easy scapegoat. "It made me livid. How could he do something like that? Harm Raoul for his own personal gain? Raoul is so dejected now because he is not physically fit enough to race and he can't remember things. He can't even remember me. We were supposed to get engaged and yet he doesn't know me. Do you have any idea how I feel?"

She exaggerated her grief to convince him of how much she hated Maurizio. Once he believed that, he would be more forthcoming with information. About Eva too. There was no way he had been inside her room to leave a red rose on her bed because he was so in love with her. He had just admitted that he had never believed it would get serious between them.

She pushed on. "I want Maurizio Dulce to pay for what he did to Raoul. If there is any way in which I can hurt him, I will not let that chance pass me by. Let me look into the murder case and perhaps I can prove that *he* killed Eva Reuter."

Franco's eyes flashed a moment with malicious glee. "You would do that?"

"Readily. But I need your help. You must tell me everything you know about the hotel guests and what happened before I arrived. How it all led up to Eva's death. You see a lot. You are perceptive and smart."

Franco flashed a self-confident smile. "There's not a lot happening at this hotel that I don't know about."

"That is what I mean. You can really help me. Or rather, we can help each other. If I prove who killed Eva Reuter, you go scot-free."

Franco nodded slowly. "That sounds fair enough. What do you want to know?"

Atalanta didn't want to ask about Franco having been in Eva's hotel room as he might feel attacked. She had to get some information from him first, about the others.

"Dieter Bergreiter. He comes here every weekend to visit Margot. He presented her with such a beautiful bunch of her favourite flowers. He seems concerned about her health, always asking people if she is doing well. Are they as devoted to each other as they pretend to be?"

Franco sighed. He tossed the cigarette to the ground and ground the stub. "I think so yes, actually. He seems to genuinely care about how she feels. He tries to make her smile, brings her gifts and all. He doesn't seem to see her darker side."

"What darker side?"

"She can be very impatient with the staff, with her own secretary, when things don't go the way she wants them to."

Atalanta nodded. "I think it is also a consequence of her secluded lifestyle. She doesn't have much to focus on so what she can control she will control."

Franco lit another cigarette. He took a deep inhale and then blew the smoke out slowly. "I do feel sorry for her. She hasn't had much of a life."

"Did she ever show photographs to you? Of her sister's travels?"

"Oh yes, frequently. I must admit I never listened closely to any of her stories. As a bartender you get used to people wanting to unburden to you. You sort of feign an interest and say 'Oh yes' at all the right moments. But most of what they share escapes you. It wasn't very interesting. Just places her sister had been to."

"Recently or a long time ago?"

"I think fairly recently. She goes down in the cart once a week to collect her correspondence at the local post office. There is usually a letter from her sister in the mail. She sits on the terrace reading it and afterwards she is always in a good mood."

"I see. How was her relationship with Eva?"

"They tolerated each other. They had vastly different personalities. And Eva could be a little mean – always making fun of people behind their backs."

"Was Eva close to Margot's husband?"

Franco seemed to hesitate. Atalanta eyed him. "You can tell me. I won't share it with Margot."

"The night before she died, when he arrived here, she talked to him in the lobby."

Atalanta nodded. She had seen that exchange herself, or at least part of it.

Franco said, "Dieter Bergreiter didn't seem eager to hear what she had to say. But when I passed by them, I heard her say something like 'You will be sorry if you don't come.'"

"Come? As in, come to a meeting place?"

"Apparently."

So he could have gone to the reading room later to meet Eva and found her body there, perhaps losing his tie clip when he leant over the body.

"Did you share this information with Inspector Tanner?"

"No, of course not. He would not have believed me. He would have thought I made it up just to direct his attention at someone else."

"How about Theresa? Was she close with Margot or Dieter Bergreiter?"

"I can't tell. Theresa is the type of woman you hardly notice. She's in the background, watching and not saying much. I think she did like Margot's books but she wasn't one of those devoted fans who idolise the author. In fact, I can't tell you much about her. She was kind of, uh ... invisible."

How convenient, when you wanted to commit a murder and blame someone else for it.

Atalanta rubbed her hands together. She was getting cold standing here in the chill. She asked, "Theresa told me that Eva often went down to the village to make phone calls. Any idea whom she was calling?"

"How could I know that? She probably worried that any calls made from here were monitored by the staff."

"Yes, but if the calls were of an innocent nature – inviting a friend to visit or reporting on her lovely holiday – she could just have called from here."

Atalanta frowned as she tried to envision Eva thinking up an excuse to spend time away from Theresa and then going to call ... the doctor who had helped her when her husband had died? She had set him up in a practice somewhere. Were they in love? Had she only pretended not to be interested because it might have led to rumours right after her husband's death?

Franco said, "I do wonder why nobody ever had suspicions about her husband's death."

"Her what?"

"Her husband's death. She marries a much older man and then he dies suddenly."

"Well, because he was that much older, he might also have been more likely to die."

"Yes, that is what people assume but he was in good health. Why would he suddenly die? What if she killed him? To get to his money and travel."

Atalanta stared at him. "And you believe a doctor might have helped her?"

"To cover it up, yes. He would have signed the death certificate."

Atalanta stood motionless. This was a huge accusation, but it also opened up interesting possibilities. Suppose Eva had indeed murdered her husband and the doctor had known. He had helped her and stayed close to her, hoping to marry her and get his hands on her newly acquired wealth. But she had rejected him. She had set him up in a practice well away from her. Perhaps an investment to ensure his silence?

But what if he had kept asking for more money? What if he had blackmailed her? Had she called him? Had she sent him money?

But if the doctor's knowledge was a threat to Eva, one would expect her to try and remove him, not the other way around. How would her death benefit him? And even if it did, how would the doctor have gained access to the hotel to poison the tea? Might he have an accomplice here?

A staff member?

Or a guest? Someone posing as an innocent visitor but in reality sent here on a mission to poison Eva and let another take the blame?

It would be a brilliant plan.

Franco said, "I have to get back inside or there will be trouble." He turned away from her and started to walk back towards the hotel, but then he stopped and said, "I should not be saying this, perhaps, as I want you to help clear my name, but you must be aware that Maurizio Dulce is a very dangerous opponent. He is not some nice businessman with an interest in racing. His uncle is … influential. He can make or break people. Crossing Maurizio is not a good idea. Please be careful what you do or it may cost you."

He took another step towards the hotel and added ominously, "It may cost us both."

Chapter Fourteen

"I hadn't expected him to be thinking of you," Raoul said with a scoff when she told him everything. "He is selfish to the core."

"Perhaps, but at least I can get some information from him. The rest I will have to investigate by myself or via Renard." She looked over at Raoul who was walking beside her. They had left the hotel after breakfast to do some sightseeing. She had convinced Maurizio it would distract Raoul from his gloomy mood and that it would be good for him. Now they were in the village and heading for the post office. Atalanta would pretend to send a few postcards home while she tried to get some information from the postmaster or mistress about the hotel guests who had been there. Especially Margot Bergreiter.

While she waited her turn, Raoul took a photograph of the post office's interior. He had borrowed the camera from Renard and it made him look like a typical tourist. A very handsome tourist. Atalanta had to smile as she imagined them sightseeing together in Rome or Paris. She would have to invite him to spend a few days with her at her home in the French capital, to unwind and recover further. In fact, she was certain that Maurizio's idea to keep him here in such a remote location was counterproductive.

When it was her turn, she handed over her cards for stamps. As she paid for them, she asked if there was any mail for Margot Bergreiter she could collect and take back with her to Hotel Alpenrot.

"She would come down herself but she is not having a good day."

Her cheeks burned at the lie and she was certain the woman at the counter would see right through her. But all she got was a blank stare. "What name did you say?"

"Margot Bergreiter. She is a guest at Hotel Alpenrot. She picks up mail here every week."

"I do not know her."

"Her sister writes to her. From all over the world. Letters with foreign stamps. You must have noticed."

"I'm afraid I do not recall the name." The woman said it with finality. "I would notice if someone named Margot Bergreiter came in here. I have read all of her books. But the mail for Hotel Alpenrot is sent straight up. No guests come here to collect it."

"I see. Thank you very much. Good day." Atalanta joined Raoul who took one more photo and then they went outside. Blinking against the bright sunshine, Atalanta told Raoul what the woman had said. "Isn't that odd? Franco assured me that Margot gets letters every week. She sits on the terrace reading them."

Raoul lifted the camera to take a photo of the bus that had just stopped to let some elderly women with purchases get on. Then he said, "Didn't Theresa also mention to you that the photographs her sister allegedly sent her from Crete were not taken recently?"

"Yes." Atalanta gave him a smile. "You remember."

"You told me the other day. I do remember recent things." Raoul answered her smile. "Every day it becomes a little easier. I don't need to strain myself quite so much to recall when it is time for dinner or what someone's name is. Perhaps I am getting better?"

"Of course you are. We will make sure you recover completely." She linked her arm through his. "So Margot is lying about getting letters from her sister." She remembered the moving dedication from the novel she had read in the reading room. *To my sister Johanna who made all this possible for me.* "Perhaps there is no sister? Perhaps she did invent the whole story to make her books seem more interesting to the public."

"That would be a risk. People could ask questions about it."

Atalanta froze. "People like Alexander Hansen. Judging by what I've heard about him, he goes after sensationalist stories and he doesn't care whom he hurts by publishing them. If he thought Margot's well-travelled sister was a mere invention, he would certainly want to write about it."

Raoul nodded. "He can't show himself at the hotel though. Dieter Bergreiter knows what he looks like."

"Exactly. So he would need someone on the inside to report to him. Theresa told me about phone calls Eva could not make from the hotel. She must have been Alexander Hansen's source. She fed him the information he needed for his articles. When she showed us the article about Maurizio wanting your spot on the team, she acted like she wanted to investigate the veracity of the report, but if she was feeding information to Hansen, she herself had suggested this angle. Why? To get the others to agree to doing a little sleuthing? If several people started digging into the mystery, it would have created confusion, and once the revelations about Margot's non-existent sister came to light at some later time, it would be difficult to determine who had leaked it. Eva would not have been suspected, or at least no one would have been able to pin it on her as she had created other suspects. She even asked Margot for help analysing the pills she took from Maurizio's office, in her bid to accuse him of keeping you sedated. Margot believed she was in the ETAM team sleuthing to get to the bottom of your accident, not because she herself was an object of interest to Eva. It was a clever and daring plan."

Raoul said, "You speak of a non-existent sister like it is already a fact. But it would be quite a risk to do something like that. People could easily check into her past, her family, to find out if she actually has a sister or not."

"Well, perhaps there is a Johanna somewhere, but she need not be delivering exciting travel stories to Margot."

Raoul frowned and then his expression lit up. "I know how to move forwards. I will call the newspaper Hansen is working for and set up a meeting. I will claim I want to tell Hansen about my accident. An exclusive interview. He will certainly fall for that and agree to see us. We can then question him about Eva and what she wanted to reveal. That way we can find out who might have been interested in killing her to keep her silent."

The newspaper had been eager to put Raoul in touch with their star reporter right away and Raoul came back announcing to Atalanta that they were going to travel to a nearby town for the meeting. The train ride took them through a lush valley with wooden houses huddled together at the foot of steep rock formations. Waterfalls rushed down in a tumble of white foaming water and birds of prey soared against the bright blue sky.

Raoul had slid the train window down and they could hear the tinkling of bells around the necks of peacefully grazing cows and playful goats.

A man pushed a cart loaded with wood slowly up a small track towards a cabin sitting high on the mountainside. Everyone was going about their daily business and it made the place seem like a tranquil and beautiful slice of the world.

But death had struck here, twice, and Atalanta felt apprehensive about the decision they had taken. Inspector

Tanner had forbidden them to leave the village and yet they had hopped on a train to go and meet an infamous gossip columnist. Nobody had stopped them, though she had seen several people get on the train at the same time as them and she wondered which one of them was an informer for Tanner. She had no illusion that she could keep much from him. And then there was the risk in meeting Hansen. They wanted information from him but the smart reporter would not let this chance pass by to learn things from them. He had a sharp pen and didn't shrink back from writing about influential people. If Raoul used the wrong words or Hansen deliberately misunderstood him and wrote a harsh piece involving the Dulces, Raoul's life could be in very real danger. She herself might also not be safe. They had to watch carefully where they trod or they would ruin themselves in the process.

As they alighted onto the platform, under the tolling of the bright bell of a nearby church, Atalanta touched Raoul's arm. "We must be very careful. If you anger Vincenzo Dulce in any way…"

"I am not going to talk about Vincenzo Dulce. We are going to confront Hansen about his use of Eva Reuter as his source and suggest that her snooping led to her death. We will make him feel guilty and that will make him reveal things to us."

"I doubt that. A man such as him will be used to accusations and reproaches. He has written pieces that have led to people's personal and financial ruin. He will not suddenly develop a conscience."

Raoul hmm-ed but didn't slow his pace. They had agreed to meet at Hotel Moser. It lay beside a clear blue lake and from the jetty a large white boat was just leaving to take tourists across to the other side. Atalanta gestured at the towering grey rock walls on the other side of the lake.

"I read in a brochure that there are caverns there you can explore. I don't know if I'd want to do it. The darkness and the idea of being locked inside a mountain... It would feel oppressive."

"Perhaps we can try it once this case is solved?" Raoul glanced at her. He ushered her past a sign advertising the various fish dishes the hotel had on offer. The fish was caught fresh in the lake each morning.

They seated themselves at a table under richly blossoming trees. There came a light breeze across the water, ruffling the heavily laden branches and causing pale pink petals to drift down and rest upon the checkered tablecloth. An elderly waiter with a pointy beard took their order for coffee and cake and then retreated.

On a bench near the jetty a man sat smoking. He appeared to be waiting for another boat, but Atalanta had seen him come off the train with them and wondered if he was Tanner's man watching them. What would Tanner think if he heard they had set up a meeting with the nosy reporter?

Raoul checked his watch. "Hansen is late," he observed. Just as he said it, they could hear the roar of a car engine. A red sportscar was parked at the edge of the lake and a tall, blond man jumped out of it. He waved off someone who tried to tell him he wasn't allowed to park there and approached Raoul and Atalanta with long strides.

He cut a fashionable figure in his light suit and several women on the hotel's terrace regarded him with interest. As he reached their table, he shook Raoul's hand with fervour. "Good to see you, Lemont. Word had it you were just about dead and buried." He focused on Atalanta with his lively blue eyes. "Hello there, who are you?"

"Atty Ford," Atalanta said. "I am a friend of Raoul's."

"I see. Alexander Hansen. But you already knew that." He winked at her, then sank into a chair. He straightened his tie with lean, suntanned fingers. "Shall we start? I am most curious to hear what you want to tell me."

"Eva Reuter is dead," Raoul said bluntly.

Atalanta saw the reporter's face stiffen. It was as though he physically recoiled a moment before slipping his mask back in place. "Excuse me?" he said tightly.

"Eva Reuter. The woman who provided you with information about everything that goes on at Hotel Alpenrot." Raoul leaned on the table. "Your source, as it is called, I believe? She died. She was poisoned."

Again, there was a twitch in Hansen's face. "Poisoned?" he repeated with a dull voice.

Raoul nodded. "Perhaps she was a little too talkative? Or too reckless in her snooping around offices and bedrooms? She did it all for you."

"No, no, she did it for herself." Hansen sat up straight. "She wanted to earn money. But most of all, she loved the excitement. She was a very insistent woman. She practically coerced me into printing her story."

"The story about me." Raoul gave him a glare.

Hansen made an apologetic gesture. "Look, you know how it is for newspapermen. We live off news. We have to bring the public something worthwhile every single day. So, when I get information about the injured driver Raoul Lemont, information every journalist on the continent is after, I take it and I print it."

"You have created a difficult situation for me with my team."

Hansen made another hand gesture. The sun glinted off the signet ring he wore. "I can't change the truth."

"The truth? Is what you write the truth?" Atalanta eyed him sceptically. "Or is it just rumours and suggestions?"

"The public don't care much either way."

"But *you* are a journalist. *You* are supposed to search for the truth. *You* should care."

Hansen laughed bitterly. "Oh, I started out like that, believe me. I was all fired up to go and change the world with my stories. But I soon found out that my editor was not interested in the real issues I wanted to address. It was all society gossip, news about famous faces. It sells papers and then I get paid. That's just how it works."

"And Eva agreed to that?" Atalanta asked, to lead him back to their topic of interest.

Hansen nodded. "Completely. She enjoyed the excitement of seeing her stories in print and watching how people responded to it. She was onto something big for me.

A sensational scoop she said. Something that would hit like a bomb."

"A bomb?" Raoul queried.

"That's what she said. She was doing her research…" Hansen scoffed a moment. "She called it that. Research. As if it were more than just picking up gossip or noticing a man come out of the wrong bedroom door. But she called it research. And I did tell her that if she had something major, she needed some proof. Something for me to go on. I wasn't about to have my career destroyed by a slander suit."

"And she thought she could deliver proof?"

"Yes. She said she'd have it for me soon. After the weekend. She needed to connect a few dots and…" Hansen spread his hands. "Then it would all be ready for me to take over."

"And you have no idea what this was about? Whom it concerned?" Raoul queried.

"No. I don't think it was about you again. She was so … I don't know what you call it. Sort of gleeful? Like she couldn't wait to see someone squirm."

Dieter Bergreiter? Atalanta wondered. During that conversation at the reception desk after Bergreiter's arrival, had Eva invited him to a meeting in the reading room later that night? A meeting in which to present her evidence and pressure him to pay her not to reveal what she knew?

But Dieter hadn't even waited for the meeting. The tea had been poisoned before he got to the room and lost the tie clip.

Had he decided to take no chances? How had he

obtained the poison? What kind of poison had it been? Inspector Tanner hadn't told them yet. Would he even share any details of the case with her? He seemed to be very self-confident. She wasn't even certain whether she could fully trust him. After all, he might have obtained his post by running his predecessor off the road!

Raoul said to Hansen, "Eva Reuter is dead, and I think you must agree it had something to do with this big thing she was looking into. Now you must help us find out what it was."

"First of all, I am not at all certain Eva was killed because of her work for me. She was a formidable character. People didn't tend to like her. She had some tensions with the woman she was travelling with – what was her name?"

"Theresa Hofer?" Atalanta suggested.

"Exactly. Something about her taking advantage of her wealth and her not liking it? I don't recall the details. I just wanted her to do her job and not whine to me about it." He gave a hoarse laugh. "It didn't seem so hard to me. A holiday at a magnificent hotel, enjoying the luxury lifestyle and doing a little investigating on the side."

"Had she worked for you before this? Did she specifically come to Hotel Alpenrot at your behest?" Atalanta wasn't certain whether the slick reporter was being fully honest.

Hansen said with a shrug, "She had delivered me some titbits before. Because of her marriage to a wealthy man, she was ideally placed to, uh ... learn things."

"So she worked for you from the start of her marriage?"

"On and off, yes." Hansen fell silent as the waiter brought the order for Atalanta and Raoul. Hansen asked for black coffee and then resumed speaking when the waiter was out of earshot. "She would call me when she had something. I couldn't even use everything. But I was glad she was at the hotel where you were recuperating."

But had Eva known where Raoul was? Or had her story on him been an unexpected extra, not what she was really there for? It seemed she had been working on something else, a major thing. The jewel theft and the disappearance, perhaps? Had she deduced the chambermaid Sylvia had never run away but had been murdered? Eva had been very interested in the grotto…

"Did she tell you anything about a jewel theft," she asked Hansen, "and a missing chambermaid?"

"No. She kept her cards close to her chest. Typical Eva. I am sorry she was murdered but … she was a very selfish woman."

"A trait you didn't fail to exploit," Raoul said with disgust.

Hansen threw his head back and laughed. "I don't pretend to be anything other than what I am. I am a working-class man who always envied the people who were born with a silver spoon in their mouth. If I can expose the dark secrets of their world then I will do it. Do I not deserve my share of the wealth they are so callously enjoying?" He stared past them a moment with a frown and then continued, "Eva was just like me. She had never known privilege. She got it by her looks, by marrying an old lecher who fancied her. She made the most of the chances she had, as she put it."

"Have you ever heard anything more about this marriage?" Atalanta asked. As Hansen did not seem very interested in Eva as a person, only as a source, chances were slim that he knew anything relevant, but she wanted to try anyway.

Hansen leaned back with a pensive frown. "As a matter of fact, I got a call a few weeks back from a man – that is all I know, because he mentioned no name – and he told me that Eva Reuter had killed her husband and was now playing the merry widow with his money. It sounded like a story I would never be able to prove and so I put down the phone and forgot all about it."

"I don't think you would have done that." Atalanta eyed him intently. "Eva was your source. She delivered interesting information to you but you never liked her. Why not use her for a story? I wager you did look into it, or at least tried to get some proof. For instance, from the doctor who signed the death certificate for her husband?"

Hansen licked his lips. "If I did, why would I admit it to you?"

"There is a murder investigation going on," Raoul said with an edge to his voice. "You could become involved in it if we disclose to the inspector that you were in communication with Eva. That she sold you information about influential people you could use for the stories you publish."

"That is not against the law." Hansen looked smug.

Atalanta said, "Herr Hansen, I do agree that your position is relatively safe. But you do want to know what Eva was working on, don't you? You still want the scoop she promised you. And we can get it for you. If you help us with what you know." She was making a risky promise here but it might be the only way to get Hansen to cooperate and share what he had found out about Eva's marriage and the death of her husband.

Hansen looked from her to Raoul and back. "How do I know if I can trust you?" he asked slowly.

Atalanta had no idea how she could convince him but before she could even start to reply, Hansen continued: "But then again, I have always taken risks and so far that strategy has paid dividends. So go on. What do you want to know from me?"

"Have you been in touch with the doctor who looked after Eva Reuter's late husband? Have you learned anything that can prove she was involved in her husband's passing?"

"Not really. The doctor said everything was perfectly normal and he sent me a copy of the death certificate. It listed heart attack as the cause of death. I could not go deeper into it from there. I mean, how would I be able to do that? I did try to contact staff who worked at the manor house when the old man died, but most of them are still employed with the mistress and they didn't want to talk. The only one who did speak to me was an old cook who had been dismissed but she was obviously drinking a lot and could not be trusted. She said it wouldn't surprise her if the mistress had killed the master, but while it might not surprise me much either, knowing Eva's greedy character, that is hardly proof of a crime."

Atalanta took a bite of her cake and chewed. This whole conversation seemed to be delivering very little by way of hard evidence of any wrongdoing.

Hansen said, "It was interesting though that the cook told me that she had been approached a few months back by a man who was looking into the death as well. She said he wasn't a reporter but had claimed to be one of the victim's children. The old man had been married three or four times and had a number of children – all grown up and robbed of their inheritance by their stepmother."

"By Eva," Atalanta said. She held the cake fork suspended mid-air, wondering if someone at the hotel was a stepchild of Eva. The questions had come from a man, Hansen said. Did it make sense to think of … Franco? During that late-night conversation in the reading room, he had told her that he had been born on a manor. He had made it clear that he was not able to profit from the wealth or position because he was but a second son, but what if he had lost everything to a new young stepmother?

Had he romanced Eva to get close to her and find proof that she had killed her husband? Theresa had mentioned that Franco had been in Eva's hotel room, allegedly to put a red rose on her bed, but perhaps he had been looking for evidence among her things? Eva had mentioned that the doctor who had signed the death certificate had changed practices and now owned a house on Lake Maggiore. Had he received money for his involvement in covering up the murder? It was an interesting possibility.

Raoul said, "Is there anything else you can tell us? Did Eva ever give you anything important? A notebook? A key to something?"

"No, like I said before, she was very secretive. I have no idea if she had any proof of anything and if she did, where she kept it."

The waiter brought his black coffee and they sat in silence for a while eating and drinking and looking at the lake. The excited voices of tourists resounded across the water and a majestic black swan sailed past. More pink petals descended on them under the rising breeze.

Finally Hansen spoke, "Look, I don't want you to think I am an unfeeling monster. I do feel sorry for Eva having overplayed her hand and paying the price for it, but I am just not convinced it was her story for me that caused her death. There must have been lots of people that hated her. Or feared her. She had a nasty way of suggesting things, of making you feel like she was just waiting to push a blade into your back when you were least expecting it."

"Did she also put pressure on you?" Atalanta asked. "If she was so unreliable, why did you keep working with her? Did you have to, because she knew too much?"

"You are seeing suspects where there are none." Hansen rose to his feet. He brushed a petal from his immaculate suit. "Thank you for calling me out here for nothing. You have wasted my precious time. You can pay for the coffee. Good day."

Atalanta watched the arrogant reporter as he walked angrily away to his car. The man on the bench at the jetty was also watching. If he was Tanner's man, he would make certain to report back quickly what he had witnessed here. Atalanta wondered if Tanner would confront her about it or retain the information for possible later use. Her heartbeat skittered at the idea that she was up against a formidable opponent, one who might not have hesitated to remove people who stood in his way.

But she had to focus on Hansen now and what he had revealed to them. He had mentioned a man who had approached the alcoholic cook claiming to be Eva's stepson, wanting justice for his deceased father. What if the cook had contact information and had provided that to Alexander Hansen? Would he not have wanted to follow up with this alleged family member? And if he had, had he ended up at Franco? The stepson looking to get close to his stepmother and … get even with her?

Or had Hansen put Franco up to the murder, thinking Eva was getting too dangerous?

Either way, Atalanta had to talk to Franco once more and see what he had to say for himself.

Chapter Fifteen

When they got back to the hotel, they learned from the clerk at the reception desk that Franco was in the cellar looking for some skis for guests. Steep steps led down into the large storage room where food and supplies were kept. Franco was standing with his back turned to them, taking down skis from where they were hung up against the wall. He checked how smooth they were by running his finger along the edge.

"It must have been hard," Raoul said, "to get absolutely nothing when your father died. To learn that he had left everything to your ridiculously young stepmother whom you had always hated for luring your father into a marriage that was the talk of the district."

Atalanta flinched under the directness of the sudden attack but Franco didn't seem to be surprised. He turned around, holding the skis. "So you found out. I supposed that you would, sooner or later." He took a deep breath.

"I thought I could stay anonymous by assuming an Italian name. I do not think Eva ever had any idea who I was. Then that murder went and ruined everything."

Atalanta asked with a frown, "Why did you want to get close to Eva without her knowing who you are?" He had used his attractive bartender role to charm her but that had obviously not restored what he had lost.

"I wanted to find a way to get money from her. My father's will was clear: she got it all. To go against it would mean lengthy lawsuits that might not deliver anything in the end. I didn't have the patience for it – or the funds to pay for all the legal costs." Franco sighed. "I came up with a different plan. I found out that she was travelling and where she regularly stayed. She has a few hotels she frequents. In Monaco, Rome and here. I applied to work at all the places she visits, and I got the job here. As bartender. I thought it would be a good idea to get close to her, maybe even … have an affair with her. She might be willing to slip me money. Or pay me to be discreet." He looked down. "I am not proud of my strategy but I just wanted a share of what should have been mine anyway. My father's inheritance."

"Did Eva give you anything?"

"No." Franco laughed softly. "She did flirt with me but she was careful not to let it go too far. She told me something about being afraid that the hotel might blackmail her if she committed any indiscretions. She said she had heard a story from a friend in which this had happened but

I don't know whether she made it up to keep a distance between us."

"You've been in her bedroom," Atalanta said. "You put a red rose on her bed. At least, that's the reason you gave for being in her room. But what did you really do there?"

"Is that so hard to understand? I was searching her belongings for proof that she defrauded my father. That she altered his will or that she was even involved in his death. I didn't put anything past her. My father may have been in his seventies but he was as strong as an ox. His sudden heart attack came completely out of the blue. It seemed to me to be very suspicious."

"I see. So you called Alexander Hansen and suggested to him that Eva might have killed her husband to get her hands on his wealth. You also contacted the cook."

Franco scoffed. "Not that it paid off. Her drinking makes her totally unreliable and Hansen would rather keep Eva as his source than look into my father's death. He did not consider it a viable story, quote, unquote."

"You underestimate him." Raoul's voice was calm. "Regardless of what he said to you initially, he did look into it. But, like yourself, he could not find conclusive proof."

Franco nodded slowly. "I began to see that it was pointless. That I could never know for certain whether Eva tricked my father, killed him, and took his money by design. I was wondering if it even made sense to continue my quest for the truth."

"Rather, your quest for money," Raoul corrected him cynically.

Franco had the decency to flush. He glared at Raoul as he said, "Of course you say it like that. You are good at something. You have built a life for yourself and earn money and can live comfortably. I am not good at anything in particular. I will forever work these low-paid jobs and am forced to please other people to stay afloat. It is not what I imagined for myself."

"I can understand that, seeing as you are the son of a nobleman," Atalanta said. She wanted to keep Franco's goodwill so she could learn more from him about the hotel. "If your father hadn't married Eva Reuter, you would have an easy life now."

"I've thought about that a lot," Franco said. There was a strange light in his eyes. "How everything could have been different if not for her."

Raoul glanced at Atalanta. She sensed that he was thinking the same thing she was: that Franco might have killed Eva anyway, not because it would benefit him directly, but because he simply couldn't stand the way in which she had changed the course of his life and got away with it.

Still, it hadn't been smart of him to poison her tea and then be present when she died, so the trail would lead directly to him. She believed Franco was not a stupid man, so even if he were vengeful, he would go about it in a careful and considered manner.

It seemed more likely that someone else had poisoned the tea and Franco had been there by accident.

"What did you and Eva discuss before she died?"

she asked. "Did she know who you were? Why were you with her in the reading room?"

"She had asked me to come and find her for the usual flirtation. She liked to see that I was interested and then keep me at arm's length. She had no idea who I truly was. She was just toying with me. She thought she could get away with it because she could always go running to Maurizio Dulce to get me dismissed." Franco took a deep breath. "But it was more than just flirting that night. She told me she was onto something, something sensational, and she wanted my help to get proof of it. Because she knew I had been in her room to put the red rose on her bed, she suggested to me that I could also go to other ladies' bedrooms and pretend to put a flower there for them but in truth search their drawers and suitcases."

"And she didn't know you had done that with her luggage? She wasn't testing you?"

"No, I didn't get that impression. I think she genuinely wanted me to search for information."

"In whose room?" Raoul asked.

"Theresa's room."

"Theresa?" Atalanta was surprised. "Weren't they firm friends? Why would Eva have wanted you to search her travel companion's room? What for?"

Franco smiled. "They were hardly firm friends, as you put it. Eva wasn't friends with anyone. She only saw her own advantage and acted accordingly."

"Even so," Raoul said gesturing to indicate that he

should get to the point, "what did Eva want you to find out?"

"I don't know. Just as she was about to tell me, she began suddenly to feel unwell and shortly after she was dead."

"So you don't know?" Raoul looked sceptical. "You claim there was something sensational she was onto, something to do with Theresa, but you don't know what it might be? She never even gave you a hint?"

Franco shrugged. "I can only tell you what happened. I was upset that she fainted, then shocked when it turned out she was dead. I placed her at the foot of the ladder to make it look like an accident. I had no idea she had been poisoned, so I didn't think there would be a police investigation and—"

"It wasn't very smart of you to think that," a voice said. Atalanta swung round. Tanner came down the steps with another policeman. He looked at Franco with a grim expression. "Cuff him and take him away."

"What? Wait!" Franco inched back, holding up the skis as if to create a barrier. "What have I done? Why are you arresting me?"

"You are suspected of involvement in the death of Eva Reuter. And possibly in a second death. Take him away."

The second policeman approached Franco and said, "It is futile to resist. You have nowhere to go. Now, put the skis down."

Franco's gaze flitted around the room as if he were frantically searching for a way out. But he was obviously cornered and with a sigh he lowered the skis to the ground. "You are making a huge mistake! It wasn't me! There is a killer here at the hotel and by arresting me you are letting them roam free to target new victims."

"I will decide whom I arrest," Tanner said in a chill tone. He gestured to his man. "Take him to the police station. Keep him under lock and key and I will be there soon to question him."

Franco stared at Atalanta as the cuffs clicked closed. "You said you would help me. You said you would prove my innocence."

Atalanta felt her cheeks flush. Fortunately, he didn't say she had promised to incriminate Maurizio Dulce in the crime. That would have been potentially disastrous for her and for Raoul.

Tanner said, "Really, Fräulein Ford? That is very interesting." As the policeman led Franco away, Tanner leaned closer to Atalanta and said softly, "And how were you proposing to do that? Do you have another suspect in mind?"

Atalanta's cheeks were on fire. She tried to look calm and collected but she feared he saw her distress clearly. "I do not think it is right to assume that the first person you come across is the killer. Franco moved the body in a panic but why would he do that if he had put the poison in her tea? Why would he even have been present? It makes no sense as he wouldn't get away with it."

"But do killers act with a lot of sense?" Tanner shook his head. "You are an intelligent woman, Fräulein Ford. You think about crime as if it were a logic problem but often that is not how it works. The criminal is eager to remove a threat, or he acts from jealousy and rage. Those emotions don't allow for good decisions. They drive a person to do the most illogical things and still believe they can get away with them. Franco is a prime example of this. He killed his stepmother to get her money and believed we would never find out who he truly is."

"You know about the deception?" Raoul asked. Atalanta wasn't certain if the awe in his voice was feigned or real. Perhaps he was playing into the inspector's sense of achievement to get more information from him.

Tanner smiled softly. "I may not have much experience with solving murders, but I do have a lot of experience as a hunter. I know how an animal behaves when it feels trapped. With people, there is always a reason for that – some secret they are hiding. I suspected Franco was hiding a secret so I made it my business to find out what it was. Now everything makes sense."

"And the dead body in the grotto?" Atalanta asked. "Is it Sylvia the maid?"

"Probably not. The doctor told me that the remains have been there for some time. Months, perhaps even years. He said he must examine them more closely to know for certain. Sylvia disappeared but a few weeks ago. It is not her."

Atalanta blinked in confusion. "So the remains in the grotto have nothing to do with the recent jewellery theft and disappearance of the chambermaid?"

"We do not believe so, but we cannot be certain until we know more about the remains." Tanner turned his back on her. "I am sorry, Fräulein Ford, to have proved you wrong. You believed in Franco's innocence, but you were deceived."

"I still believe in his innocence," Atalanta said. She stood straight with her feet planted apart. "You obviously have the advantage of me as you know what poison killed her and how the murderer got their hands on it, but I can use my common sense to draw conclusions. Eva Reuter was a woman who made enemies wherever she went. There must have been more people than just Franco eager to see her dispatched."

Tanner seemed to want to go but still he lingered with his foot on the first step. He turned back to her and said, "Why do you want so badly to clear his name, Fräulein? Are you also deceived by his good looks? I have heard from the other staff that Franco was very friendly with all the female guests."

Atalanta flushed again. "I don't care about his looks. I am concerned that he has been wrongly accused because you grabbed the first suspect at hand."

Tanner's eyes flashed a moment. "And why would this concern you? You are merely staying here for a few days to look after an injured friend. Are you not?"

Atalanta took a deep breath. "Let us not play games. If you know already who Franco really is, you also know who I am. The moment you found out I was travelling under an alias, you wanted to know why, and you looked into me.

You found out all there is to know about Atalanta Ashford. Including the cases I have solved." She spoke boldly, as if it was all self-evident. "You know who I am and what I am capable of. I don't expect you to appreciate my skill because police officers are never keen on amateurs mixing in their business, but you can at least stop insulting my intelligence by suggesting that this is a clear-cut case."

Tanner blinked a moment. Then he smiled again. "Very well. You go *en garde*. I offer you counter charge. I do know who you are and from what family you come. I am therefore very surprised to find you here enjoying the hospitality of a man such as Maurizio Dulce. You ask me not to insult your intelligence, but surely if you were that insightful, you would have stayed far away from here?"

His eyes probed her, trying to see into her very soul. Atalanta took a deep breath. "I came here for Raoul, to see how badly injured he was. I have no connection to Maurizio Dulce or his uncle."

"Don't deceive yourself, Fräulein. If you are so worried for your friend, you do have a connection. One they can easily abuse." He stared her right in the eye. Then he said, "Let me go about my business and you about yours. I would advise you to leave this hotel. Leave the region. Go and holiday somewhere else."

"That is rude," Raoul remarked as Tanner took his leave. But Atalanta didn't agree. The inspector hadn't been rude or condescending. He had been warning her. He had made it very clear that she was getting tangled up in things that would harm her. He had given her friendly, yet very urgent, advice to leave and extract herself from the situation while she still could.

But she would never leave Raoul. She loved him, even if he didn't remember her. How could she leave him when his accident might not have been an accident at all, but an attempt on his life? If she did leave, to save herself, her good name and her sleuthing career, and then something happened to him, this time fatal, she would never forgive herself. No, they were in this together and they had to get out of it together.

Or not at all.

Chapter Sixteen

After a delicious dinner of mustard soup, fish with vegetables and *Karamel Kupfli* – caramel pudding – Atalanta retired to the reading room where she found Margot standing at the bookcase staring at a shelf. Her finger was running along the spines and when Atalanta looked closer, she saw it was her own books she was studying. There was a wistful expression on her face and Atalanta tried to read her mood. Was she dejected because she was running late for her new deadline? Was she uncertain whether she could create a new masterpiece like the others had been? Had the murder affected her creativity? Atalanta asked, "Are you not well? You look pale and distracted."

Margot smiled at her. "I feel a little out of sorts after everything that's happened here. I love this hotel ... and then these sudden murders. Not just Eva but those remains in the grotto... Dieter wants to leave this place as fast as he can. He'll never buy it for me now, like I've wanted for so long." She sighed. "Oh well, one cannot control fate. I write about that a lot in my books. That life takes the turns it has to take. For good or ill. We believe we have a lot of influence, but in the end we really don't. We're just kidding ourselves."

Atalanta took a seat in one of the leather chairs by the fireplace and stared at the painting over it. Then she said softly, "Your sister is not writing letters to you. You supposedly go to the post office every week to collect one and you read them on the terrace. But it's all a big lie. There are no letters arriving for you."

Margot stood quietly at the bookcase. She didn't respond with anger at the assertion. She just frowned and looked down at the floorboards. "How did you find out?"

"I was at the post office to send some postcards to friends. I asked whether I could collect the mail for the hotel. The woman at the counter had never seen you there. She knew for certain because she is a firm fan of your novels."

Margot smiled. "That's nice to hear." She began to stroll around the room, absentmindedly running her hand across objects. "It's true. My sister hasn't written to me in over a year. We had an argument. She said she wouldn't help me with the books anymore. She walked away in anger. I thought it would be a passing thing. Johanna was always very easily offended, even as a child. But she was always eager to make up again and play like nothing had happened. She never held a grudge." Margot swallowed hard. "I don't know what I did wrong to make her so angry with me, but she kept her word. She never wrote to me again. Dieter saw her at a party, I think around Christmas last year?" She bit her lip. "He asked her to make up with me because I was so upset about not hearing from her anymore."

She took a deep breath. "Johanna scolded him to his face, saying he was always defending me and that he didn't want to see who I truly was. That I was taking advantage of her and that she had never felt loved." Her voice broke.

Atalanta said gently, "I'm sorry to hear that. It must have upset you very much."

"I can't make her change her mind. I've written countless letters apologising. I've sent them all over the world, to every hotel she's ever stayed at during her travels. I also wrote to the magazines she writes articles for, hoping they would pass on my letters, but they were returned unopened. Or they called me to say I should stop writing." Margot raised a hand in a gesture of despair. "I didn't know what to do anymore."

"But you keep up the pretence that you are still corresponding?"

"Yes. For my books, my career. It's not just my own reputation I'm thinking of. My publisher would also not be happy if the truth came out. Sales might be affected and... Well, to be honest, my books haven't been doing so well lately and... The novelty has worn off, I assume." She smiled sadly. "To me it's my whole life. For the readers it's just another book. They discover new favourites and I don't blame them for it, but ... it does leave me feeling a little dejected. Not as inspired as usual to write something new."

"I see. But how can you even write something new without your sister's input?" Atalanta inquired.

"I've collected a lot of material over the years. She sent me lots of photographs and stories. I can fall back on those. At least, I have been able to so far." Margot sighed. "I can't keep it up forever of course. I have been thinking about ... not signing another contract. Retiring. Dieter always says I'm overexerting myself with the writing. That I should take it easier. He'll be glad when I eventually decide to heed his advice."

Atalanta nodded. "Do you think Eva knew that your sister was no longer writing to you?"

Margot chewed her lip again. "Yes. She told me to my face that she had been to Crete and that the photograph I showed her couldn't have been taken recently because the site had changed."

Atalanta nodded to herself. Theresa had told her about that. She had visited Crete and noticed the discrepancy but Eva had taken credit for it, pretending to Margot that she had been to the island. Had that led to her death?

Margot said, "I felt terribly caught out. I didn't know what to say. I made up some lie about having confused things but ... Eva was not convinced. I was worried about what she might do with her knowledge."

Worried enough to kill her? Atalanta wondered.

Then again, she herself had found out about the lies surrounding the letters fairly easily so it would not have been very smart of Margot to kill Eva to keep something hidden that was not exactly difficult to find out once you knew where to look for the truth.

Margot said, "You only met her briefly, Atty, but Eva wasn't a nice person. She seemed to delight in making other people look bad. She was always finding ways to expose their little mistakes or failures and make them look like gigantic flaws. Take my husband Dieter. When he is here at the hotel, he plays cards with Maurizio. He often loses and sometimes it is quite a lot of money. But he is a wealthy man and I won't deny him a pastime he enjoys. Eva, however, made it look like Dieter was addicted to gambling and losing a fortune to Maurizio. She even suggested that he was wagering with his clients' money."

Was he? Atalanta wondered. He wouldn't be the first person to act irresponsibly with money entrusted to his care and then have to resort to even worse actions to keep that guilty secret hidden. Had Eva been pressuring him?

Margot said with a smile, "Dieter is such a dear, he can't keep silent about anything to me. He told me straight away what Eva was accusing him of. How manipulative she really was. I told him not to worry about it because she would not succeed in driving us apart. She was flirting with him, you know, when others were watching. Then when she got him alone, she threatened to expose him as a gambler and a thief. It was terrible."

"But you never believed that her threats were serious? That she could indeed ruin him?"

Margot looked at the floorboards again. Her expression

was pensive. "I didn't think it was serious at all. Dieter told me he believed her to be in contact with Alexander Hansen, the newspaper reporter, but he only told me that after her death. I just thought Eva was the kind of person who liked to make herself look important. She wanted attention, one way or another." Margot looked up at Atalanta. "Now that you know about my sister, what will you do with that knowledge?"

"Nothing, I suppose. I just wanted to tell you and…"

"Gauge my reaction?" Margot held her gaze. "Or do you want money to stay silent about it? Now I expect anything from anyone." She laughed nervously. "The atmosphere has been so strange since the murder. As if there's something in the air. We're all watching each other and … no one can be certain who's friend and who's foe."

"I don't want money," Atalanta assured her. "I feel sorry for the situation you are in. I do hope your sister will come to her senses one day and write to you again. I mean, she may not want to deliver material for your books anymore, but she could at least write to you as a sister to let you know what she is doing and that she is well."

Margot nodded. "I wish she would. Dieter told me that at that Christmas party where he saw her, she was quite drunk. Johanna has always had a problem with alcohol. She started drinking from a young age and by the time she left home to travel, she was already quite dependent on it. I have tried to get her to see a doctor about it, but she won't hear of it." Margot sighed. "I guess one has to let go, but it's very hard."

Atalanta nodded. She had always thought it would be wonderful to have siblings but of course there were also challenges attached. You might not get along, or the other party might not want to have the same bond as you.

"I'll leave you to read in peace," she said and retreated to the door. In the corridor she ran into Renard, who seemed visibly relieved to spot her. "There you are, mademoiselle. I have someone you should speak to. He is waiting outside."

"Outside?" Atalanta queried in surprise. "But it is evening and cold. Can he not come inside to speak with me?"

"He doesn't want to be seen. Dress up warmly and then go out the back door across the terrace. We will be waiting at the shed where they keep the deckchairs." Renard added softly, "And make sure no one follows you."

Intrigued by this mysterious behaviour, Atalanta went to her room to get her coat and then managed to sneak outside unseen. She stayed in the shadows while traversing the terrace towards the dark silhouette of the shed. As she came around the side of it, she almost collided with two forms. Renard and another man.

Atalanta froze and whispered, "Good evening. Why do you want to meet?"

The man said something to Renard in German. Atalanta said, "You can speak German with me. I taught in a school in Switzerland for years."

"I am Sylvia's father."

"The chambermaid who went missing?"

"Yes. She ran away because she was accused of theft but she didn't do it. She is innocent."

"You have spoken to her since she disappeared?"

The man looked at Renard who gave him a reassuring nod. The man said, "I spoke to her, yes."

"Do you know where she is now?"

"Yes."

"So she is not dead?"

"Most certainly not. I heard about the body found in the grotto and I wanted to talk to someone about it. To make sure people are not thinking..."

"I see. Should you not go to the police?"

"No. They will want to know where Sylvia is. They might still arrest her for the theft. But she is innocent. I know it."

"What about her boyfriend?"

The man grimaced. "He was a coward. As soon as she was accused, he ran. He didn't stand by her. He didn't believe in her innocence."

"Was he the thief?"

"Possibly. But I don't fully believe it. I think it was a hotel guest."

"A hotel guest?" Atalanta asked, perplexed.

"Yes. The jewels disappeared from the lady's bedroom. It was thought that a staff member had done it because they have a key to the bedroom doors. But Sylvia told me that there was a pass key that went missing a few days before. She's certain a guest took it in order to steal the jewels."

"Did she have anyone in mind in particular?" Atalanta asked.

"There are a few guests who stay in the hotel for long periods at a time. She said it was most likely they were involved."

"Meaning Margot Bergreiter," Atalanta said.

"And her secretary." The man nodded. "Sylvia said the woman had a furtive look about her."

Atalanta nodded thoughtfully. She had only seen her in passing on a few occasions. She was an inconspicuous, middle-aged woman. Someone you wouldn't look twice at. A thief?

She had to find out more about her and her circumstances.

The man said, "I was told you are a detective investigating the case. You must clear Sylvia's name so she doesn't have to hide anymore. The police will do nothing for her. But your butler told me you are a person who is determined to see justice done."

Atalanta glanced at Renard. He said, "You were working on the other cases anyway, and I thought it couldn't hurt to try and solve the theft as well."

Atalanta said to Sylvia's father, "The dead body in the grotto, do you have any idea who this can be?"

The man shook his head. "We aren't missing anyone in the village. Perhaps a guest?"

"A guest? Surely not. If a guest went missing, the hotel staff would have..." Reported it? To whom? The manager, no doubt. Would he have covered it up to protect the hotel's reputation? Acted like the guest had left? But what about their belongings? Did that even make sense? She had to look into that matter further.

But first she had to think of a way to find out whether the jewel thief was still at the hotel and if they could be caught in a trap.

Chapter Seventeen

Atalanta smiled at Raoul as they left the dinner table the next day. She hadn't told him about her plan to lure the jewel thief into a trap but still it seemed like he had picked up on the tension and was extra alert. It surprised her that he was so attuned to her feelings that he had noticed her mood, even without her telling him something was bothering her. Was it possible that their connection had survived even though he had no active memory of their earlier encounters? She felt very comfortable in his presence and he was supportive of what she was trying to achieve. Perhaps he felt the same way. Even if he could not logically explain it, he might be able to feel their bond and rely on it.

Her hand came up to finger the emeralds around her neck. The necklace was part of a set that also included a bracelet and drop earrings and she had decided to wear them all this evening. It was a bit much for the informal setting of a hotel dinner with other guests, but she wanted the thief, should they still be present, to notice and see her as a potential target.

It felt rather dangerous to put herself up as a target for a robbery attempt like that, but on the other hand she couldn't even be certain the thief was still at the hotel, and if they weren't then she was in no danger at all.

Raoul leaned over to her. "Shall we go out on the terrace to look at the stars?"

"What a lovely idea. Let me get a cocktail first. Do you want one too?"

"I had better not. Alcohol makes my head worse." He grimaced. "But you go and get one. I will wait for you here."

Raoul stood at the doors leading onto the terrace, waiting for Atalanta. Ever since she had walked into his life, something inside him had shifted. The terrible darkness of his fate – stumbling about with no memory of who he was or what had happened to him – had lifted a little and he began to feel more hopeful about the future. He was not spending his entire day trying to regain some sliver of memory, by looking at photographs in books or talking to people, forever feeling for any small hold of the slightest thing that felt familiar. At first he had imagined it to be quite simple, like unlocking a door, and then everything that was hidden behind it would come flooding back to him like a dam released. But it wasn't simple at all. Sometimes there was a sound or a scent that struck him as highly important and he perked his head up and waited for something to happen inside of him, for an awakening of memories that would lead him back to the past that eluded him. But nothing happened. He could not catch the meaning, and it felt like when somebody's name won't come to mind. It's right there on the tip of the tongue, but what is it?

He smiled ruefully. These days, everything was hard like it had never been hard before. He couldn't remember much about his past but at least it seemed like it had been an easier existence than what he had now, trying to make sense of a world that was foreign to him.

At least now he could retain the new memories he was making. He recalled Atalanta's arrival, their first meeting and the sadness in her face when she had learned that he couldn't remember her. He knew the names of some of his fellow guests and remembered snippets of conversations he had had with them. He remembered that one of them had been murdered and that the bartender Franco had been arrested for the crime.

A shiver of anxiety went down his back and he turned to see whether Atalanta was on her way back yet. The idea that death had struck at their hotel gave him goosebumps. Poison was such an insidious thing. It struck out of nowhere and it didn't matter how strong one was or how smart. It could not be avoided.

The bartender was behind lock and key now so the place

should be perfectly safe, but he didn't feel safe. He had even asked Maurizio to please take him to some other hotel and let Atalanta come with them. But Maurizio had said it was not necessary as the culprit had been caught and the case was closed.

"I'm surprised," he had said with a crooked smile, "that that total idiot Tobias Tanner managed to catch the killer, but then Franco handled it in such a terrible way that it was destined to go wrong. To think he was actually with her when she died... That he moved the body, further incriminating himself..." He had clicked his tongue.

"Most people have no experience with murder," Raoul had responded cynically. As he had said it, something had stirred in his mind. As if his words were true, but not for himself. Did that mean he had experience with murder? Atalanta claimed they had solved cases together. Was that true? Were there memories locked away in his brain about chasing dangerous men? About confrontations with murderers? She had told him he had saved her life, on multiple occasions.

He shook his head almost impatiently. Pain stabbed behind his temples. But this was all so unreal. If she had told him they had danced together, laughed together, conquered the world together, he would have believed her. There was a connection, a bond, a closeness he sensed even without being able to recall what had happened between them.

If she had told him he had kissed her and professed his love for her, he might even have believed her. Because she was special, different from anyone he ... had ever known? Of course he could not be certain as he didn't recall those other people, but ... she was special anyway. He smiled to himself as strange feelings ran rampant inside him. He hated being so helpless and having to depend on others; it must be this that made him feel a little more open to emotions.

But her insistence that they had fought crime together ... it was so unbelievable. That she, a beautiful, kind, innocent woman, would deal with murderers? And be able to outwit them too?

He didn't think she was lying but ... the story seemed to be part of this entire surreal episode in his life. Perhaps he would wake up some day and discover it was all a long and difficult dream. That none of it had been real.

He opened the terrace door and felt the night air on his face. That seemed very real. He could see the moon rising over the mountains. The white light on the snow. It was all so ... tangible almost. Could dreams be like that?

Atalanta appeared by his side carrying a glass full of a red liquid. "Franco is not here of course," she said, "so another member of the staff had made the cocktails. He had made a blue one for me but Theresa wanted that one. She claimed I had already had the blue one before. I hope this one is also nice." She sniffed the contents. "It has raspberry in it, I can smell that. I do hope it doesn't have too much alcohol. I don't like drinking a lot before bed. It makes my head spin."

"You like to keep your head level," Raoul observed and

suddenly he felt like he was standing not on a terrace among snowcapped mountains but in a sunny garden at some large country house. There was a scent of flowers on the air. They had been talking and he had called her a very sensible and controlled young woman or something to that extent.

"Provence," he said to her, "where we met. Was it at some estate?"

"Yes, the house of the comte…"

"De Surmonne," he added.

She stared at him with wide eyes. "You remember?"

"I saw a flash of an image, a sunlit garden, flowers and having a discussion with you in which I called you too sensible. I am sorry if it is offensive."

Atalanta laughed. "Not at all. I am so happy you remember."

"Just that one image."

"And the comte's name. Do you also remember the name of his first wife? You were firm friends with her."

Raoul thought for a moment, but where the memory had briefly been very vivid, it was now dark in his mind. A darkness in which he could do nothing but feel blindly around and become desperate.

"I don't. And it doesn't matter really. Let us enjoy the beautiful evening." He looked her over. The stones around her neck seemed to be alive. "May I say how lovely you look with those jewels?"

"Thank you. I feel they are a bit too much. Everyone seemed to be staring at them."

"They look perfect on you. I should perhaps be jealous, thinking of who bought them for you."

"My grandfather. He purchased several sets of jewellery before he died, for me, as part of my inheritance." She said it with a smile but there was sadness in her eyes.

"You wish you could have known him. Had an hour of his company rather than these precious stones." He knew as if she had told him. Perhaps she once had?

Atalanta nodded. "I feel like I was cheated out of so much that I desperately wanted. To know him better and speak to him about my father, my mother, my life when I was a little girl. I know too little."

Raoul made a dismissive hand gesture. "We always feel like we know too little. I feel right now like I can't move a foot without knowing first who I was and what I did. But look at me. I am here in a beautiful place with a lovely woman by my side. What else do I need to know?"

He stopped to look her in the eye.

"What more do I need to know, Atalanta, than that I am happy to be with you?"

Atalanta stared into Raoul's deep brown eyes. He had never said anything like that to her before. He had complimented her and they had flirted and there had been tension in the air. But tonight it seemed to be different. He was pensive, more open, and suddenly also willing to let his emotions show. It might be part of his condition but ... it was still very nice.

Raoul kept smiling as he leaned down to her. She should stop him, she knew that, but she didn't want to. His lips touched hers, brushing them in a light caress. She had never been kissed before. It was like the mere touch went to her head faster than any cocktail could. She felt like the whole world was spinning and she was floating in a universe full of stars.

Raoul locked his arms around her and kissed her again. Now she wasn't floating anymore, adrift and tumbling, but she was secure in his arms, feeling his warmth and the tenderness in his kiss. This was as it should be.

"I am sorry." Raoul rested his forehead against hers. His breathing was rapid. "I shouldn't have done that."

"Why not? It was wonderful."

"I don't remember who I am or what I want from life. I don't know if I will ever fully recover from my accident. Kissing you is irresponsible. I can't make any promises..."

"And I am not asking for any." Atalanta brushed her fingers across his cheek. "I know the situation and I understand it may change when your memory comes back. Then you will remember all the reasons why we can't be together. All the reasons you told me before. But tonight you don't remember them. And I don't *want* to remember them." She hid her face against his shoulder and they stood there holding each other for a long, long time.

Maurizio Dulce stood at the window of his office and watched how the two shadowy figures melted into one. He didn't know what he should feel. Relief that the burden of cheering Raoul up after the accident and memory loss was no longer on his shoulders? His uncle was a demanding man. He expected Raoul back healthy and able to race. That was a distant dream right now. But with Raoul feeling revived by the presence of this woman for whom he seemed to have feelings, something good might be around the corner. If his recovery kept progressing like this, Raoul might be ready to race again in late May.

Maurizio frowned hard. Who was he deceiving? His uncle would not be pleased. Late May was not soon enough. And this woman... What did she want from Raoul? Could she be dangerous to his uncle's enterprises?

The telephone rang. It was hidden in a drawer of his desk. He recoiled a moment, desperate to pretend he was not here and could not answer, but fear drove him to open the drawer and pick up the receiver. "Si?"

A voice began to explain things to him in rapid Italian. Maurizio listened with growing discomfort. This was not good. Not good at all. Raoul was on the terrace kissing a woman who was doing him the world of good, but the voice on the other end of the line was telling him things that destroyed that idea completely. His uncle would never want her near his charge. What could he do? Urge her to leave?

Could he use the kiss as an excuse? "You will have to do something about it before Vincenzo hears of it. You understand?"

Maurizio's heart was like a stone in his chest but he replied in a calm voice, "I understand. Consider it done."

Chapter Eighteen

Atalanta awoke to sounds of turmoil in the corridor. There were doors banging and voices speaking in an agitated manner. She even heard a female voice cry out in shock.

For a few moments she thought she must be dreaming, but then she realised she was indeed fully awake and this was real. What was happening?

Heart racing, she got out of bed, put on her dressing gown and went to the door. Pulling it open a crack, she peered outside. *Police!*

Her heartrate shot up even more. This made no sense. Franco had been arrested for Eva's murder. The case was closed. Why would the police be here now?

Her mind suggested a possibility but she didn't want to think of it. She had to ask some questions before she drew any hasty conclusions.

She went out into the corridor and asked a

chambermaid what the matter was. The maid said between sobs, "In the reading room. Another body. Another death. This hotel is cursed! I don't want to work here anymore."

Another death... She had feared it but not wanted to let the thought materialise. Now it had been said. Murder, all over again.

Steeling herself, Atalanta quickly went to the reading room. She could not get beyond the door but spying inside she saw Tobias Tanner speaking to a man who knelt over a body on the floor.

It was ... Theresa.

Atalanta backed away immediately. Her head was spinning. Theresa had tried to blackmail Dieter Bergreiter with the gold tie clip she had found beside the body. Had he decided to silence her? But why? Franco had been arrested and the police had seemed satisfied that he was the killer. Why risk a new investigation and take the chance that the two deaths were seen as connected? Franco was locked up and could not have done this. The police would have to find a new suspect.

She returned to her room with hasty steps. She had to think about this, thoroughly.

As she approached her bedroom door, it flew open wide and a woman stepped out. She stared at Atalanta with wide eyes. She wore a thick white bathrobe and clutched it closed at the neck with both her hands. "Oh, there you are," she said. "I peeked inside to find you. What's going on?"

Atalanta now recognised her as Margot Bergreiter's secretary. She tried to recall her name. Raoul had mentioned

Trouble in the Alps

it in passing but she couldn't remember it. "Theresa is unwell," Atalanta said. "The doctor is here for her." She didn't mention the police. Not yet.

The woman nodded and retreated. "I will tell Margot. She must not get upset. The deadline for the new book is approaching and it is not nearly finished. I will have a lot of typing to do in the next few days. But we will be away from here."

"Away?" Atalanta queried.

"Yes, we are leaving this morning. Herr Bergreiter insisted on it and since the murder was solved, the police agreed to it. I will continue packing the bags." The woman walked away.

Atalanta stared after her. It was odd that the woman had gone into her room to look for her. But at stressful moments people did unexpected things and the secretary was obviously under pressure with the Bergreiters's imminent departure. Atalanta doubted that the Bergreiters would indeed be able to leave today. If Theresa was dead...

She sat on the edge of her bed and stared ahead of her. This was so strange. Why another murder? Who had been afraid of Theresa? Was it something she knew or something she had only alluded to?

There was a brief knock on her door and Atalanta went over to open it. It was Tobias Tanner. He looked her up and down and said with an apologetic smile, "I am sorry to be intruding at this early hour, but I thought you should know. Theresa has been found unconscious. We don't yet know what she has ingested but the doctor says it seems she is just fast asleep, not near death."

"Was it poison?"

"He doesn't think so. There are no outward signs of poisoning such as rashes or blueness around the lips."

"Perhaps she took a sleeping pill herself?" Atalanta wondered.

Tanner nodded. "If she did, she overdosed. She cannot be roused. The maid who found her in the reading room assumed she was dead and created a stir."

"I can imagine she was frightened as it was the same place where Eva Reuter was found murdered." Atalanta frowned. "It is strange. Is there a connection?"

"I do not know. But I am not happy with this development. It might persuade me to rethink whether I indeed have our murderer under lock and key."

Atalanta nodded. She herself had immediately drawn that same conclusion. "I understand."

Tanner said, "Did you notice anything strange last night? Tension? An argument? Who did Theresa speak to?"

"I don't know. I spent a lot of time with Raoul Lemont on the terrace." Atalanta flushed at the memory of their kiss. "I have no idea where Theresa was or what she did."

Tanner pursed his lips. "That is unfortunate. Herr Bergreiter had asked me for permission to remove his wife from this environment. She loves this hotel but he feels like it is not good for her nerves to be here after the murder. I gave him that permission. They are supposed to leave in…" He looked at his watch. "An hour. They are catching an early train to go to Lugano. They have some friends there with a villa where she can finish her book in peace." He grimaced. "It was intimated to me that the book is most important."

Atalanta said, "It must be to her."

"Yes, yes, but the question is, can I let them leave?"

"Are you asking me?" She tilted her head. "Why would you?"

"You are staying here at the hotel. You see and hear more than I do. You are best placed to make a judgment. I am not so pig-headed as to I think I can do this all by myself." Tanner eyed her. "You have formed an impression of me, I know, but you might be wrong. And I would really appreciate your help in this matter. Should I let the Bergreiters leave?"

He stared at her with intensity, as if to draw the answer from the depths of her soul. But Atalanta didn't know. How could she tell? She had no idea what had happened between the others last night because she had been preoccupied with Raoul and their relationship.

"I will give you a few minutes to think about it." He turned away from her. "I will be in the reading room. Do come and tell me when you have made up your mind."

She didn't know why he was asking her this. Was it just to teach her a lesson? To show her it was not easy to make such decisions and you could always go wrong?

Or was he genuinely interested in an outside opinion? Did he think she might know something vital?

Did she?

She sat down on her bed again and closed her eyes. Her stay here was connected with so many emotions. She had come here in tears thinking Raoul might be dying. Then, when she had found out he was very much alive, she had suffered a new shock on discovering that his memory was gone and he didn't remember her or their relationship. Everything she had done here was overshadowed by the awareness that she might never get back what she had lost. She had been distracted, not paid close attention to what people were saying, doing, or how they were acting. She was here for Raoul and not for a case.

Still, Franco had asked her to clear his name and now there might be a chance. If the person who had sedated Theresa was the same one who had killed Eva…

But why?

Atalanta massaged her temples as she tried to go back across things Theresa had said and done that might have made her a target for Eva's killer. She was the one who found the body so she might know something else that she wasn't saying. Was it connected to the gold tie clip? Or was it something different?

Theresa was a selfish woman who had tried to use Eva's wealth for her own gain. Now, after Eva's death, she needed more money to continue her lifestyle. She had tried her luck with Dieter Bergreiter but had she had more irons in the fire?

Maurizio Dulce? Shortly before her death Eva had searched his office. Had she told Theresa what she had found there? Did Theresa know more than she had let on?

But why sedate her and not kill her? Had it been a mistake on the killer's part?

Atalanta tried to breathe slowly as she played out the events of the past days, scene after scene in which Theresa had participated. Was the key information among it? Or had something happened to which Atalanta had not been a witness? Was this whole exercise pointless?

Her reel of images ended with Theresa picking up the blue cocktail that had been made for Atalanta and toasting her with it. "Thanks, but I'll take this one. You've already had one. It looks delicious. Cheers. To a wonderful night!"

It had been anything but a wonderful night for Theresa. *Cheers.*

Atalanta sat up and stared ahead. *Cheers.* Theresa had toasted her with her glass. Her glass? No, Atalanta's. The cocktail had been meant for her.

The sleeping pill had been meant for her.

Not to kill her. Just to make her sleep deeply. For the entire night.

To what end?

She suddenly jumped off the bed and looked around her. The jewels! The emeralds. She rushed to her dressing table and pulled away the silk scarf she had tossed, rather too carelessly, across the set. It was there. The stones glimmered reassuringly.

For a moment her tight shoulders relaxed and she scoffed at her own anxiety. What had she expected? That the thief had come into her room overnight to steal the jewels? How could they have? She had not been sedated. The theft had not taken place. The thief had observed that it was Theresa who drank the cocktail and the plan had gone awry. The emeralds were safe and she was left to wonder who...

She froze anew. Margot's secretary. She had been inside her room. Allegedly to look for her to ask what the commotion was all about. But why come into her room to ask her when she could have walked further down the corridor to ask other people who were milling about?

And the way in which she had held her bathrobe... As if to keep it closed, but in reality to conceal something hidden underneath it?

Atalanta opened the drawers of her dressing table one by one and then she saw it. In the bottom drawer she had put an ivory box. It held her collection of postcards and magazine clippings which she had held onto during her lean years, wishing she'd one day be able to travel. To the casual observer such a box would suggest it held something of value, and it was gone.

Stolen.

Taken in haste.

She could just picture the scene. The woman had entered in a rush, walked over to the dressing table and decided not to take the emeralds as Atalanta would immediately miss them. The party was leaving in an hour so if something was found to be missing after they had left, they would be long gone. And perhaps such a box kept in the lower drawer would not be missed for days and then it could also have been the chambermaid or the valet or—

Atalanta quickly dressed herself and went to look for Tobias Tanner. She needed his help.

Half an hour later, Atalanta was ready to take action. Margot Bergreiter was already downstairs waiting for her husband to settle the bill with Maurizio Dulce before their departure. Only the secretary was still upstairs, collecting the last things needed for the journey.

The door to the bedroom stood open and Atalanta knocked briefly and entered at once. "I wanted to wish you a safe trip."

The secretary turned to her. Her face was already flushed, thus hiding any shock at being faced with the person from whom she had stolen.

She forced a smile and said, "Thank you. That is very kind."

"It is, isn't it, considering you stole my jewellery box." Atalanta had decided to go for the direct approach. "You took it from my dressing table while you were in my room."

The woman stared at her a moment, her eyes wide and frightened, then she produced a hoarse laugh. "Honestly, you must be mistaken. I was inside your room for but a moment to look for you and ask what the commotion was all about. I didn't touch anything."

"You went through the drawers of my dressing table and took my jewellery box." Atalanta held her gaze. "You made a mistake though. The box looks valuable, but there is nothing of worth in it. Nothing of material worth, that is. It holds private papers that are very dear to me. I want them back."

The woman rocked back on her heels. "I don't have them. Now let me pass, for I am running late."

"The box is of no value to you. I want it back. If you do not give it to me, I will go downstairs and tell your employers what you have done."

"They won't believe you."

"Oh yes they will. I am an influential person. I have important friends. I will tell them that I want my box back or I will make a scene and it will be very painful and awkward for them. The great author Margot Bergreiter, involved in common theft."

The woman seemed to hesitate. Atalanta said, "I don't judge you for your actions. Perhaps Margot doesn't pay enough to sustain the lifestyle you feel you deserve?"

"She wants to dismiss me. I need money to live. Not in luxury. No, just for survival." The woman seemed anxious now, clutching her hands together. "I am at an age where I won't find another job easily. I can't do much more than typing. I felt I was so secure here…"

"Why would Margot dismiss you?"

"She has decided to stop writing books and instead travel more with her husband. They spend a lot of time apart and apparently she feels it is not good for their marriage."

Or was it because Dieter wasted too much money

playing cards and Margot wanted to keep an eye on him and his spending?

The woman said, "I am needed no more. She is throwing me away like a used handkerchief. Not even an extra month of wages. No, just dismissal as soon as the current book is done. I feel helpless. Desperate."

"You also stole jewellery in this hotel a few weeks ago. The maid and her boyfriend were accused."

"They vanished. They aren't in prison or suffering for what I did." The woman tried to keep her chin up but her lips were wobbling. "I didn't hurt anyone. Rich people have so much. Their jewels are well insured. They suffer no loss. And I must have something to provide for myself."

"My box really does contain nothing but papers – just old postcards and magazine clippings. I want it back. Please?"

The woman eyed her and then leaned down with a sigh to extract something from a bag she carried with her. "Here it is."

Atalanta accepted it and opened it to let the woman see inside. "There, you see, it is as I said. It holds nothing of monetary value. Just a lifetime of dreams."

"Dreams," the woman scoffed. "They are worth but little. They don't pay bills. I need money. And lots of it."

"Did Eva find out what you've been doing? Did you kill her for it?"

The woman blinked. "Eva? What does she have to do with it?"

"You put something in my cocktail last night. To ensure I

slept deeply so you could come into my room with the passkey you had taken earlier. You wanted to go through my things while I slept and steal something valuable. But Theresa drank the cocktail and your plan was thwarted. You were forced to improvise."

"It was only a harmless sedative."

"But Eva died of it."

"No, I never wanted to steal from Eva. She was too shrewd. I was worried she would work it out and… I didn't put anything into her drink, I swear."

"I have heard enough." Tobias Tanner appeared at the door that Atalanta had left open so he could overhear the entire conversation from the outside. He said to Atalanta, "You handled the situation well. I will take her in for questioning. Who knows, if I can get a confession that she killed Eva Reuter, I can release Franco later today."

"I didn't kill Eva," the woman protested. Her face had now turned a deadly pale. "I only put a sleeping draft in the cocktail to steal some jewellery but I never mixed anything in Eva's drinks. Please believe me. I will give back the jewellery I have taken. I will make up for it as best I can. I will even go to prison for theft if I have to, but not for a murder I did not commit."

Tanner took her arm. "You are coming with me. We will have a long talk and you will tell me everything."

"I didn't kill Eva! I didn't!" The woman kept protesting her innocence all the way down the corridor.

In the lobby, Margot rose from the sofa and looked at them, perplexed.

"What is the matter? Why are you holding her arm?"

"I am sorry to inform you that your secretary has been stealing from hotel guests. She put sleeping drafts in their drinks so she could do her work undetected. We assume now that she also put something in Eva's nettle tea to sedate her, but it went wrong and she died."

Margot stared in horror as Tobias Tanner handed her secretary over to one of his men who cuffed her hands behind her back before taking her away to the funicular.

Dieter Bergreiter appeared with Maurizio Dulce. He saw his wife standing there in shock and disbelief and asked sharply, "What is wrong, Margot?"

"They have just arrested Karin. But surely they must be mistaken? She is no thief or murderer." She raised a hand to her mouth as she continued in a small voice, "Or is she?"

Dieter put an arm around her shoulders. He looked at Tobias Tanner. "You can tell us all about it on the way down. We are leaving. Goodbye." The last word was addressed to Maurizio Dulce who also looked quite stunned at the recent developments.

Tobias Tanner raised a hand. "I am sorry to say this, Herr Bergreiter, but under the circumstances I cannot permit you to leave. Not today. I must first speak with the secretary and ascertain the truth."

"You can let us know what you find out via correspondence. We are not staying here a second longer. This hotel has not been good for my wife. Look at her. She is close to fainting." Dieter Bergreiter pulled his wife nearer. "We are leaving and whatever the secretary is guilty of,

I will support your investigation in any way I can. But we are not staying here because my wife does not feel safe here anymore."

Tanner said, "If I say you are staying, then you are staying here. The doctor can give your wife a pill to calm her down, but you are not leaving and that is my final word. I will have my men watch the hotel and the cable car. No one is leaving until the matter is resolved to my satisfaction."

"This is outrageous!" Dieter Bergreiter turned red in the face. He glared at Maurizio Dulce. "Are you allowing this to happen with guests? Important guests, I may add. Well-respected people who do not wish to be associated with crime of any kind."

Maurizio raised both hands in the air palms up. "I am powerless to do anything when the police have decided that the guests must stay. We must adhere to the inspector's wishes until we know more."

"They are not wishes," Tanner said slowly. "They are commands."

Maurizio's eyes flashed at this insult to his authority in his uncle's hotel but he didn't respond.

Bergreiter huffed. "I will not tolerate this! I will call my lawyers!"

"You do that," Tanner said and turned away, leaving with the policeman who had cuffed Karin.

Margot said to Atalanta, "Do you know why this is happening? I can't make sense of any of it. This morning it was said Theresa was unwell in the reading room and now my secretary is a thief?"

"I am afraid it was a mix-up. Theresa drank a cocktail last night that was meant for me. She was sedated instead of me so your secretary was unable to search my room for valuables. I caught her this morning stealing this." She held up the box she was still holding. "I am sorry but there is no mistake. She took this from my room. She has also confessed to the jewellery theft that happened earlier, of which the maid Sylvia and her boyfriend were accused."

"But why? She earned a decent salary." Dieter Bergreiter looked confused. He was still holding Margot close.

Atalanta kept looking at Margot as she said, "You dismissed her, she claims, at short notice and without an extra month of salary."

Bergreiter winced. "Is that true? You mentioned nothing of it to me."

"I was waiting for the right moment to discuss the situation. But with all the events here at the hotel…"

"What situation?"

"I don't want to continue writing. It has become torture for me. I can't make up new stories. I am worn out." Margot burst into tears.

Bergreiter patted her back. "Now, now, calm down. No one is forcing you to write. If you want to stop then you must stop. I didn't know it was so hard on you. You always seemed to enjoy it so much."

"I did, before. But the past year…" Margot kept sobbing.

Maurizio Dulce said, "Perhaps a glass of strong liquor will help? Do come into my office."

Bergreiter supported his wife in that direction. Atalanta was left clutching the ivory box with her papers and sentimental trinkets. Her box of dreams. It had now played an ominous role in the mysterious happenings at the hotel. The secretary had admitted to having put the sleeping draft in the cocktail which meant that Theresa had not been poisoned. She had simply consumed the drink meant for Atalanta. But how did this all relate to Eva's murder? Or was there no connection at all? Franco could still have killed Eva. Or he was innocent, as he claimed, and the murderer was still free?

Was it Dieter Bergreiter? He had been about to leave the hotel. He might be acting like his concern was all for his wife's wellbeing, but what if he himself could not wait to get away?

She followed the little group to Maurizio's office. Dieter Bergreiter had settled Margot in a chair and was feeding her sips from a glass as if she were a little child. Atalanta gestured to Maurizio to come to her in the corridor. She made certain they were not overheard when she asked, "Is it true that Herr Bergreiter plays cards here and often loses?"

Maurizio tilted his head. "That is a private matter, Fräulein Ford. I cannot go into it."

"But there are so many strange happenings here at the hotel. One must find out how they are all related."

"Why must one?" Maurizio held her gaze.

"For Raoul's sake. He is supposed to be enjoying a quiet stay here but there is so much commotion. How can he ever recover this way? And your uncle... He is a decent businessman who just wants to have a quiet hotel here in a beautiful remote spot. He doesn't deserve to have criminals use his business for their ill-gotten schemes."

She saw the change in his features for just a flash, a brief glimpse of humour almost. He knew she was playing him. He knew more about her than he let on. He knew that she wasn't thinking about his uncle as the injured party here, but as ... a possible accomplice?

He said, "Your concern for my uncle is commendable, but you need not worry. He has always been able to take care of his own business. He is a man who knows what he wants and usually gets it. No matter who stands in his way."

That sounded rather ominous.

Maurizio continued, "Herr Tanner has enough suspects to choose from. He can solve the matter whichever way he likes. The hotel has now been rid of a malicious bartender and a thieving secretary. I am sure we will all be very safe."

He leaned closer to her and said softly, "Isn't there an English saying that it is better to let sleeping dogs lie? Well, I am certain that after today's arrest, the dogs will go back to sleep again and we ought to let them enjoy their slumber."

She wanted to respond but before she was able to, Maurizio continued. "Raoul is doing much better now that you are here, Fräulein Ford. I can see that your company revives him. I would hate to harm his recovery by taking him away from here, but I might be compelled to do so if the peace and quiet of this place doesn't return. You understand?"

He was threatening to remove Raoul from her influence. And she knew he could. He could take him somewhere she would not be able to find him. For all his improvement, Raoul was still in no condition to escape the Dulces's clutches on his own. She had to be very careful what she did here, both for Raoul's sake and her own.

"I am certain," she said with more calm than she felt, "that Inspector Tanner is more than capable of solving this case to your satisfaction. I just want to enjoy my holiday with Raoul."

"Then we are agreed." Maurizio smiled at her, but his eyes were guarded. "I will go back in to see if Frau Bergreiter is feeling better. It seems we must entertain her as a guest a little longer."

Chapter Nineteen

Later that day, Atalanta was pleased to learn that Theresa was recovering steadily from the sleeping draft that had been administered to her. At least there was no new murder to deal with.

But it was daunting to think that the draft had been intended for Atalanta. It could have been *her* lying in bed. She felt lucky to be walking about and at the same time she knew she was far from lucky as the case was not solved. The secretary had insisted that she had not killed Eva and Atalanta was inclined to believe her. Her gut feeling told her that the puzzle pieces fit together in a different manner. If only she could understand the connections.

She caught up with Dieter Bergreiter as he was walking through the lobby. "How is Margot?" she asked. "Is she still very upset? It must have come as such a shock to her that her trusted secretary was stealing from people."

"Yes, she had no idea Karin was capable of anything like

that. Margot is too gullible. She always thinks people have her best interests at heart."

"People like Eva?" Atalanta queried softly. "I had the impression that their friendship was a little ... unequal? It was mainly Eva profiting from Margot's fame." This was not at all how the relationship had struck her, but she wanted to draw him out and see how he reacted to this suggestion.

Dieter Bergreiter sighed. "Margot will never suspect anyone of having bad intentions. She enjoys meeting new people and spending time with them. I never liked Eva. She always seemed ... predatory somehow. Perhaps this was a hasty judgment on my part because I knew she had married a much older man and acquired his fortune but..." He shrugged.

"Eva was also unpleasant to you, wasn't she? I couldn't help but notice that there was tension between you."

Dieter Bergreiter's eyes became guarded. He said, "Why would you say so?"

Atalanta shrugged. "I can't really explain it, but ... perhaps it was my own feeling that Eva was a little manipulative? She told Margot that she really liked you and it made Margot feel insecure."

Dieter Bergreiter huffed. "I can assure you, Fräulein Ford, that there was absolutely nothing romantic between Eva Reuter and me. I considered her a leech and I was determined to stay far away from her."

"Oh, I believe you." Atalanta did her best to sound convincing. "I wish Margot had been as determined but she was easily fooled by Eva's charm. She could turn it on whenever she wanted."

Dieter Bergreiter nodded pensively. "Yes, she could be very friendly. I assume it is only natural that people act a certain way around a celebrity. That's what Margot is really. People want to get into her good graces and—"

"Into her good graces or into her chequebook? Did you believe that people were taking advantage of her?" Atalanta waited a moment to place the next question. "Her sister?"

"Her sister?" Bergreiter seemed genuinely surprised by the suggestion. "Why would she? Johanna has a successful career as a travel writer. She doesn't need Margot's money. Or her approval of her lifestyle." He grimaced a moment. "Despite their good relationship when they were younger, they grew apart over the years. People always assumed they were very alike because of their almost identical looks, but they were at heart very different. Margot was always quieter, perhaps because of her lung condition. Johanna is the opposite: lively and adventurous. A real risk taker."

"That means she probably also takes risks with money. Perhaps she is not as well off as you assume and she needs money to sustain her lifestyle? To pay for the travelling?" Atalanta waited a moment and added, "Margot seems very sad that they have become alienated. She pretends the letters are still coming, but … you must know the truth, after you bumped into Johanna at that Christmas party last year."

Dieter Bergreiter stared at her. "Margot confided in you about that?"

"It has been a very stressful time for everyone here." Atalanta put her hand on his arm. "You need not worry. I can assure you I will be very discreet about this. Until I came here, I had not heard of your wife or her novels. I have no intention of speaking about what I have learned here and ruining her career. I am just sad for her that the basis for her books, the information her sister provides her with, seems lost. I assume that is also why she wants to stop writing. Not so much because she is worn out but because her source is no longer delivering what she needs."

Bergreiter sighed. "Margot has been distraught about it for quite some time. In fact…" he fell silent a moment and then continued. "I lied to her about meeting Johanna at that Christmas party. I never met her. But I wanted to give Margot some reason for the alienation, the lack of letters. I wanted her to believe it was because Johanna was drinking again and all that so Margot would not blame herself. It's hard enough for her that the letters stopped coming and she has to make things up for her books."

Atalanta nodded. "She was showing people photos with dates scribbled on the back and Eva was able to figure out that these were not accurate because the places depicted had changed since then. You must persuade her to stop. Once people realise and rumours start flying, she could lose her reputation entirely."

Bergreiter nodded with a serious expression. "I will talk to her about it. But as she has already decided to quit writing, this won't be a problem anymore. We can do more travelling together. I am actually glad she wants to leave this place. She has been badgering me for so many years to buy it for her and now she is not at all interested in it anymore."

"The murder must have deterred her. It is not nice to live somewhere with a shadow hanging over it." Atalanta wondered whether she could address the other matter with him – his spending, the losses in the card games. But Maurizio's warning had been very clear. She should not poke around, because if she did, he would take Raoul away from her.

Dieter Bergreiter said, "Now that we have to stay here for a few more days, until the matter about the thefts is settled, we might as well make the best of it. I am glad you are such a good friend to my wife, Fräulein Ford. She needs all the support she can get."

Atalanta felt a twinge of guilt. She had not been honest about her identity or her reasons for asking so many questions. Did she really have Margot's best interests at heart? Or was she, in a way, just like Eva, acting purely with her own needs in mind? For a commendable reason – to solve the crimes committed here – but still… Would that make a difference to Margot once she discovered that yet another person of her acquaintance had been dishonest?

Atalanta caught sight of Renard making eye contact with her as if he was signalling. She took her leave of Bergreiter, wishing him well in getting Margot over the recent shocks, and met Renard in the dining room. He led her outside so they could be private.

Once they were removed from the hotel in the crisp

mountain air, he said, "I have been able to learn a bit more about Margot's sister. Johanna Laub is a well-known travel writer. She has been published in major magazines on the continent and across the Atlantic. She used to work with an agent in New York to get her assignments but a year ago she suddenly ended the partnership, arguing that she could do better on her own. Since then, things have been going downhill for her. She has been published a few times but in less important magazines and she has not had a new piece out for quite some time now. Her agent admitted that sadly she had always had a weakness for alcohol and he feared she had become so addicted that she is no longer able to deliver quality material. He could not tell me where she is living now or how I might reach her. I did think it could be worthwhile to talk to her, to get more insight into her relationship with Margot."

"Yes, that would have been nice, but I can imagine how hard it will be to locate her when she is no longer in touch with that agent. She leads a nomadic existence and we cannot expect to find her at such short notice." Atalanta frowned as she stared ahead. "Perhaps it is not necessary either. Margot is determined to quit writing. We should be happy that she has realised she cannot keep up the pretence forever. Still, it is sad for her that she has to stop doing what she loved because her sister ended the cooperation. I wonder if there would be a way for her to continue if..."

Renard studied her with narrowed eyes. "Are you contemplating delivering material to her?"

Atalanta flushed as if caught red-handed. "Well, I did

think that because I am travelling so much, it would not be difficult at all to send her some information about places I have been to. She doesn't need to get it from her sister specifically."

"But part of the charm people find in her novels is the idea that the adventurous sister travels the world and the sister who cannot go places herself uses her stories as inspiration for her beautiful books. There is a sort of romantic allure to it."

Atalanta nodded. "I suppose you are right. Well, who knows, the sister might come to her senses and reconnect."

"Before Margot lets her publisher know she will not write another book?" Renard looked doubtful.

Atalanta bit her lip. "You are right. Her decision that she cannot go on anymore has made it all the more urgent that we find out if their bond can be rescued or not. Could you do some more research to locate Johanna Laub? Draw on all those wonderful contacts you have everywhere? Even if she is always travelling, she must have favourite hotels like Raoul's hotel in Rome."

Renard sighed. "It will be difficult but I can try if you think it is important."

"I do want to help Margot. She has lost so much during her stay here. Especially her trust in other people. Eva flirted with her husband, her secretary was stealing jewels. She must feel totally let down. If we can salvage something for her..."

"I will do my very best." Renard was now smiling in

spite of his frustration. "You can never resist doing a little good."

Atalanta sighed. "I wish I could do something good for Raoul. His memory loss is not getting much better. He tells me that he can recall things he experienced a few days ago so there is some improvement but ... he still does not remember having met me in Provence or the other occasions on which we were together. He had a brief flash of recollection in which he remembered the comte's house in Provence and his name, but when he tried to elaborate on it, the image faded and it was all blackness again. It dejects him so."

Renard studied her with a frown. "Perhaps you need to take him away from here, to places where you have been before. That might restore his memory."

"I wish I could, but I am afraid Maurizio Dulce will not let me." She looked around her to ascertain they were indeed all alone and added, "He actually gave me a subtle but very real warning that if I interfere with anything, he will remove Raoul from here and I won't be able to see him anymore."

Renard looked grim. "Then we must make a move before he does."

"You actually propose to take Raoul away from his influence? But how could we? He controls this environment. His men operate the funicular. Besides, Tanner and his policemen are watching the hotel to ensure everyone stays in place. They are not at all convinced that the case is closed to their satisfaction."

Renard nodded. "I see." She saw by the workings of his features that he was not ready to simply accept this as a reality. He was thinking up some plan. She hoped he would come up with something brilliant to resolve the stand-off.

Just before dinner, Tobias Tanner arrived and drew Atalanta aside. "The secretary confessed to both the theft of your ivory box and the earlier theft. She put the jewels in a deposit box at a bank in Basel and we have arranged for a local policeman to pick them up. Now that we have them, we can charge her officially and it seems like I can close the case of the jewellery thefts to my satisfaction."

"But how does Eva's murder fit in?" Atalanta asked with tension in her stomach.

"To be honest, I don't know." Tanner eyed her directly. "She denies having poisoned the nettle tea but the doctor confirmed that Eva Reuter died because of a strong sedative being added to her drink. The same sedative that was used to sedate Theresa. The one that was originally meant for you."

Atalanta shivered. Theresa had taken her glass and thereby saved her from ingesting the sedative. Could it have killed her?

"It seems obvious that the secretary used the sedatives to ensure she could steal without anyone noticing. But with Eva Reuter it went wrong. She gave her too much or Eva reacted to it in a bad way. Some people have a weaker heart than others. And it is never safe to combine sedatives with alcohol."

Atalanta nodded. "I am aware of that. But you have Franco in custody for Eva's murder and now the secretary. You cannot charge both of them. You have to decide who is actually responsible."

Tanner nodded. "I have searched the secretary's luggage and the bottle with the sedative was found among her things. With her fingerprints on it – hers alone."

"Wealthy people have gloves." Atalanta said it pensively.

Tanner nodded. "I cannot determine whether anyone else used the bottle. I only have the evidence that she used it. I have her admission that she sedated hotel guests to steal from them. It would be easy to argue that she sedated Eva Reuter as well and it went tragically wrong. She probably didn't want her to die, but—"

"Still, it is particularly convenient for a few people that Eva died." Atalanta eyed him squarely. "She was very curious and even said to us that she wanted to investigate certain matters." She waited a moment and added, "But you must have found that out already yourself."

"If this is your way to check whether I have been thorough, I can assure you that I have been." Tanner puffed up his chest. "I have discovered via the staff that Eva was asking a lot of questions about the card games being held here. Apparently she had a theory that it was not merely innocent gambling but a way for Vincenzo Dulce to earn money from the rich."

Atalanta blinked a moment. "You mean it is a form of criminal activity?"

"It could be." Tanner held her gaze. "Your friend Raoul Lemont is a driver in Vincenzo Dulce's team. I do not want to cast aspersions on his sponsor. I am merely saying that the staff informed me of Eva's interest in the card games."

"I see. Have you asked Maurizio about those card games?"

"Not yet." Tanner kept watching her. "I first wanted to get your opinion about them. You have been staying here for some time now. Have you noticed anything strange going on?"

"As a woman, I am not invited to the card games. I have no idea what's happening with those. I do know Dieter Bergreiter is always losing money when he is here. But perhaps he's just a bad card player?"

"Yes, who knows?" Tanner seemed disappointed by her lack of information for him. He rubbed his hands together. "I must focus on the matters at hand. At least with the jewel thefts solved I have a success to my credit, one that will please the hotel manager and the owner."

He sounded a bit cynical. Atalanta frowned as she watched him. What was Tanner really after? Why had he joined the police force? Was he hoping that the Dulces would pay him for the successful solving of a crime that ensured the hotel's name would not be tainted? Did he think this job could make him rich?

But why then mention to her that the card games might

be a cover for criminal activities? She could easily tell Maurizio he had said so.

Or was he hoping she would do some discreet sleuthing for him? Why would she, considering the risk? If Maurizio had poisoned Eva's tea ...

Tanner said, "You were so certain that Franco was innocent. Do you think I should let him go? Can he come back here to resume working?"

"I don't know if Maurizio would want him back. That is not my decision to make." Atalanta took a deep breath. "There is, of course, the matter of Franco being Eva's stepson. He had an interest in her death seeing as she robbed him and his siblings of all their money."

"And he happened to use the same sedative as the secretary?"

"Perhaps the prior theft got him thinking. Perhaps he had figured out that although Sylvia and her boyfriend fled, they were not guilty and it had actually been a guest. He is the bartender. Perhaps he witnessed the sedative being administered? It could have given him the idea to use the same method to kill Eva and have another be blamed."

Tanner nodded slowly. "It sounds possible but is it likely he would have gone anywhere near her after he poisoned the tea?"

"Perhaps she kept him there too long? Or it worked faster than he anticipated? We don't know." Atalanta thought a moment whether she wanted to share the information or not, but then decided that she had to, because of her own conscience. "Theresa found something else beside the dead body. A gold tie clip. She believes it belongs to Dieter Bergreiter. She is blackmailing him with the knowledge. I know she drank the cocktail with the sedative by mistake, but ... I do think she is playing a dangerous game. You should warn her to stop it."

Tanner tilted his head. "How long have you known this?"

Atalanta flushed. "Longer than I should have. I mean, I should not have kept quiet. I should have informed you straight away."

"Why?" Tanner kept looking at her. "You are not with the police. You are not obliged to report to me. You can hear things and consider them ... pointless gossip?"

"What she is doing is dangerous."

"Dangerous? You think Herr Bergreiter would kill her to keep her quiet?"

"If he is Eva's murderer then why not?" Atalanta decided to stand her ground. "Theresa is playing a game with him to get money to fund a luxury lifestyle, but I wonder if it is worth it."

Tanner seemed to suppress a smile. "Your concern is commendable. But you are selective in your reporting. You share with me that Theresa is blackmailing Bergreiter, but you don't tell me that Eva Reuter handed Alexander Hansen the information that your friend's accident was in fact sabotage so another could get his seat on the team."

Atalanta flushed deeply. She had suspected that one of Tanner's men had followed her and Raoul to their meeting with Hansen at Hotel Moser by the lake. Perhaps Tanner had subsequently contacted Hansen and put pressure on him to reveal all he knew about Eva?

"I can only assume that you are protecting your friend," Tanner said. "That you do not want to believe any of this sabotage story, because it would mean he is in actual danger. You dismissed it as pointless gossip by Eva Reuter to make herself important with Hansen and get money or something like that. I have to assume that this is the case or else I would be forced to assume that you are shielding Maurizio Dulce."

He took a step back before adding, "I would rather not think so."

She felt a niggle of guilt that she had not told Tanner about the pills Eva had taken from Maurizio's office. The ones Eva had wanted Margot's doctor to analyse. It suggested that she had been onto something shady concerning Maurizio. He could very well be Eva's killer. But she still wasn't convinced that Maurizio would really take the chance of murdering someone at his uncle's hotel, thus drawing police attention onto them and their activities. It was illogical.

Still, she had to give him a reason why she had been so reticent to alleviate his suspicions of her intentions. Atalanta cleared her throat.

"I have been looking into a few points because I thought I should be thorough and not come to you with half a story. Raoul's accident might well have been a genuine accident. I do not know as of yet and I don't want to accuse people without proof."

"I understand." Tanner touched his hat to take his leave. He turned back to her and said, "But there is a saying that a dog never bites the hand that feeds it." Then he walked away.

Atalanta was left perplexed. Did he mean to imply that she was shielding the Dulces because they were the hand feeding her? Or indirectly through Raoul's spot on the new team? His meaning could also be far more ominous. He might have been using this conversation to make it clear to her, subtly, that he was himself on the Dulces's payroll; that he was a bought policeman who would protect their interests. He might have been implying that it would be better for her to steer clear of any shock revelations about what was really going on at the hotel, because if she did decide to go against the Dulces, she would discover that there was no one on her side.

Chapter Twenty

Renard knocked discreetly on the bedroom door. He had waited until it was quiet and everyone had gone to bed to come to his mistress's room to speak to her. He felt that the information he had received was urgent enough to warrant a conversation, but had to make certain it was done in absolute privacy.

She opened the door a crack and looked out. When she recognised him, the tension left her features and she gladly invited him in. As he entered and stood waiting for her to make herself comfortable on the sofa, it hurt him to think she was under such strain. She was staying with the enemy, so to speak, and she knew it. Handling murder cases was always difficult and dangerous because she was usually under the same roof as a ruthless killer who, when cornered, might strike at her. But here it was even worse. This hotel belonged to the Dulces who had Raoul Lemont dangling like a puppet on a string. Mademoiselle Ashford would not forsake him, but perhaps for her own safety she should. He wanted to convince her of this, but at the same time knew it served no purpose. She would never abandon Lemont.

Renard felt the tension between his shoulder blades. He had to protect his mistress. That was his assigned role even if his deceased master had never told him in so many words. He had initiated her into the sleuthing business, step by step, and ensured she didn't risk too much. But where it was possible to advise her when it came to cases, it was so much harder to direct her in her personal life. He had never thought that someone as pragmatic and logical as her would get carried away by emotions and yet, in a strange way, it also made sense. She had no one in her life – no one to care for, no one to care for her. She was all alone and she ached for closeness. To Renard's mind, she was attempting to find it with someone unsuitable, but his ideas did not matter. Her safety did.

She said, "You look very serious."

"Yes, I'm afraid I have bad news." He was not normally so dramatic but he felt that now he should paint the danger in the strongest possible colours. "I have spoken with a few people. It was difficult as the community here is very guarded and no one wants to reveal anything about the Dulces. But finally I spoke to a man who was very frank. It is no wonder, since he is the father of the previous police officer in this region."

"The one who was killed in the car accident?"

"It was no accident. He was run off the road on purpose

because he was getting too close to revealing the criminal activities of Vincenzo Dulce and his nephew." Renard held her gaze. "That man was a danger to them, and they did not hesitate to remove him. Even though it looked suspicious, they wanted him gone and they acted."

"That's what the father thinks," she countered. "He is distraught because he lost his son and he is looking for reasons why the accident happened. He cannot accept it was just an accident, a pointless death."

Renard would normally have applauded Mademoiselle Ashford for always looking closely and considering all angles of a case. He would have agreed that it was possible for grief to make people assume things that were not in fact reality. But today he wanted her to assume it was true and make sure she got away from here unharmed.

He said, "I think he is not an emotional or vindictive man. He knows what he is talking about. His son was investigating serious crimes and he was killed to stop that."

"What does this have to do with the murders here? Do you think he worked out who had been killed in the grotto? The unidentified remains?"

Renard shook his head impatiently. "I don't know anything about that. I am trying to explain to you how hazardous it can be to cross the Dulces."

She leaned back against the sofa. "I am not crossing the Dulces. In fact, I have done Maurizio a favour by exposing the jewel thief who was plaguing the hotel. With her arrest, things can settle down." She held his gaze and continued, "Inspector Tanner will likely charge her with the murder as well. Or if he thinks he cannot prove it, then he has Franco as a backup."

Renard felt anger rise in his chest. "So with two eligible suspects the case is closed to everyone's satisfaction?"

"I cannot see how I can change much about it. Tanner made it very clear to me that he is not willing to stir the pot."

"*Non*, of course not." Renard raised a hand in agitation. "He is on the Dulces's payroll. He was appointed shortly after the car accident that killed the previous police officer! He has been put in place by them as their puppet! He must keep them away from the limelight. He does not care who he has to arrest for murder in this hotel as long as it is not a Dulce or anyone associated with them."

His mistress did not respond. Normally her ability to refrain from immediate judgement struck him as making her perfect for investigative work but now he was growing increasingly agitated at her lukewarm reactions.

He said sharply, "Do you not see what position you are in? The Dulces are free to do what they want in this region because no one will stand in their way. They are like medieval lords."

"With the power of life and death?" she queried. "Do you really think Maurizio killed Eva Reuter and is certain Inspector Tanner will never arrest him for it?"

Before Renard could reply, she continued, "Eva made it very easy for Maurizio to assume that he would get away with it because she made so many enemies around the hotel. She was manipulative, unkind, flirted with married men, led the bartender on, leaked information to an outside source... So many motives to choose from! Maurizio could easily have killed her and been confident of a dozen likely suspects, even if Tanner had not been bought."

Renard blinked at her persistence in going against him. "What are you saying?"

"That I am not convinced Maurizio did it." Atalanta eyed him quietly. "Yes, he may have wanted her dead because she was snooping and leaking information to a journalist, but other people also had compelling motives to remove her. I cannot take the fact that Maurizio is part of a crime family as proof that he is a murderer. It is too easy."

Renard blinked in confusion. Her words made perfect sense, but he so wanted her to believe him and leave this place. How could he convince her?

Atalanta continued, "There is something decidedly odd going on here. And I have a feeling it is all connected to the dead body in the grotto. Remember that Eva went there, repeatedly? Did she know that something was hidden there? Was she on the trail of something much bigger than just Raoul's accident or Dieter Bergreiter's gambling? Was she looking into a murder that had already happened here? Did she know who it was being hidden there? Did she perhaps even come here specifically to look for this body because she knew someone had disappeared in this hotel?"

Renard stared at her. "You think Eva came here in order to look into a disappearance?"

"Why not? We are distracted by so many things, but we must keep our focus on the primary cause. What started it all? *Before* Raoul came here and I followed. Who was here previously? Eva, Theresa, Margot and her secretary Karin. Her husband Dieter came to visit every weekend."

Renard let his arms dangle by his side. He began to see what she was driving at. "You think that the remains in the grotto have something to do with one of the hotel guests? But surely if someone vanished from the hotel, the staff would know? It would not be a total secret."

She shook her head. "The person who died and whose body was hidden need not have been a guest here. They could have come to visit one of the guests. Perhaps they were killed in an argument and hidden. The grotto was a clever place to choose. It is large and although guests take a peek inside, they do not explore it thoroughly."

Renard nodded. "That makes sense."

"So the body would never be found. At least, that's what the murderer thought."

"Until Eva came looking."

She nodded. "Exactly. So we only have to figure out who stood to lose if the body in the grotto was found."

"But it has been found now. Eva's murder did not prevent that." Renard began to pace the room. "If her murder was carried out in order to keep the body from being found, it failed spectacularly."

"But the killer could not know that in advance." She seemed determined to pursue the point. "They simply thought that Eva's snooping was annoying and had to stop. The sedative used to kill her was the same as the one used to sedate the jewel-thief victims. So it makes sense to see a connection there."

"The secretary? Who can she have killed?"

"Or Margot. She must have known about the sedative her secretary took, and she was well placed to acquire it. Dieter Bergreiter perhaps?"

Renard shook his head. "We are back to pure speculation. There are too many options. Tanner has not given us any information about the body in the grotto. We do not even know if the remains are male or female."

"I wager they are female." She stared at him with narrowed eyes. "Because I have a strong hunch I know who the body in the grotto is."

Renard eyed her perplexed. "Who then?"

His mistress stared past him. Her expression became troubled. "If I am correct, it is really sad. I don't want to…" She sat in silence for a while, thinking. Renard did not dare disturb her. He waited until she was ready to speak. She chewed her lip and then snapped her head up as if she had come to a decision. "I must find out. Will you help me?"

"Help you with what?" Renard felt a twitch in his stomach. "You're not going to do anything dangerous, are you? I don't want to see you in danger again."

"I cannot help it, Renard. If you are right that Tanner is a bought man, he might not want to help. I will have to do it myself. In my own way. And you are the only one who can help me. Raoul is not in a position to—" The pain in her eyes was visible. "I don't want to ask him to involve himself with something like this. He has to be careful and get better.

It is bad enough that he ended up like this. With no prospect of regaining his memory any time soon."

Renard's own heart hurt because of her pain and her sadness that the bond she had built with Raoul had been erased by his memory loss. Renard might never have liked their intimacy, but he only wanted to see Mademoiselle Ashford happy.

And safe. So what could he do but agree to help her? He would not leave her to act alone.

Chapter Twenty-One

Atalanta took a deep breath before she approached Margot Bergreiter. The woman was standing on the terrace, her fur stole wrapped tightly around her narrow shoulders as she gazed up at the star-filled night sky. She cut a lonely figure and, suspecting what she did now, Atalanta understood just how lonely Margot had been for the past year. It was hard to go up to her and confront her, but it had to be done. For the sake of the truth. For innocent people who were incarcerated for crimes they had not committed.

"Good evening." She came to stand beside Margot. "It is so beautiful out here. So peaceful and serene. Almost like there is nothing worrying in the world."

"It must be the snow on the mountains," Margot said. "Always when I look at it, I feel like it signifies purity. New beginnings." She smiled softly. "I think I've written something like that in my books a few times. People like hopeful statements."

"They do," Atalanta agreed. She turned her head slightly in the direction of the grotto. That was where Margot's hope had died. Her hope of a new beginning.

She said softly, "I heard from your husband that you are no longer interested in buying the hotel. It surprised me as you seemed so adamant earlier that you wanted it. To stay and relax and … write."

"I changed my mind. Writing is taking its toll on my health. I have done it for years because I love it so much, but now it is time to have other priorities. My life with Dieter. I want to travel with him, see the world. He is the love of my life and yet I have taken so much time away from him to write about love. Ironic, isn't it? But I see it clearly now. The book I have to deliver shortly will be my last one. And then I can enjoy life. Together with Dieter."

Atalanta said, "But if you love this place so much, why not buy it and use it as your base? To come to in summer and at Christmas time? It is a wonderfully unique location."

"Yes, but…" Margot seemed to look for her next words. "Dieter is not as rich anymore as he used to be. We have to put everything into travelling. We cannot afford to buy this place. Maurizio is asking an outrageous sum for it." She forced a smile. "Because he knows I want it so much."

"Really?" Atalanta looked up as if she were innocently enjoying the night sky. She could make out so many stars here. Her heartrate would normally slow when enjoying natural beauty like this but now she was intensely aware of what she was heading towards.

Margot said, "I am not troubled by the loss of the hotel."

"Nor by the loss of your secretary?"

"I have a deadline so it is inconvenient, but I can find someone else, I suppose."

"I wasn't thinking of your deadline but of the shock of finding a trusted employee is a thief."

"Oh yes, of course. I had no idea she would ever do anything like that. And then she had the gall to blame it on me for dismissing her. If everyone who was dismissed started stealing, where would we get to with the world?"

Atalanta nodded. "It is terrible." She wanted Margot to believe she was sympathetic until she had achieved her goal. "I thought she was far too sensible to ever commit a crime. I mean, something like that must come to light somehow. To think she believed she could take the box from my room and run away with it without consequences…"

"I suppose the desire was stronger than she was." Margot sounded wistful. "It would work well in one of my novels. Readers sympathise with tragic characters."

"Even if they do wrong?"

"If it is for the right reasons… My secretary stole to get money for herself. We tend to find that rather despicable. But suppose she was stealing to buy medicine for her sick mother. Would we blame her as much? Probably not. We would still think theft is not right, but we would find her motivation praiseworthy."

"I agree." Atalanta shifted her weight. It felt like the

night air was ice cold on her damp skin. She wasn't enjoying this. In fact, she would rather avoid it, but it was inevitable. "Reasons matter so much, don't they?" she said softly. "Reasons why we do things. We can try to convince others it was the only way out. Or even ourselves."

Margot didn't stir. She stood there like a statue, her face calm as if it were cut from marble.

"It was such a nice arrangement," Atalanta continued. "Your sister Johanna travelled and supplied the material for your books. You thanked her in the dedication and readers thought it fascinating how you, with your weak health, could still write these engaging books about faraway places to which you had never been. It added to the allure of your writing and increased your sales. But your sister became more and more unstable and unreliable. She didn't deliver materials. Then she left her agent in New York. She was drinking. She sought a confrontation with you."

Margot stood motionless. Atalanta could not tell whether she even heard her or understood what she was doing here.

"She came to the hotel to tell you she was no longer going to deliver anything for your books. She was angry with you. She blamed you for many things. It turned into an ugly argument. Perhaps even a struggle? And as a consequence, she died. You hid her body in the grotto. You tried to buy the hotel to keep the secret hidden. No one could ever be allowed to look closer and find something there."

Margot slowly turned her head to Atalanta. Her

expression was still calm but her eyes shimmered with unshed tears.

"Yes, she died in the grotto. She was very drunk when she came to see me. She was shouting all these terrible things about me having abused her, having made millions with my books off the back of *her* work. She wanted money from me, lots of it. I told her I would not let her drink herself to death. She clawed at me. I shrank back. She came for me again. I stepped away and she lost her balance and hit the grotto's wall. She fell to the ground and ... she never got up again. I could not believe it. She always seemed so strong and full of life. How could she die like that?" Tears now rolled down her cheeks. "How could she leave me? Think of me what you will, but I loved her. In spite of everything, I loved her."

"Why did you not tell anyone what had happened? Why hide the body?"

"I saw her lying at my feet and I ... realised I could just go on like nothing had happened. I could hide her body and go back to the hotel and pretend she had left whole and well. There were several people controlling the cart and if one thought he had seen her go up, another could have let her down. It would never come out. I didn't want to admit to myself that she was dead. I pretended to receive letters, I continued writing, I..." Margot bit her lip. "I deceived myself into thinking it could go on like that. But it couldn't. The writing became so much harder. I didn't feel the joy of it anymore. I just ... wanted to quit. To do something different. Have Dieter by my side and—"

"But then Eva interfered. She was interested in the grotto. She could have found out your secret."

Margot looked at her with surprise. "No, Eva had no idea."

"She told you she had been to Crete. She knew you had lied about the photographs. The date on the back."

"That…" Margot shrugged. "It was nothing serious. I wasn't worried about Eva."

"So you didn't kill her?"

"No, of course not! How can you think something so horrendous?" Margot wiped at her tears. "Eva was playing a dangerous game. She wanted to find out information about Maurizio Dulce. She pretended to you that it was about Raoul Lemont's accident but she was onto something completely different." Margot stopped and shivered under her stole.

Atalanta watched her carefully. "What then?"

Margot rubbed her hands together. "I shouldn't tell you. It will only cause harm."

"Harm for whom?"

"Everyone involved."

"Everyone?" Atalanta suppressed an incredulous laugh. Margot was trying to deflect attention from herself by suggesting some big conspiracy.

Margot seemed to sense her disbelief and leaned closer. "It is blackmail. They let Dieter pay outrageous sums. Every time he comes here, he has to lose card games in order to hand over money. But it is really a payment."

"Payment for what?" Atalanta asked.

Margot took a deep breath. "When the Dulces bought the hotel from the previous owner, he told them that Dieter also wanted it. That he was quite persistent about it. He joked to Maurizio that if they ever wanted to get rid of it again, they could get a good price by offering it to him. Maurizio wondered why Dieter wanted it. He ... examined the property carefully. Including the grotto. He thought that ... it was perhaps a site where you can find those mountain crystals that everyone is so keen on."

Atalanta nodded, thinking of her visit to the gem museum.

"He found Johanna's body. He realised that Dieter wanted the hotel in order to keep something secret and confronted him with his find. Dieter realised that it was my sister and ... he has been paying blackmail money ever since."

Atalanta frowned hard. "Why would Maurizio not go to the police?"

"Him?" Margot laughed bitterly. "He's a criminal. A gangster. He hates the police. There are whispers he even had the previous police officer killed, in that so-called accident. I put nothing past him. He is blackmailing more and more people. With secrets. He killed Eva and he's trying to pin it on my secretary. Or that bartender Franco. He doesn't care who goes down for it as long as he and his uncle go scot-free."

Atalanta was processing all she learned here.

Margot continued. "Dieter asked a private detective to look into the Dulces. He didn't intend to pay blackmail money, at first, and he wanted me to confess to the police what had happened so they could establish that it had been an accident, and it would all be resolved. But the detective found out about Vincenzo Dulce's past. That he has amassed a fortune via criminal activities, even assassinations."

This was the same information Renard had gathered when he had looked into Dulce as Raoul's potential new sponsor. Her breathing grew shallow as she realised, anew, what her dear friend had ended up in.

Margot said, "Dieter feigned wanting to do business with Dulce to explain why he asked the detective to look into him. The detective urged him in the strongest possible terms to stay away from Dulce unless he wanted to get himself killed. Those were his exact words."

New tears formed in her eyes.

"Dieter told me that he didn't dare resist Maurizio and thus he began paying money. Every time he is here, he pays. And pays and pays. It would never have ended. So you see, I am actually glad the body has been found now, because Maurizio has lost his hold over us and we can finally go free."

"But will Tanner not work out who the body is and what happened?"

Margot took a deep breath. "Dieter suggested I tell Tanner the truth but I don't trust him. I think he takes bribes. Whoever pays most will get his cooperation. So I told Dieter to pay him to get the case closed without the body being identified. I think it will work."

"But Maurizio knows the truth."

"That's why we have to leave as soon as possible. We can go to South America. He won't be able to get to us there. We can finally be together and be happy."

Margot stood up straighter.

"I am sorry for the troubles my sister had but her death was an accident. I am to blame for hiding her body, I do see that, but—"

"And Eva? You didn't kill her because she was getting too close?"

"Maurizio killed her. He knew she was uncovering his blackmail operation. He didn't want her to spill the beans to that reporter."

Margot shivered anew.

"I want to go inside. I assure you that Eva's death is Maurizio's doing. Just wait and see."

"Wait and see what?" Atalanta called after her, but Margot was walking away and she didn't look back.

Atalanta felt a little lost. She had expected plenty of reactions to her suggestion that the dead body was Margot's well-travelled sister Johanna, but not this admission. She had even asked Renard to watch closely in case Margot tried to attack her to silence her. Had the threat been a little exaggerated? Margot was a kind and quiet writer of romance novels. She had never shown any violent tendencies. When thinking about a confrontation between her and her bolder sister, especially when the latter was intoxicated and angry, it seemed more likely that the sister would have attacked her. If she had indeed stepped aside and Johanna had taken an unfortunate tumble against a piece of solid rock...

But what about Eva? Had she found out about the dead body in the grotto? Or had she been out to expose Maurizio? She had searched his office...

Atalanta wiped her forehead. What should she do next? How should she best act? She felt like she was getting no closer to the truth, like every piece added to the puzzle only made it more complicated and impossible to solve.

Chapter Twenty-Two

The following morning, Atalanta came down to find Raoul waiting for her in the lobby. He walked over to her with hurried steps and said in a shaken tone, "They have arrested Maurizio."

"What? When?"

"Tanner came to the hotel at first light and they searched the premises, especially Maurizio's office. He found something significant because he arrested him right on the spot. Maurizio said he would be sorry as his uncle has very good lawyers, but Tanner replied that no one could get him off now." Raoul looked pale under his tan. "What can he mean? Do you have any idea what Tanner is up to? Has he told you? You have been so silent. Yesterday evening..."

Atalanta flushed as she recalled the meeting with Margot and how she had kept Raoul in the dark about her suspicions and actions. "I was just tired. So much has happened and ... it seems to keep on happening. I want to go to the police station to hear what Tanner has against Maurizio. Will you join me?"

They went outside to the funicular, but upon arrival they were told they were not allowed to go down, on Inspector Tanner's orders.

"But it is Inspector Tanner I want to see," Atalanta protested. The officer shrugged. "You must stay here. You could call him, I suppose."

Reluctantly, Atalanta and Raoul retraced their steps. They found the lobby empty. It seemed like the staff had gathered in the kitchen to discuss the new developments. Raoul gestured for Atalanta to follow him into Maurizio's office.

"There is a phone in here. I once saw Maurizio hide it away in his desk when I came in. I suppose he uses it for private business. You can place a call to the police station. That way the receptionist won't overhear, should he come back while you are speaking."

Atalanta was surprised that there was an extra phone but sat down to place the call. She had to wait a few minutes before Tanner came on the line. "What is it?" he snarled.

"I want to know why you arrested Maurizio Dulce."

"He poisoned Eva Reuter. I found the vial of sedative hidden in his desk. His fingerprints were all over it. I am arranging for him to be transferred today to a prison where his uncle's friends cannot reach him. I don't want him to escape." He sounded grim. "Finally I have something against them."

"Why did you come back to carry out this search?" Atalanta asked. "You looked around before. Did you not find the vial then?"

"I was told that there was a secret compartment in the desk. I came back to see if I could find it. There was lots of money and the vial."

Atalanta's head spun. "Who told you about this secret compartment?"

"Does it matter? I have him under lock and key now. I will release Franco later today. The secretary must of course face charges for the thefts, but she will be happy to hear the murder will not be blamed on her." Tanner waited a moment and added, "Not bad, for a glorified gamekeeper." Then he disconnected the call.

"What did he say?" Raoul asked with tension in his voice. He leaned over her, looking at her with wide eyes.

"He is very smug and pleased with himself." Atalanta stared ahead. She still wasn't certain that Tanner had arrested the right person. Some detail was nagging at her brain: the secret compartment that had been uncovered; the money inside; the vial. All the evidence he needed. So convenient. Almost too convenient. Too neat.

She looked at Raoul. "Do you think Maurizio is capable of murder?"

Raoul leaned back on his heels. "How can I know that? I have not known him for long. He is a strong-willed man and he has an uncle who won't take no for an answer."

"You think he may have killed Eva under his uncle's orders?"

"I wondered before if he keeps that extra phone"—Raoul pointed at it—"especially to hear from his uncle. I'm sure they don't talk about the weather."

Atalanta shied away from the phone as if it had suddenly turned into a snake. If Margot had told the truth about the blackmail scheme, this phoneline had been used to take the orders to extort people and lure them to this hotel; to this beautiful place where evil lurked around every corner.

She stood up. "I want to get out of this room. I don't feel at ease here."

Raoul nodded and agreed. In the corridor, they saw the hotel manager coming towards them. He cast them a suspicious look. "What were you doing in Signor Dulce's office?"

Raoul shrugged. "I called the inspector to ask what I can do to help Maurizio. As the team's driver, I feel it is my responsibility to support him at this difficult time."

The manager seemed doubtful but could not do much but let them pass.

Once in the lobby again, Raoul asked, "What do we do now? We don't know whether Maurizio is guilty or not. We should hardly go to the trouble of acquitting him if he did kill Eva. What do you think?"

"I'm torn. The whole sudden discovery of evidence pointing at his guilt? It feels too convenient to be real. There has to be something behind it. But what?"

She looked up at the mounted deer heads along the wall. The range of statements that people had made were whispering through her mind: Theresa's story of how Franco used the same line from one of Margot's books with every female he wanted to woo; Margot claiming he had also tried it on with her, but not recognising the line she herself had written; the photographs of Crete with buildings that had been torn down in recent years; Dieter's lie to Margot that he had seen her sister at a Christmas party. But why lie if they both knew full well that she was dead? After all, he had been blackmailed with the truth.

Or had he?

Atalanta raised a hand and massaged her temple. She was missing something. Something that would make everything come together. The last piece she needed. Or the aha moment. In the past, it had often come via a letter her grandfather had written her. But in this entire case there had been no letter. Perhaps it was logical that he could not have prepared her for every eventuality. That there would come a day when she had to do things on her own, whether she felt like she could or not.

Raoul said, "This morning I woke up and I remembered your last name. It is Ashford, isn't it?"

It was strange because earlier she would have been livid at the idea that he would ever not know her last name. But now, it made her so happy that this was a sign of his memory returning. She nodded enthusiastically. "It is."

Raoul frowned. "That is very odd because I am certain that I received a letter the other day from someone named Ashford. Clarence Ashford?"

Atalanta stared at him. "That's my grandfather. He is

deceased. How could he ever write to you?"

Raoul turned away. "I will go and get it. Wait here for me."

Atalanta stood with a nervously drumming heart. Raoul sometimes mixed things up so he might be mistaken. Still, he had seemed alert as he had mentioned it, and the name Clarence Ashford was probably not that common. What could she expect?

Raoul appeared again and handed her the note. It was not addressed to anyone, but the sender was indeed Clarence Ashford. She opened it and took out a sheet of paper. Seeing her grandfather's familiar, strong hand, made tears burn behind her eyes.

This letter may come as a bit of a surprise to you, for you do not know me and I do not know you. I am sitting here writing this letter to the man who has become important in my granddaughter's life. A man who I hope deserves her adoration and loyalty. I know that when Atalanta sets her mind to something she will not easily be swayed. I must therefore ask you not to take her feelings lightly and to search within yourself for certainty about whether you reciprocate her feelings. For it will certainly pain her greatly to discover that someone who pledged allegiance to her has let her down. I know I cannot keep her safe from every hurt that might come her way, although I wish I could do just that. Having lost both her parents, she has suffered quite enough. But that is in the past and you have no dealings with it. You are in the now and you can make her happy. Ensure that you do. By

this I do not mean to say you must profess love for her that you do not feel. Quite the contrary. Profess nothing until you are absolutely certain that she is the one, even if it takes time. Because once you are certain and you have her love, it is a treasure that will never lose its worth. I hope you will value that treasure and that you will be worthy of it. I hope you can bring her the happiness she so deserves.
   Yours truly,
   Clarence Ashford

"How did you get this letter?" she asked breathlessly.

"It was pushed under my door."

Atalanta stared at the words.

Renard. It had to have been him. But why? He didn't like Raoul. He didn't want them to be together.

She gestured at Raoul. "Stay here. I have something I must do." She went to look for Renard in the kitchen with the other staff. She drew him aside to a private corner where they could not be overheard. He wanted to tell her something about the staff's observations after Maurizio's arrest, but instead she merely showed him the letter. He fell silent and hung his head.

"You put this under Raoul's door."

"Your grandfather asked me to keep that letter for the man who would win your heart. To give it to him at an appropriate time."

"And you thought this appropriate? I am so confused and out of my depth and... I wished for a letter from Grandfather to help me in the case and get on, but this only makes it harder."

Renard wanted to say something but she didn't give him the opportunity.

"Raoul doesn't remember that we met let alone anything we might have shared and then you drop this letter on him with my grandfather's words to the man who—" *Should marry me?* She shook her head, angry and upset. "You had no right to do this. You should have discussed it with me first. I would have told you now is not the right time. It had to wait."

Renard shook his head. "No, it could not."

"Why? Raoul is confused. He has lost everything he loves. His career, his health. He doesn't know anything for certain. He must focus on finding his way back to what he was and then you do this. It only makes it harder."

Renard said, "For him perhaps, but not for you."

"Not for me? I don't follow. Are you trying to use Raoul's vulnerability to get him to marry me? I won't have it. I want him to choose me, of his own accord. Not because he is forced to do it." She was so angry she wanted to kick something!

"I have no idea what the letter says." Renard stood up straight. "But knowing your grandfather, it will be something this young man needs to hear. Your grandfather loved you very much and he was also open to loving whoever would catch your fancy. He wanted you to be happy with someone who stole your heart. With whom you could share a love like your parents had."

Atalanta stared at him. "My parents? But my father

chose my mother when he had walked away from his birthright. Grandfather can never have wanted that."

"He was disappointed in your father's choice of career, but not in his choice of wife. He thought your mother was marvellous. He admired the love they had for one another."

Atalanta recalled that one of the things that had prevented her grandfather from reaching out to them earlier had been his reluctance to drive a wedge between her parents or between her and her father. He had truly cared for their little family.

Tears burned her eyes anew. "And what am I supposed to do with this? I am always hearing that he loved me so much but I never heard it from him. I feel so alone and … how can this letter help me?"

"The letter was not written to you," Renard pointed out kindly. "It is not for you to act on it, but for Monsieur Lemont."

Atalanta wanted to say more but suddenly she froze and stared at him. "You do not like Raoul. You have never wanted us to get together. Why give him the letter? Why not keep it for a later occasion in which I have severed my unwanted ties with Raoul and am open to a new love prospect?"

"Indeed, why?" Renard said, holding her gaze. She saw a little twitch around his lips as if he had trouble controlling himself.

The anger left her then, and she stood there trying to gauge what he had wanted to achieve. Had his action been an attempt to show, to her and to Raoul, that he was taking them seriously? That he was no longer opposed to them getting together?

She held the letter uncomfortably. It had indeed not been for her to read. It had been meant for Raoul. For him to understand that if he wanted to pursue her, there were people who were cheering him on. Who wanted him to love her, if he felt that he could.

It still didn't answer the question of whether he could – that was something Raoul had to determine for himself, but at least she now knew that the two people who meant the most to her – Grandfather and Renard – had her back. She could count on them to want the best for her, to want her to be happy. Even if it required her to choose a difficult path with a man she loved, a man she also found infuriating at times because they were so very different.

She released her breath and the heavy weight lifted off her shoulders. She could suddenly smile at Renard. "Thank you. You have done the right thing. I will give this back to the rightful recipient." She turned away and then said again, "Thank you. It means a lot to me. After all, of all the things in the world, like justice and truth and loyalty, the most important must be love."

She took two more paces and stopped in her tracks. What had she just said? Of all the things... The most important... Love.

Images flashed through her head. People together. People apart. Jealousy. Rivalry. Laughter. Love. The ideal of love. The beauty of romance. What had Margot called her secretary's motivation? Not greed. But desire. It had a different ring to it. These two things were not the same.

And this could be the answer to everything.

If only she could see a way to unravel the web and catch the killer in their own snare.

Chapter Twenty-Three

Atalanta watched Margot and Dieter Bergreiter skating on the frozen lake behind the hotel. They held hands as they went in slow circles, constantly looking each other in the eye. There seemed to be something special about this ice dance, and the way they saw no one else but each other. Was this what true love looked like?

True love or ... obsession?

Atalanta crossed the terrace and stopped at the edge. She waved at the happy couple. They came over to her, their faces warm from the exertion and the cold wind. Dieter Bergreiter smiled at Margot before focusing on Atalanta. "Fräulein Ford, good morning. How are you? Isn't it a beautiful day?"

"It certainly is," Atalanta said. "You look very happy. Carefree."

"Yes, well, the situation is resolved, and we are all

packed and ready to go," he said. "As soon as the inspector gives the green light, we can depart."

"Now that I have decided to stop writing, I feel so much better. We can travel together and see the world," Margot said, smiling up at Dieter.

"But how will you support yourself if there is no more money coming in from your books?" Atalanta asked.

Dieter said, "There are still royalties from older titles. And there are a lot of older books. They will supply a steady income."

"And I will make sure Dieter doesn't play cards as much as he does now," Margot said in a teasing tone. "That will save us money which we can spend on doing nice things together."

"Yes." Atalanta kept her expression friendly as she continued to speak. "You are in a much better position now than you were before. With Maurizio Dulce in prison, you are no longer being blackmailed about the body in the grotto. You can keep all that money in your pocket. For travelling."

"You make it sound like a crime," Dieter said with a sharp look at her. "I admit that we should not have kept Johanna's accident in the grotto a secret, but we were very afraid of what it might mean if the truth got out. I was only eager to protect Margot."

"And her writing career, which brings in so much money," Atalanta said.

Margot put a protective hand on her husband's arm. "I was devastated when Johanna died. Dieter did everything he could to help me. To keep me from harm. I am sorry that I made him lie for me, but it was not our fault that the Dulces began to blackmail us. We have been so afraid." She shivered. "Finally it is over."

"Yes, it is." Atalanta took a deep breath. "Because you planted the sedative and the money in Maurizio's desk."

Margot looked at her and began to laugh. "Excuse me?"

Atalanta said, "Wasn't it a coincidence that these items were suddenly found by the police after they had searched the desk earlier and found nothing?"

"Because he had a secret compartment." Dieter gestured. "For the blackmail money. I could not tell them before the truth about the body had come to light but afterwards it seemed to make sense to do so. And you see how vital it was for the investigation."

Atalanta felt a chill at the deviousness of the two people standing opposite her. "Yes, and it came at the exact right moment. Maurizio is now under lock and key, arrested and charged with Eva's murder. He is the best possible scapegoat. Better than Franco or your secretary. Eva's murder will not be blamed on you and the blackmail is over. How perfect. Was that the idea from the start? Or did it only develop as time went on? I assume you know how to improvise. After all, you had already covered up the death of Johanna and hidden her body in the grotto. You were there when it happened." She nodded at Margot. "And Herr Bergreiter agreed to keep the secret. For your sake."

"I only wanted to avoid an unpleasant investigation."

Bergreiter was turning redder and redder. "Margot had nothing to do with Johanna's death. It was an accident."

"Oh, it might have been an accident. We will never really know, will we? Because one person is dead and the other is telling us the only story there is about what happened."

Margot's face was pinched. She hung her head and said softly, "I was afraid no one would believe me. That's why I didn't tell the truth. I never let anyone in on it, but Dieter. At least he believed me. Because he knows who I am."

"Yes," Atalanta said, "he knows who you are. Not *what you are like*. But he knows who you truly are. Because you are not Margot Bergreiter."

Bergreiter froze.

Atalanta continued, keeping her eyes on Margot, "You are her sister, Johanna Laub."

Margot laughed softly. "That's ridiculous. Where do you get such nonsense?"

"Johanna Laub disappeared about a year ago. She stopped writing travel articles and parted ways with her agent. No one ever saw her again. Letters written to her were returned unopened. You"—she looked at Dieter Bergreiter—"lied that you had seen her at a Christmas party. Allegedly, you lied to reassure Margot. But Margot – or should I say, the woman posing as Margot – knew full well that Johanna had not been to that party. Because Johanna was here, pretending to be Margot."

The two watched her with frozen expressions but Atalanta continued. "Margot was staying here as she often did and you came to visit her. I don't know what you wanted. To severe the ties perhaps? To stop providing details for her books? Or to get paid more money for them to support your lifestyle? Anyway, you met up and there was an argument and Margot died. You were left in a very serious situation. If you had notified the staff at the hotel, you would have been arrested. But if Margot didn't come back, they would also perk up and start looking for her. Johanna was just a day visitor who could have left again unobserved. But Margot was such an important guest here... You thought up an audacious plan. You dressed like her and pretended to be her. And it worked. Then Dieter came to visit his wife. Of course, he was not to be deceived. He would realise right away that his wife was someone else..."

Margot held her gaze. "This is the most ridiculous nonsense I have ever heard. Dieter is devoted to me. He would never just accept a switch. Please stop harassing us with this nonsense."

"It is true that the story went that Dieter Bergreiter was devoted to his wife, that he came to see her every weekend and he even wanted to buy this hotel for her. But was he really doing all of that out of genuine affection? Or was it a token of his guilty conscience because he had been deceiving her by having an affair with another woman? With her own sister!"

Dieter Bergreiter opened his mouth to say something but nothing came out. "We can even assume that the argument that led to Margot's death was about you, her husband?

About her discovery that you had been unfaithful to her? That you had betrayed her?"

Margot shook her head. "You are lying! Johanna is dead. She died in that grotto. I'm sorry I never told anyone about her accident, but—"

"Stop!" Atalanta raised a hand to underline her order. "You have betrayed yourself on numerous occasions. When Franco flirted with you, he quoted a scene from one of your novels but you didn't recognise it – because *you* had never written it. Margot did. You're having so much trouble writing a new book because you're not used to writing fiction. You have experience as a travel writer but that's not quite the same thing, is it? You tried to rework material that you already had from your travels to look like Johanna had sent it to you from abroad. But Eva found out. She mentioned she had been to Crete and the site show in the photo looked different now. She was out to expose you. I don't know if she realised the full truth or if she merely speculated that maybe your sister wasn't helping you or the sister was an invention, but the big scoop she wanted to sell to Alexander Hansen had to do with exposing the famous romance writer Margot Bergreiter as a fraud. People would hate you for the deception and stop buying your books. But that wasn't the main thing, was it? By drawing attention to your sister, the whole situation was on the verge of exploding. There was always the possibility that the death in the grotto could come to light. And you couldn't risk that. Eva had to die, but someone else had to take the blame. That's why you drew my attention to the pills Eva allegedly stole from Maurizio's office. The ones she supposedly asked you to have your doctor analyse. That way, when Eva died, I would be thinking that she was investigating Maurizio's involvement in Raoul's accident. Eva's suggestion to us to start ETAM was an unexpected gift to you. It would inevitably steer me in the wrong direction."

"No, Margot has nothing to do with it," Dieter said quickly. "She was even afraid when Eva died that *I* had done something drastic."

"Then she has cleverly deceived you with her concern. *She* killed Eva Reuter."

Dieter shook his head. "She did not. Margot is no murderer."

"Why do you keep calling her Margot?" Atalanta asked sharply. "She is Johanna."

"No, she is Margot." Dieter said it without flinching. "She is the Margot I once had. The woman who was light-hearted and flirty and funny. Not the woman she later became when she was so obsessed with her fame and her books and her health. All of those so-called cures she ran after to get better. While they were only costing a lot of money and delivering nothing good."

Atalanta looked at "Margot". Her expression was worried now that Dieter was talking. She put her hand on his arm again. "Say no more. This woman knows nothing. She cannot hurt us. We are leaving today. It will be fine." She kissed him on the cheek. "It will be fine, darling."

Dieter shook his head. "No, it won't." He sounded

suddenly weary. "This sword of Damocles will keep hanging over our heads. You keep telling me it will all go away, but it won't. This conversation proves that's not true."

"This conversation proves nothing. We will go away and be together. That is all that matters."

"We are not the only two people in the world." His voice had an edge now. "There are others, and they will always interfere with us." He reached up and rubbed his forehead. "It has to stop somewhere. I am tired of it. I cannot go on."

"Yes, you can. For me you can." Her voice was insistent.

Dieter Bergreiter stood taller. "No, I cannot. It has already been too much. I was willing to lie for you to keep it all alive. The books, the career that brought us money. I was selfish like that. I thought we could make it. But then Maurizio started to blackmail me. He thought he knew something even though he knew but a part of it. I had to keep paying. Then Eva came snooping around. And now this woman knows." Despair lined his voice. "You said it would just be a matter of keeping our heads down and no one would notice. That time would pass and—"

"Don't be stupid! We can still get away. Do you see a police officer here? Anyone to arrest us? I don't." She glared at Atalanta. "I don't know what you want from us – money, probably, like everyone else. But I won't give it to you. You have to be silenced in a different manner." "Margot" looked at her husband. "Were we not just remarking on how risky it is to skate on this lake? With the warmth of the sun on the ice it is getting thinner. There could be cracks. Before you know it, there is a hole and someone can disappear beneath the surface."

Dieter turned pale. "No," he said softly. "We are not doing it again. We cannot do it again."

"What difference does it make? Just once more. To get to South America safely. You get an axe and make a hole in the ice then we shove her under. She won't be found for hours. By the time her body is discovered, we will be long gone."

Dieter Bergreiter flinched. "You're mad." He said it under his breath. "I should have stopped you before, but I was too much in love with you to do it. You look so much like her. I made myself believe you were her. Margot."

"I *am* her. I *am* Margot." Johanna wrapped her arms around his neck. "I am whoever you want me to be, darling, just as long as we are together. We are all that matters, remember? Our love."

Dieter Bergreiter shrank back from her. "Love, you call it," he said in a dull tone, "but how could it be anything like love? Love is kind and forgiving and gentle. It does not hurt others. It certainly does not kill."

"Oh yes it does." Johanna stared at him with a strange tightness in her features. "Jealousy is part of love, whatever you may say. The need to have a person all to yourself. It burns like a fire within. It cannot be tamed. It is all-consuming. You belong to me. I won't let anyone or anything get in the way."

"I have belonged to you long enough," Bergreiter said. "I cannot go on with it. I will not commit another murder to continue this insanity."

"How dare you call it that? I love you. I love you and you love me."

"At the time I did, and it seemed to make sense, but … things have changed now. You have become unrecognisable. You killed Eva and you are contemplating killing this woman and I cannot help but wonder if you ever told me the truth about Margot. Was her death really an accident? Or did you come here fully intending to dispose of her?"

"Does it matter? You wanted to be with me. You said so. You said that you would be with me if you weren't married to Margot. You could not divorce her, you said. She would not survive. Well, guess what? She didn't survive, so you could marry me. Or stay married to me, as I was your wife already. Your dear, devoted wife." She wrapped her arms around him again and leaned her head on his shoulder. "I don't care if you call me Margot or Johanna or whatever as long as I can be with you. I need to be with you. I need you, more than oxygen."

"You really are mad." He tried to push her away, a disgusted look on his face. "How can I have ever believed that I loved you?"

"What? Now you deny everything? I did all of this to be with you and you deny having feelings for me?" Johanna gave a piercing scream and pushed Dieter away from her with all of her might. He staggered backwards and fell on the ice. There was a dull thud and then a creaking sound as cracks appeared in the shiny surface. Before Atalanta realised what was happening, a section of the frozen lake imploded, dragging Dieter Bergreiter into the freezing water below.

"Noooooo!" Johanna screamed. "No, my love!" She threw herself into the water.

Atalanta raised both hands to her face in shock. "Renard!" Her butler was already by her side. She had asked him to keep an eye on the situation and to come to her aid in case things got out of hand. But she had not expected this.

Renard looked her in the eye. "Run to the hotel and get help. We need a ladder and ropes. Quickly!"

Atalanta ran across the terrace, waving her arms and shouting for help. Two staff members came out of the doors and she told them to go to Renard at the lake. She went inside to call out more people and told them to bring ladders and ropes and other things that might be useful to get two guests out of the lake. "They have fallen through the ice while skating—"

As the turmoil outside grew with more people involving themselves in the rescue, Atalanta stood with her hands still up to her face, her breath shallow as she realised what had just happened. No matter how incredible the scenario seemed, it was the truth. It all made sense now. She even recalled the words that "Margot" had said to her when they had spoken about finding love. She had said, *"It goes to show that you should never let yourself be guided by fear. If you are in love and you think he is the man of your dreams, the one you want to spend the rest of your life with, you must act. Regardless of the consequences."* That was what she herself had done.

She had fallen in love with her sister's husband, and she had first seduced him and then, not satisfied with an affair and his protestations that he could not divorce his wife because it would be the end of her, she had decided to kill Margot and pass herself off as her to the outside world. Dieter Bergreiter had participated in the ruse by saying he had bumped into Johanna at a Christmas party and that his wife got letters from her and so on.

"I remember now," Raoul's voice said softly by her side. He looked at the consternation at the edge of the lake. "We have chased someone together. It was in a garden. And there was something else. A fire?"

"I am sorry you are recalling all the dangerous situations." Atalanta forced a smile. "I assure you, we have also done nice, innocent things together. Things that had nothing to do with criminals and murder cases."

"I'm glad to hear it." He turned his gaze away from the frantic scene to look at her. "I hope we can do it again."

"What?"

"Spend time together away from criminals and murder cases. I've made a plan. I want to travel through Italy, along the Amalfi coast. I'm not allowed to drive right now but your butler can be our chauffeur. We can see all the sights, eat delicious food and have a quiet time together." He waited a moment, a smile lighting his deep brown eyes. "What do you think? Do you have the time and the inclination to join me?"

Atalanta's heart missed a beat. "You really want to do that?"

"Yes. I want to get away from here. I need to recuperate in a different environment. With you. I am certain Vincenzo will understand. I will tell him how you rescued his nephew from a murder charge. By getting the right people apprehended you have pulled Maurizio's neck from the noose. That will mean something to Vincenzo. Family is everything to him. Now that you have saved a member of his family, you will be like family to him."

Atalanta grimaced. "I don't know if that's good or bad."

"He will never hurt someone to whom he owes loyalty." Raoul put an arm around her. "Believe me. Now, what do you think of my offer? Do I need to include more reasons in order to persuade you to accept?"

"No. Being with you for a while, exploring beautiful Italy, is reason enough."

"I knew Italy would do the trick," he said with a wink. But his eyes were serious and Atalanta had the breathless feeling that for the first time in their relationship, she was really hopeful they could be together. That they could somehow overcome their difficulties and become more to each other than they had ever been before.

There were raised voices outside and Raoul drew her along to go and see what was happening. Both "Margot" and Dieter had been pulled out of the lake. She was sitting on the ground with two staff members wrapping blankets around her, but Dieter Bergreiter lay on his back, pale and unmoving. The hotel doctor was leaning over him looking grim.

"Margot" shook off the blankets and crawled over to

him. "Dieter..." She put her hand to his face. "Dieter, please. I did not mean it. Come back to me. Please come back to me!"

The doctor looked at her. "He has swallowed a lot of water. His pulse is very weak. I am afraid he won't make it."

"But he has to make it. He cannot die. Dieter!"

Raoul wrapped an arm around Atalanta and led her away from the scene. "We don't need to be part of this," he said. "Either he will live and go to prison, or he will die and she goes to prison alone."

Atalanta looked at him in surprise. "You know that they killed Eva Reuter?"

"It makes sense, doesn't it? Margot was obsessed with her husband all the time I saw her here. She cannot stand anyone getting close to him. Eva flirted with him and Margot killed her for it. Dieter helped her, or at least he knew she had done it and didn't tell the police. They will consider him an accomplice."

"It is even more complicated than that." Atalanta took a deep breath. "That is not Margot Bergreiter, but her sister Johanna Laub. The real Margot was killed and her body hidden in the grotto. Johanna took her place. Dieter knew and accepted it because Johanna was, to his mind, the Margot he had lost when her career took over her life. They had a twisted obsession with one another that was bound to lead to heartbreak."

"And bloodshed," Raoul said with a grimace. "So they

are guilty of two murders? Margot Bergreiter and Eva Reuter?"

"Indeed. Tanner will have a hard time proving exactly what each of them did. At first Bergreiter pretended that he did not believe Johanna had killed Eva, but later in the conversation he did state that she had killed Eva. Remember Theresa found his gold tie clip beside Eva's dead body? That suggests Bergreiter went to the reading room during the night. Possibly to check whether Eva was really dead. Perhaps he was worried that Johanna had felt compelled to do something about her? I do remember that he cast her worried looks during the evening. I assumed it was because she was drinking a lot of wine over dinner. Johanna seemed to have had a fondness for alcohol since childhood. At least, that's what 'Margot' told me. But was she telling me the truth, or only projecting all the weaknesses onto Johanna to glorify her blameless Margot persona?"

Raoul frowned and grimaced. "That is too complicated for my sore head. And I wager Tanner will not be happy with this resolution either. He will have a hard time proving everything. And he seemed so pleased when he arrested Maurizio." Raoul looked across the lobby and said, "Speaking of the dear inspector, there he is."

Atalanta watched Tanner close in on them. He wore the same old hat with the feather from the first day she had seen him. But she knew better now than to underestimate this man. He was intelligent and persistent. And apparently not on the Dulces's payroll or he would not have moved against Maurizio.

Tanner said, "I was on my way up here with news when I heard that there was something going on. Can you fill me in?" His tone was ironic.

Atalanta gestured to a few chairs in the corner. "Shall we sit? It's quite complicated."

Tanner listened without interrupting her. Finally he whistled. "That will cause a stir. The famous author Margot Bergreiter murdered at a luxury hotel by her own sister and the body hidden and the sister taking her identity… It could almost become a novel in itself."

"But not a romance novel," Raoul observed. "I doubt readers would find the affair between Bergreiter and the sister very palatable. Or consider their love romantic."

"Probably not," Tanner agreed. "Anyway, I will take them away for questioning as soon as they're ready to be moved."

"Could you keep Maurizio locked up just a little longer?" Raoul asked. "You see, I'm planning a trip with Atalanta, and I doubt Maurizio will like it. If he's locked up, he can't stop me from going."

Tanner suppressed a smile. "I can do that, I suppose. I have to investigate his part in covering up Margot Bergreiter's death, it seems. Once he discovered the dead body in the grotto, he should have reported it to the police but instead he used it to blackmail the Bergreiters. I will keep him under lock and key until I have ascertained what he knew and how much he earned by extorting them."

"Fantastic." Raoul rose to his feet. "I will go and find Renard to discuss everything with him. He also has to pack our bags." He looked at Atalanta. "You do not mind him packing my bags, do you? I am not allowed to do much, you know."

She laughed out loud, shaking her head at him. "Go and find him. But don't squabble. I want it to be a wonderful light-hearted and restorative trip."

"Will do." Raoul tipped an imaginary hat and left.

Tanner regarded Atalanta. "I do hope your friend has a full recovery from his head injury. He does seem better when you're around."

She flushed. "I hope he will enjoy the Amalfi Coast."

Tanner raised a hand. "Don't tell me where you're going. Maurizio may ask me about it and if I don't know then I can't lie." He was silent a moment and then continued, "You probably think I don't mind lying."

Atalanta studied his serious expression. "I distrusted you at the start. I believed you were working for the Dulces. I have even … wondered if they arranged for you to become a policeman here in the place of the man who was run off the road."

"And what was your conclusion?"

"If you were on their payroll, you would never have arrested Maurizio. You would have made the evidence of his involvement in Eva Reuter's death disappear."

"Exactly." Tanner leaned back with a sigh. "I wish I could hold Maurizio Dulce much longer than just for the time you need to get away to Italy. I wish I had grounds to charge him and lock him up for good. Him and his uncle. But I fear there will be good lawyers swarming in to get them off the hook for the blackmail. After all, it is only the Bergreiters's claim that they were being blackmailed at all, and they are a couple of murderers. Why should we believe them? I will need solid proof, but if the money was paid via card game losses, it will be difficult. With a Dulce involved it is always difficult to prove any wrongdoing."

Atalanta studied him. "The death of your predecessor, was it murder?"

"I suspect so. The other car, the driver were never found. But ... we locals have our suspicions."

"Then you took a risk accepting the job."

Tanner looked her over. "Why did you feel compelled to solve Eva Reuter's murder? You came here for your injured friend. You need not have involved yourself at all."

"I guess ... I cannot stop myself from caring about justice being done."

Tanner nodded and rose to his feet. "Then we understand each other." He reached out his hand and shook hers. "It was a pleasure to work with you. Good luck and all the best to you and your friend."

She watched him walk away. He was on their side. He was a fighter, for law and for justice. He had taken the job in order to oppose the Dulces not to support them. She hoped he would be able to stay the course and keep the region crime-free.

Raoul came back to her smiling from ear to ear. "Renard for once agrees with me. He is very keen on this idea of taking a trip and ran off to start packing. Your things, my things, his own things. He doesn't care what things as long as we can get away from here. I totally understand his feelings. This is a beautiful place but it has become quite oppressive. I have seen enough snow. I want to walk in the sunshine and eat the best pizza."

He reached out his hand to her. "Come on. We have so much exploring to do. We will make new memories. Together."

Preorder the next instalment in the Miss Ashford Investigates series taking Atalanta to Italy's breathtaking Amalfi Coast.

PERIL IN POSITANO
COMING JUNE 2026

Acknowledgments

As always, I'm grateful to all agents, editors and authors who share online about the writing and publishing process. Special thanks to my fabulous editors Charlotte Ledger for believing in Atalanta from the start and Helen Williams for the thoughtful feedback on this story and enthusiasm for the series as a whole; to Lucy Bennett and Gary Redford for the gorgeous cover illustration which captures the glory of snowy Alps brilliantly; and to the entire One More Chapter and wider HarperCollins teams, especially the Rights Department. A special mention to the fabulous narrator of the audiobooks, Jessica Whittaker, who brings Atalanta and her world to life!

This story takes place in one of my favourite environments: the Swiss mountains. The majestic sights, the delicious food and the varied activities on offer, whether it's skiing, hiking or boating on the lakes, make it a perfect holiday destination. And fascinating titbits like the search for gems and the history of hotels that began as health resorts inspired part of the plot. Of course, it is also intensely personal for Atalanta as she faces the scheming Dulces in her quest to save Raoul from their clutches, and from the memory loss following his accident. By now these characters feel like friends to me and I hope they are also to you, reader, as you follow their adventures.

If you haven't done so already, do check out all the other instalments in the series, which always have Atalanta visiting gorgeous locations where baffling mysteries await her. Happy reading!

Have you read the rest of the Miss Ashford Investigates series?

Miss Atalanta Ashford suddenly finds herself the most eligible young lady in society when she inherits her grandfather's substantial fortune, but with it comes a legacy passed down from her grandfather ... sleuthing discreetly for Europe's elite.

Not one to back down from a challenge, Miss Ashford must depend on her sharp wit and charm to solve her first case, which takes her to the lush lavender fields of Provence and a wedding at the mansion of the Comte de Surmonne.

Miss Atalanta Ashford is sightseeing near Venice when a mysterious veiled lady approaches her with the urgent request to look into her daughter's mysterious death on the idyllic Greek island of Santorini. Whilst working as a companion for the eminent Bucardi family, the unfortunate girl took a plunge from the dramatic cliffs during a walk alone. But is all as it seems?

Sailing to Santorini and going undercover as the new companion, Miss Ashford soon discovers that her client hasn't told her the full truth. Someone is watching her. Now she must unravel the mystery and prevent the breathtaking azure sea views from becoming the last she too will ever see...

When novice detective Atalanta Ashford is whisked away to Italy by her friend, race car driver Raoul Lemont, she anticipates a happy holiday under the Tuscan sun. But a chance meeting on the Orient Express with Italian heiress Catharina Lanetti leads to a party invitation…and front row seats for a mysterious murder!

With their new friend under suspicion Atalanta and Raoul set to work trying to discover who really murdered Catharina's father. But with more than half a dozen suspects – all with compelling motive – Atalanta may just be facing her toughest case yet!

After accepting an invitation to attend the ballet in snowy Salzburg, Atalanta is shocked when a convicted jewel thief is found dead in the concert hall where the theft occurred a decade ago.

Did he return to the scene of the crime because he wanted to prove his innocence? Is the real culprit among the high-society guests? In her quest for the truth, Atalanta uncovers dangerous secrets about the European elite that put her own life in mortal danger…

The smell of Glühwein and spiced Lebkuchen from the Austrian winter markets fill the air, but for Atalanta there's an intriguing puzzle to be solved.

A luxury cruise
Hidden family secrets
A body on board…

A birthday trip to Bonn sees amateur detective Atalanta Ashford drawn into the scandalous will of a wealthy grandmother during a scenic cruise down along the Rhine.

But growing tensions lead to a sudden and shocking death. Facing suspicion all around, Atalanta must unravel a deadly web of family secrets as treacherous as the river they voyage on, to find the killer.

Books available in paperback, eBook and audio!

ONE MORE CHAPTER

The author and One More Chapter would like to thank everyone who contributed to the publication of this story...

Analytics
Imogen Wolstencroft

Audio
Fionnuala Barrett
Ciara Briggs

Contracts
Laura Amos
Inigo Vyvyan

Design
Lucy Bennett
Fiona Greenway
Liane Payne
Dean Russell

Digital Sales
Laura Daley
Lydia Grainge
Hannah Lismore

eCommerce
Laura Carpenter
Madeline ODonovan
Charlotte Stevens
Christina Storey
Jo Surman
Rachel Ward

Editorial
Rosie Best
Kara Daniel
Charlotte Ledger
Lydia Mason
Laura McCallen
Jennie Rothwell
Sofia Salazar Studer
Caroline Scott-Bowden
Helen Williams

Harper360
Emily Gerbner
Ariana Juarez
Jean Marie Kelly
emma sullivan
Sophia Wilhelm

International Sales
Peter Borcsok
Ruth Burrow
Bethan Moore
Colleen Simpson

Inventory
Sarah Callaghan
Kirsty Norman

Marketing & Publicity
Chloe Cummings
Grace Edwards
Katie Sadler

Operations
Melissa Okusanya
Hannah Stamp

Production
Denis Manson
Simon Moore
Francesca Tuzzeo

Rights
Ashton Mucha
Alisah Saghir
Zoe Shine
Aisling Smyth
Lucy Vanderbilt

Trade Marketing
Ben Hurd
Eleanor Slater

The HarperCollins Distribution Team

The HarperCollins Finance & Royalties Team

The HarperCollins Legal Team

The HarperCollins Technology Team

UK Sales
Isabel Coburn
Jay Cochrane
Sabina Lewis
Holly Martin
Harriet Williams
Leah Woods

And every other essential link in the chain from delivery drivers to booksellers to librarians and beyond!

One More Chapter is an award-winning global division of HarperCollins.

Subscribe to our newsletter to get our latest eBook deals and stay up to date with all our new releases!

signup.harpercollins.co.uk/
join/signup-omc

Meet the team at
www.onemorechapter.com

Follow us!

@onemorechapterhc

Do you write unputdownable fiction?
We love to hear from new voices.
Find out how to submit your novel at
www.onemorechapter.com/submissions